"You're going to bawl me out, aren't you?"

"Yes, I am," she assured him.

"Don't bother. I shouldn't have questioned your authority. I won't do it again."

"Until tomorrow, anyway. I'm not kidding, Connor. These men work for me. If I went to your staff without talking to you, you wouldn't like it."

"No, I wouldn't. I've already apologized, Rowena."

"Yes, you have."

"You want me to repeat it?"

She almost smiled at the thought of Connor Wingate apologizing twice for the same misstep. "No… What is it about me that's so hard for you to trust? Do I look like a crook or something?"

"Hardly. You look like a beautiful woman."

Beautiful? With mud and dirt oozing from every pore? "Now you're just being mean."

"Mean?" Confusion darkened his eyes.

She *so* was not going to argue about her un-beautiful self.

Books by Lois Richer

Love Inspired

Love Inspired Suspense

LOIS RICHER

Sneaking a flashlight under the blankets, hiding in a thicket of Caragana bushes where no one could see, pushing books into socks to take to camp—those are just some of the things Lois Richer freely admits to in her pursuit of the written word. "I'm a book-a-holic. I can't do without stories," she confesses. "It's always been that way." Her love of language evolved into writing her own stories. Today her passion is to create tales of personal struggle that lead to triumph over life's rocky road. For Lois, a happy ending is essential. "In my stories, as in my own life, God has a way of making all things beautiful. Writing a love story is my way of reinforcing my faith in His ultimate goodness toward us—His precious children."

Spring Flowers, Summer Love
Lois Richer

Steeple
Hill®

Published by Steeple Hill Books™

STEEPLE HILL BOOKS

Steeple
Hill®

ISBN-13: 978-0-373-87428-6
ISBN-10:   0-373-87428-6

SPRING FLOWERS, SUMMER LOVE

www.SteepleHill.com

Printed in U.S.A.

So humble yourselves under the mighty power of
God, and in his good time he will honor you.
Give all your worries and cares to God,
for he cares about what happens to you.
—*1 Peter 5:6-7*

For Josh. With love.

Prologue

"A toast, girls."

Piper Franklin lifted her iced tea high in the air.

"To what?" Rowena Davis frowned, certain neither of her best friends knew her secret yet.

"To the Bayside Trio, of course." Piper giggled. "It seems like only yesterday that we left Serenity Bay. Here's to coming home."

"Hear, hear." Ashley Masters clinked her glass against Piper's.

Rowena took a sip, and grimaced. Tea of any sort didn't appeal to her. But this place did. Serenity Bay. Home. Piper had been back for two years, Ash for one. Finally she was back, too.

Rowena took in the view of the shimmering blue water and the surrounding hills decked out in autumn's blazing hues. She had done the right thing, hadn't she?

"I wish we could think of a way to get Row to move back, Pip. Then the Bayside Trio would be back on the Bay, together again." Ashley sighed. "That's my dream."

Rowena allowed her smile to creep out. "Then your dream just might be coming true, Ash."

"What?" Piper jerked upright, stuck out her pink-tinted

toenail and jabbed Ashley's foot. "Did she say what I think she said?"

"I'm not sure I heard right." Ashley cleared her throat. "Does that mean you're thinking about moving back here, Row?"

"Come January, if things work together as I plan."

"Yes!" The other two enveloped her in the group hug ritual they'd perfected through six years of boarding school. Once her two best friends were again seated, Rowena noticed their exchange of funny looks.

"What?"

"Oh, nothing." Ashley's gray eyes opened wide innocently.

Rowena wasn't buying it. "Tell the truth."

Ash held out her left hand and let the sun light up the diamond facets on her rings. "I was just thinking that Pip and I both found our Prince Charming here. Maybe the same will be true for you."

"The Wingate brothers are sixty-five if they're a day. I don't think they qualify, Ash."

"At least they have a kingdom." Piper smirked.

"I don't want someone else's kingdom. I'm going to get my own back. You two already know that." Rowena leaned back, closed her eyes and wondered if she'd finally bit off more than she could chew.

"Maybe you'd better explain what coming back to the Bay has to do with Wingate Manor."

"The Wingate brothers hired me to redo the Manor's landscape." She leaned forward, a picture forming in her mind. "You know how they're always trying to expand their reputation, be more than a fine place to dine or host wedding receptions and anniversary parties?"

"Of course." Piper frowned. "Henry's held garden tours for the last two years. And now Wingate hosts summer stock performances for a couple of months. They have a great space for private birthday parties, too."

"Last year they started patio barbecues," Ashley added.

"They're going to expand even more." Excitement skittered up and down Rowena's spine. "They intend to reorganize the patio spaces for more private functions, make a tearoom to generate afternoon traffic from the garden tours— lots of new things."

"Wow. I've heard rumors but nothing of this scope." Piper was probably thinking how this would impact the town. As economic development officer, Piper liked to know about everything that affected Serenity Bay.

"Michael and I went there for dinner not long ago," Ashley told them. "The chef is fabulous. But how do their plans affect you, Row?"

"I came up with an idea to revamp the grounds, make them an attraction in and of themselves. Henry wants fountains, little vistas where artists can paint, a summerhouse where the horticultural society can meet, or rent for private parties. Once I'm finished, Wingate will offer the perfect backdrop for couples to take their wedding pictures, winter and summer."

"It sounds like it will cost the earth," Pip mused.

"That's the best part."

"You've got a funny look on your face, Rowena. Spill it."

"I've agreed to handle the landscaping in exchange for the land once owned by Davis Nurseries."

"So you are moving back!" Ashley crowed.

"Next January, yes."

Piper frowned. "Wait a minute. This revamp—it's coming out of your pocket?"

Rowena nodded. "I get the land free and clear in exchange for the job."

"Which means you'll quit at Yelland Gardens."

"Yes. If everything at Wingate comes together as I've planned, I can decide whether or not to return to my old job later." Their doubts echoed her own. "The opportunity to get the land back was there. I couldn't ignore it."

"Because of your father," Piper murmured.

"Yes. If I can just get him back on the land, I'm sure he'll finally be able to shake off this depression. It's my fault Dad had to sell Davis Nurseries' land to the Wingate brothers for pennies on the dollar. It's my duty to get it back."

"But how are you going to pay for it, find workers, the equipment?"

"I'm not saying it will be easy. But I am going to do it."

Ashley hugged her. "If you need any help, you just ask."

Ashley—with her elegant hair, three-inch heels and designer clothes—up a tree, limbing? Rowena had to smile.

"I mean it." Ash's gray eyes pinned her. "I'm here for you, Rowena. You're my friend and I want to help."

"Thank you both. In the meantime, does our annual birthday bash include food? I'm starved."

"You're always starved." Piper rose, headed for the kitchen. "I'll be back in a minute."

Rowena let herself daydream of better days and a thriving nursery. It would be that way again, she promised herself. And it would be worth giving up her career for. It had to be.

"Moving back is perfect, of course," Ashley mused. "It will be wonderful to have both you and Pip nearby. But I think it would be even nicer if you could meet someone."

Rowena tucked her ragged nails under her thighs and wished she'd found something more stylish than jeans and a T-shirt for the weekend. "Forget it."

"I'm going to pray about it." The glint in Piper's eye promised she'd do exactly as she said.

"Me, too," Ash agreed. "You just never know what God has in store."

Rowena opened her mouth to protest, then closed it. She knew what lay ahead: months of backbreaking work at Wingate Manor and sweat equity in a nursery left untended too long—with nary a prince in sight.

But that was exactly what she owed her father.

Chapter One

Wingate Manor had never looked so pathetic.

Well, not the actual house. The stone structure built by some wealthy industrialist as a lavish vacation villa in the 1920s stood enduringly solid and sturdy. But the grounds were a disaster.

Connor Wingate stepped out of his BMW, closed the door and winced as his Italian loafers sunk deep into the mud.

"Why did I agree to this?" he asked himself out loud.

Because the uncles took care of you when you needed it and it's time to reciprocate.

Connor shut down the voice of his conscience, glanced sideways at the yapping dog with his face pressed against the passenger's window and shook his head. No way was he letting Tobias run free in this muck. He'd be filthy in two seconds flat. Ignoring the animal, he turned his attention back to his surroundings.

Winter had caused much of the damage. The ice storm Uncle Hank had mentioned was probably responsible for felling those big oaks behind the house. He saw evidence that lightning had sheared off a massive pine he'd once climbed.

There were also signs that something combined with gravity had helped sag the flower beds.

But the marks on the spruce trunks in front of him were not caused by weather. Those trunks had been chipped at by an ax.

"A very dull ax," he muttered grimly, aghast at the damage.

A small shed stood to one side of the house. The place where his uncles kept a stock of firewood to supply Wingate's charming but voracious fireplaces lay completely barren when it was usually bursting with logs ready to burn.

"It's a mess, isn't it?"

He wheeled around and found himself staring into a pair of almond-shaped hazel eyes fringed by the longest lashes he'd ever seen. He was quite sure they weren't artificial, given that the woman's only makeup was a streak of mud decorating one cheek and a sprig of pine needles perched atop her flattened auburn hair.

"Somebody's been helping themselves to wood while the brothers have been away," she said, lifting a chip from the soaking ground and rubbing it between her fingertips as if she could tell from that who the culprit might be.

Connor took one look at her Goodwill coat and the ancient rubber boots that swallowed her legs to her knees and narrowed his gaze.

"You don't happen to know who would have done such a thing?"

"No idea." She shook her head, glanced right, then left, as if she were assessing the damage. "It looks really bad but it's reparable. If this moisture would ever stop, that is."

The rain droplets became sleet. Connor winced at the sting against his cheek. He'd be in Australia right now if Cecile hadn't—

"Does that dog want out?" his visitor asked, head tilted to one side as she studied the drooling beast.

"No."

"Oh." She blinked the spiky bangs out of her eyes. "What's his name?"

"Tobias." He did not want to talk about the dog.

"The Lord is good."

"Pardon?"

"Tobias. It means the Lord is good." Her eyes twinkled when she grinned. "Names and their meanings are a fascination with me. What's yours?"

"Connor." It slipped out without thinking.

"Hmm. Gaelic. It means high longing, I think."

High longing. Well, that about covered his recent past. Conner huffed out an indignant snort to cover his frustration.

"You're the brothers' nephew."

Clearly the meaning of names wasn't her only gift.

"Great-nephew. Look, Miss, er, Ms.—what is *your* name?"

"I should have introduced myself." She wrinkled her nose and chuckled. "Sorry. Rowena Davis."

This was the landscape designer? Connor choked on his disbelief. She was all of what? Nineteen? Twenty? Maybe a hundred pounds if she stayed out in the rain all night?

This elf was going to cut down trees and carry them away?

"Don't worry, Mr. Wingate," she said after studying his face for several moments. "I can do the job. That's why Hank and Henry hired me. They know my work."

"I see." The dog had started up a mournful howl that made conversation difficult. On second thought, maybe he should let Tobias out before he wrecked his brand-new car. "Excuse me."

"Sure."

Connor turned and opened the door, but before he could step out of the way, Tobias, in his usual blustering way, jumped against him, knocking him to the ground. Mud oozed through Connor's fingers, splatted his coat and began to seep through the seat of his trousers.

The dog licked his face in apology.

"Perfect." He shoved the chocolate lab's muddy paws aside and rose, disgusted with everything to do with his life.

The landscaper, on the other hand, seemed to welcome the dog's affection. She knelt, let him swipe his pink tongue across her face as she ruffled his fur and smoothed his ears.

"Oh, you're a beauty. Thank you for the welcome. Do you know how to fetch?" She picked up a stick and tossed it. The dog raced after it, grabbed it in his jaws, but after one last look at his new friend, took off into the bush.

"He doesn't know how to do much except eat and sleep. And run away." Connor stopped, reading her expression. *Dog hater.* He wasn't, but she couldn't know Cecile had died because of Tobias.

"Does he belong to your children?" she asked sympathetically.

"I'm not married." Struggling for composure, Connor cleared his throat. "Look, Miss Davis…"

"Rowena."

"Miss Davis," he repeated, wishing he'd waited another day. Or week. Till the rain had stopped. Or until the trees were cleaned up. Until he'd figured out his future and life made sense.

"I realize my uncles made an agreement with you to do the work around Wingate Manor and restore it to its former glory."

She smiled at that, her lips spread wide across her face in a grin that lit chips of gold in the green of her hazel eyes.

"Maybe not glory," she agreed. "But at least I can make it look a whole lot better than it does now. In return for the nursery," she added, her smile disappearing like the sun behind a cloud.

"Nursery?" Connor struggled with that for a few moments.

"Oh, you mean that land they bought years ago. Yes, I believe it did used to be a nursery. Don't worry. They told me about your, er, understanding."

Why did she want that hunk of overgrown bush?

"The thing is, Connor, your uncles and I made that agreement last summer. Before I'd seen all this damage." She glanced around, frowned. "I should warn you that the job may cost more than I'd originally estimated. The ice storm was bad enough, but all this hacking—"

"How much more?" he asked. Suspicion feathered its way across his nerves in a warning he'd made a fortune listening to. If she thought she was going to soak two old men who were recovering from an accident she was in for a second thought.

"I don't know yet. I've poked around a bit. Those terraces don't look stable. The bottom layers of bricks are crumbling. They've been repaired piecemeal, shored up for a lot of years but—"

"Look," he interrupted as the wind whipped through his wet pants. "We're both going to catch cold if we stand in this sleet, chattering. Maybe you could conduct your assessment and give me the overrun figures. Then I'll decide whether or not we'll go ahead."

She stared at him for several moments while her eyes brewed a storm, turned to green daggers. When she spoke frost edged her words. Her voice was low, determined and showed not the slightest hint of apology.

"Make no mistake, Mr. Wingate. This project *is* going ahead. I turned down a year's worth of designing to come here. Your uncles and I signed a contract. It's too late for you to back out now."

They'd signed something? Even after he'd warned them to let him handle things? Connor shoved his hands into his pockets but refused to show his frustration in any other way. He was here now. He'd protect their interests.

"I've already begun pruning," she told him. "If the weather clears up I'll be back on-site tomorrow morning with a helper to continue. But the grounds are too wet to work. I'll have to hold off on the flower beds until they dry out."

"Fine." He turned to leave.

"Mr. Wingate?"

"Yes?"

The dog came racing up, flopping down at her feet. She glanced down.

"I'm going to have some heavy equipment in here. The dog can't be loose for that. If you could construct a pen or keep him inside, he'd be a lot safer."

"Fine. Anything else?" He lifted one eyebrow as a wet drop slid down his neck.

"Yes."

Connor waited, shifted. When she didn't speak he fixed her with a glare. "Well?"

"Could you lose the attitude?" she asked quietly. "I'm not here to harm you or ruin Wingate Manor. I'm here to make it look fantastic. It's going to take some time and a whole lot of work but you can rest assured that I will get the job done to your satisfaction."

"Before June 1?" he demanded. "There's a large wedding reception scheduled here that night. My uncles want the place to be in shape by then."

"It will be."

Connor had his doubts about that, but now was neither the time nor the place to second-guess the old boys' decisions. He'd let her go at it for a couple of days, wait for her to admit it was too big a job and then he'd find someone else. Someone who looked able to lift a fallen tree, not dance across the trunk.

"Fine." He turned away, put one foot toward the house.

"Just one more thing."

Ensuring his sigh was loud enough for her to hear, he turned back. One look at her expressive face and he wished he hadn't. His bad attitude wasn't her fault. He struggled to change his tone. "What is it?"

"I've also begun work at the nursery. If you see lights up there, it's me. The power's on and I've moved into the house." Her lips lifted but nobody would have called it a smile. "Don't worry, Mr. Wingate, the electric bill's in my name."

She bent, patted the dog's head, then walked away, her boots slogging through the mud with an ease he envied.

"I wasn't going to—"

She gave no sign that she'd heard a thing. Connor gave up, closed his eyes and exhaled. When he opened them she was gone and only Tobias stood looking at him as if he'd lost his senses.

"I probably have," he admitted as he headed for the house.

As expected, Tobias was filthy. And not averse to sharing the mud. Connor was halfway up the steps when he noticed just how much of it the animal was plastering over his uncles' pristine white stairs. Tobias couldn't possibly be allowed inside.

Connor grumbled, turned and squished his way back to the car for the leash. Of course Tobias took forever to heel. Only when Connor was soaked and dirtier than he'd been before, if that was even possible, did the dog finally stand to attention so the leash could be snapped onto his collar.

"You need a bath," Connor told him, tying the leash to a rail at the side of the house. "But I need one more. Stay here and I'll come back and clean you up in a while. Then we'll talk about dinner."

His hands were frozen, his backside was sopping and his head ached like fury. Connor felt no compunction when the dog let out a woof of argument.

By the time he'd turned on the water, lit the water heater, got the furnace up to seventy and shed his clothes, the place was warm enough to take a shower. Only after he emerged from it did he realize his suitcase was still in the car.

Whatever humor Connor had begun the morning with had long since dissipated. No way was he putting those filthy garments back on. Instead, he dug through his uncles' belongings, scrounged up a pair of pants six inches too large around the middle and six inches too short on the legs, a flannel shirt with seven different buttons and a pair of wooly socks that did nothing for fashion but kept his feet and ankles warm.

Two pairs of rubber boots sat at the back door. Resigned to wearing the odious footwear, Connor slipped on one of them, squinching his toes to fit. Then he went to find the dog.

Tobias was gone, the leash dangling on the ground.

"I should have known," Connor grunted, trudging back toward the house. "If it weren't for bad luck—"

A rumble overhead warned him the day wasn't going to get better anytime soon. He hauled himself inside as the heavens unleashed a mixture of snow, rain and sleet, and caught a glimpse of his reflection in the hall mirror.

"Dogs know how to take shelter," he told it. "Animals have a sixth sense about self-preservation."

Animals that have resided inside posh New York apartments for their entire lives? A picture of Cecile's face—chiding, sad—wavered through his mind.

Guilt was a terrible thing. And right now it had a choke hold on him.

Connor sighed, pulled on a yellow slicker, dragged the hood over his head and squeezed his feet into the other pair of boots. They were no bigger. His toes ached painfully.

Grimacing, he headed outside to hunt for the dog.

Cecile had died saving Tobias. After their conversation that day he was probably the last person she'd have chosen to take care of her beloved pet, but there wasn't anyone else. The least he could do was make sure her dog got a bath and some dinner.

Chapter Two

Rowena's fingers moved nimbly over the twigs she'd received from Oren Yelland's personal nursery. With any luck she'd get the cuttings finished and into the rooting compound tonight. Ash, elm, poplar. She counted mentally, nodded. Three thousand so far.

It was a start.

A noise outside made her pause.

Not that there hadn't been noises before. Every night she was out here she heard something. So different from living in the city. She'd forgotten that. If the rain ever stopped she'd take a walk, see what else was sharing her land.

A soft "woof" made her smile.

"Hello, Tobias." She opened the door, let him inside. "My goodness, you're soaked." She stepped back as he shook himself off, then bent to rub his ears. "Does your master know where you are?"

He gave her a soulful look then flopped down in front of the heater she'd turned up just enough to take off the chill. The cuttings wouldn't be in here long enough to notice.

"Make yourself at home." She chuckled. "Are you hungry?"

His ears lifted as if he understood that word. Rowena tugged the lunch bag from her coat pocket, took out the half sandwich that was left and tossed it to him. It disappeared in a millisecond.

"Wow! You're starved. Either that or you're not very polite." She held up her hands to show they were empty. "Sorry, chum, but that's all I've got."

Rowena turned back to her work, musing about the dog's owner. Connor Wingate had been stressed today. She'd noted the weary lines beside his eyes, the tired droop he'd tried so hard to hide. It couldn't have been easy to put his own life on hold and move up here to take over while his uncles recovered from their accident. From all reports the brothers were healing nicely but it would be a while before either would be able to manage on their own, let alone run Wingate Manor.

Another noise. More like a loud thump this time. Then she thought she heard a voice. Somebody was out there.

Rowena set down her knife and moved to the door. She glanced at the dog. His head was up, his ears perked. A low growl rumbled from his throat.

"Quiet now, Tobias," she murmured. She dragged on her coat, pulled up the hood, switched off the lights then yanked open the door.

The night was dark. She'd deliberately left the yard light off to save on power. But a ripple of lightning illuminated two figures racing away from her. A moment later they disappeared behind the greenhouse structure which the Wingates had erected years earlier.

Rowena walked to the end of the planting shed, aware that the dog padded along beside her. But though she watched in the pouring rain for several minutes, she saw no one else.

"Probably teenagers sneaking back from Lookout Point," she mused. Turned back toward the shed, she stopped.

"You'd better go home, Tobias. Your master is probably wondering where you are."

The brown tail swished happily back and forth at the words but the dog never moved.

"Go home, Tobias." She ignored him, slopping over the grass.

At the door Rowena paused, peeked over one shoulder. He'd followed her. She stepped inside, closed the door and went back to work. But her conscience made her check outside the door five minutes later. He was still there, sitting, waiting.

"Oh, all right," she mumbled. "Come on in and get dry. But when I leave you have to go home. Got it?"

A funny squawk of sound emerged from the dog. Apparently he'd accepted her terms. He flopped down in front of the heater and closed his eyes. Rowena picked up her knife and resumed cutting. It was rather nice having company, even if it was just a dog.

By the time she'd finished, her stomach was complaining bitterly. That half a sandwich would have come in handy about now. She carried the bundles into the adjoining room, thrust the fragile stalks into the rooting compound.

A rap on the door scared the wits out of her.

Tobias, on the other hand, didn't seem too bothered. He was on his feet, but he didn't bark or growl.

"I sense that being a watchdog is not your forte," she scolded as she opened the door.

Connor Wingate glanced over her shoulder, shoved down his hood and stepped inside. "I might have known."

"Pardon?"

"That animal is in here safe and warm while I've been slogging through acres of mud, worried that he was hurt." He looked as if that was her fault.

"He showed up here a while ago. I tried to send him home but he wouldn't go."

"I'm sure he wouldn't." He glanced around. "Oh!" His eyes glowed like topaz.

"Oh?" What on earth was wrong with him?

"I've just put two and two together. Davis Nurseries. You're Davis Nurseries."

Rowena motioned him inside, closing the door to shut out the cool air.

"Actually that was my father."

"And now it's you."

She grinned. "Yes, I guess it is. For now."

"What are you doing here?"

"Cuttings." She showed him. "Most of the trees on the property are too large or too old to sell as nursery stock so I have to start new ones. These will root and I'll plant them this summer. By next year I'll have some to ship out."

"It's a long time to wait for a return on your investment."

She nodded, surprised by his knowledge.

"Yes. But I have to start somewhere. Besides, I'll have a few other sources of income this year. I've got bedding plants going in the greenhouse. I'll use some for Wingate, sell the rest. I've also got a contract to do some baskets and stuff for the town, so that will help."

He didn't look impressed. Why would he? Compared to him she was small potatoes. According to Henry's call yesterday his great-nephew was a stockbroker who'd just sold his brokerage. For a mint. Rowena knew that was true. She'd checked the Internet at the library.

She studied Connor, wondering what it was like to be able to buy anything you wanted, anytime you wanted.

"Do you have employees, Miss Davis?"

It was the one hole in her plan and Rowena knew it. There

was no way she could tackle Wingate without help—and that would cost money. Though she'd prayed and prayed about it, she hadn't yet found an answer.

"I'm planning to begin hiring tomorrow," she told him. "Why?"

He shrugged.

"If they weren't your employees, I suppose there's nothing you can do about it," he muttered. "I just assumed that since I followed them here they—"

"Wait a minute." Rowena blinked at the memory of two figures, backlit by a shaft of light. "You followed someone onto this property? From Wingate?"

He nodded. "The northern edge. Wingate has a high spot that sits above the rest of the property. I thought if I could get a look from there I'd find that st…Tobias," he corrected with a sideways glance at the dog. "Two people were leaving that area. That animal seems to like people so I thought maybe he'd be with them."

"Where did you follow them to?" she asked quietly, bothered by the notion of someone sneaking around her property. Well, almost hers.

"I don't know." He looked embarrassed. "They were way ahead of me. I caught a glimpse of them near the greenhouse. Then they were gone. I came here because I saw your light."

"I see."

"You look upset." He raked a hand through his precisely cut dark hair, rumpling it so he looked less forbidding. "Is anything wrong?"

As if he cared. But then she stared into those golden eyes, and Rowena sensed his concern. It was reassuring.

"I don't know. There's an old mine shaft at the back of my property. I haven't been to check on it since I've come back, but tomorrow I'll make sure it's boarded up. I don't want anyone getting hurt." She shrugged. "Or it could have been trespassers. Years ago we used to get transients that stole food from our garden."

"But there isn't any garden to steal from now."

"True." She held his gaze.

Rowena hated being short. People towered over her and they often assumed her size made her incapable of doing her job. Connor Wingate's height was different somehow. She guessed he was about six foot one but instead of feeling puny his height made her feel a sense of daintiness she'd always wished she possessed and knew was about as far from her style as possible. Landscapers were not dainty.

Stop daydreaming, Rowena.

"So what are they doing here?"

"I don't know." She closed the door of the rooting room, locked it. "I'll take a look around in the morning when the rain stops."

"Don't you mean *if* the rain stops?"

Rowena caught her breath at the transformation a grin made to his face. His forehead smoothed out, his deep-set eyes twinkled, his Roman nose seemed less haughty and the belligerent chin pulled back as his lips parted, showing strong white teeth.

He looked like a hero from an action movie.

He looked like he was in pain.

"Do you have a chair I can use?"

"Excuse me?"

"A chair," he repeated patiently. "I need to take off these boots. They're killing me."

Rowena remembered the way he'd hobbled into the room.

"A stool." She drew it out from under the counter. "Will that help?"

"Anything. Ooh," he groaned, closing his eyes and

sighing with relief as he massaged toes clad in the most bilious purple socks Rowena had ever seen. He glanced at her, reading her expression. "I borrowed some of my uncles' things. We're not exactly the same size," he muttered defensively.

"Yes, I can see that."

She tried to swallow her laughter, but when he opened his slicker so he could more easily free his other foot, she gave up.

"Stop laughing at me. It's the dog's fault."

"*He* picked the shirt?"

"Funny girl." He made a face. "Actually it's Uncle Hank's. I gave it to him for Christmas one year. I was ten, I think." He stood, rested his feet flat on the cement floor. "Oh, the relief. I thought they were broken."

His pants dangled just below his knees showing a smidgen of hairy leg before the purple wool took over. Rowena lifted a hand to her mouth.

"Oh, go ahead. Make fun of me. At least I'm warm and dry. Or I was." He shifted the hood away from his neck, grimacing at the water that trickled down his cheek. "If I can just get home in these things without maiming myself I'll be ecstatic."

"Actually, I'm usually the one plastered in mud or fertilizer. I'm sure you had a good laugh at me earlier today."

"I wasn't laughing."

"Oh." An awkward silence fell between them. Rowena glanced around, scrounging through her brain for something to talk about.

"I didn't know landscape designers got dirty."

"This one does."

"Good for you." After a moment Connor grabbed a boot and began trying to squeeze his foot back into it. Rowena had an idea.

"Wait a minute." She tugged open a cupboard on the wall, pulled out the old boots that had sat there for so many years. "These were my dad's. Maybe they'll fit better. He's tall like you."

"I guess you didn't inherit his genes," Connor murmured. He accepted the boots, thrust one foot inside. "Wonderful," he pronounced with a broad grin. "I promise I'll return them tomorrow."

"Don't bother. My dad won't be coming down for a while. There's no rush."

"He's going to be helping you?"

"I hope so." But she didn't want to talk about her father, so Rowena took her raincoat from the peg on the wall and thrust her arms inside. "I'll give you a ride home. No reason you should get any wetter."

Conner rose, too, and shook his head.

"It's all right. There's no point in dirtying your vehicle."

"It'll clean. And I want to check the mailbox, anyway." She waited until Tobias followed Connor out the door, then locked it. She pulled open the door of her truck. "Get in, Tobias. Sit."

He sat very politely until Connor got in beside him. Then he laid a paw on the too-short pant leg.

"Get down!"

Rowena closed the door, walked around to the other side and climbed in. She started the motor, turned on the fan. Man and beast were still vying for supremacy.

"Is Tobias a purebred?" she asked.

"I don't know. He belongs—belonged to my fiancée."

The one who'd died. She'd read about that, too.

"Why are you asking?"

"I had a friend who had a chocolate lab like Tobias, only she was a cross between a lab and a springer spaniel. The way Tobias jumps and bounces reminds me of Corilla."

"That's a dog's name?" His disgust was obvious. "I thought Tobias was bad."

"Corilla Barker Dog."

"Aren't you going to tell me the meaning of Corilla?" His eyes glinted golden with barely suppressed humor.

"Don't ask." She laughed at his expression. "Anyway, the only thing that worked with Corilla was to lay your hand on her head. She rode perfectly fine as long as she felt that hand on her head. Try it."

Connor sighed then lifted his hand and set it on the dog's head. Immediately Tobias put his paw on the floor and sat perfectly still. Connor lifted his hand; the paw went back up.

"Amazing." He grinned at her.

When he let go of his stuffiness, Connor Wingate would be fun to know. Not that she was likely to be around to watch. Rowena got the sense that once he'd done his duty to his great uncles, Connor would hightail it out of town faster than a rabbit chased by a fox. She didn't blame him.

She shifted gears, pressed the accelerator and eased her way out of the mud toward the paved road.

"Look! Over there. By the cliff."

She followed his pointing finger, saw a flicker of light through the trees.

"Is it a campfire?"

"Looks like it." She turned onto the main road and headed toward Wingate.

"What are you going to do about it?"

"I'll call Bud Neely tomorrow. Ask him to come out and take a look around. If somebody's camped there, he'll suss them out. He's the chief of police around here."

"Good."

Rowena dropped Connor and the dog at the door of Wingate, then headed for the big bank of mailboxes at the top of Hill Road. Nothing but fliers, certainly no responses to her ad for landscape assistants.

Sighing, she climbed back in the truck and drove up the hill toward home. Home. It was a funny feeling after all those years of living in tiny apartments in Toronto. Here there was so much space, so much silence. And yet there was noise; it was just different. The whisper of the wind through the giant spruce pushed out the cobwebs and freed the mind for reflection.

She reflected on her new neighbor and how his presence would impact her life for the next few weeks. Connor Wingate was rich, handsome and no doubt grieving. But he in no way resembled the shattered shell of a man who'd lost the most precious person in his life. Of course he wouldn't wear his heart on his sleeve, but still—something was off.

Rowena pulled up in front of the house, telling herself to forget about him. The most pressing problem in her life wasn't Connor Wingate's broken heart, it was how in the world she could possibly accomplish all that needed doing at Wingate Manor without a crew.

And what her father would say when she told him she'd done this so he could get back on the land he'd once loved.

"Please heal him," she prayed, staring at the black outlines of the buildings that made up Davis Nurseries. "Please make him well."

She waited for something, anything. But God was silent on the subject.

All she could do was keep going. It was too late to back out now.

Chapter Three

〜

"April showers may bring May flowers, but this is only March and we're drowning. Lord, can't You put an end to this rain?"

The downpour splashed even harder against her yellow slicker as if to chide her for her complaint.

With a sigh of acceptance that she'd be soaked in less than an hour, Rowena set her chain saw inside the truck bed, added a handsaw, a couple of shovels and some rope. A movement to the left caught her eye. Somebody was here and they hadn't arrived in a vehicle. She froze, waited for the husky figure in jeans and a thick rain jacket to approach her.

"Are you the woman who's been looking for help?"

"Yes. You have experience in landscaping?"

"Some." He glanced around. "Place needs a lot of work."

Her bristles went up. "And it'll get it. But this isn't the job I'm worried about. Can you tell me about your experience? And your name. I'm Rowena Davis, by the way."

"Kent Ardell. Pleased to meet you." He shook her hand, his grip strong, powerful. "Ever hear of Ardell and Son?"

"Sorry. I haven't been around the Bay for a long time."

"Our place was farther west." He named a small town

about three hours west of Serenity Bay. "My son and I started it up about five years ago. He got into some financial trouble and we lost our business. I've been doing odd jobs ever since. Felled trees for the forestry service. Worked for the federal parks department for a while. Did a couple of jobs in Toronto, too. I saw some of your work. You're good."

"Thank you." Rowena described the basics of what Wingate needed. "Is that going to be too heavy for you?" she asked.

"Meaning am I too old?" A slanted grin tilted his mouth. "I'm fifty-eight. Not quite in the grave."

Two years younger than her father. "I'm sorry. That was rude. It's just that—"

"Don't apologize. You're about the age of my son and I'm quite sure he'd have asked the same thing if some fellow had waltzed into his yard the way I just did yours."

"You don't have a vehicle?"

"Broke down halfway up the hill."

"I see." It took only a couple of minutes for her to think it over. "Why don't we go to the site and you can show me what you can do? Maybe you'll change your mind when you see the place."

"Not likely. I like the challenge of making a difference."

Exactly her sentiment. "I can't pay you city rates."

"It's fine."

This was better than she'd expected. "Okay. Hop in. I was just about to leave."

They rattled toward Wingate with Kent sitting silently in the cab. That was all right with Rowena. She preferred to get her thoughts organized. They passed his truck on the way down. The lettering on the side backed his story. She turned through the gates of Wingate, slowing down, waiting for his assessment.

"Wow! Somebody did a number on this place." Kent

surveyed the grounds and whistled. He climbed out of the truck, waved one hand. "You'll want to start in the east and work your way down, I'm guessing."

"Yes. We'll take out as little as we have to, but make sure every tree that stays is healthy."

"You got any other help?" he asked, one eyebrow raised.

"Not yet."

"Then I'd best get to limbing. One person can do a lot of that without help. Specially on those evergreens." He pulled on a helmet from the box in her truck bed, checked the gas tank on the power saw. "Are you looking to hire more people?"

"Eventually." She frowned. "Why do you ask?"

"My kid's out of work and he's got a baby on the way. He's a big, tough guy who could give you a good day's work, if you want."

A solid month of praying and advertising had turned up no one with the skills and experience she needed. Maybe this was God answering her prayer.

"Give him a call," she said, handing him her cell phone. "I don't know about accommodations around here, but—"

"I rented an apartment in town, above the florist's shop. It's got two bedrooms. Quint can bunk in with me. The owner, Mrs. Michaels, is really sweet. She even packs a lunch for me."

"I don't mean to pry, but what about your own home?"

"My wife died." His voice dropped but he cleared his throat, continuing, "When the business went bust, all I had left was the land. I turned that over to Quint and his wife. Now I go where the work is."

"I see." She waited while he talked to Quint, who promised to be there after lunch. Maybe the deadline she'd agreed to wasn't quite as impossible as it seemed. She hoped. "You ready to start?"

"Just tell me where."

She did, then used her phone to contact a disposal company who would bring a Dumpster to the site. That arranged, Rowena put on her hard hat and ear protection, grabbed the second power saw and began work.

They stopped for lunch at noon, sitting on the tailgate as they basked in the few rays of sun peeking from behind dark clouds.

"Got a few more minutes?" Connor Wingate appeared, holding out two steaming mugs of coffee. "I thought this might warm you up. Looked like you were going at it pretty hard."

How long had he been watching them?

"Connor, this is Kent Ardell. Kent, meet Connor Wingate. He's holding down the fort until his uncles are back."

"Pleased to meet you." Kent shook his hand. "This is a beautiful place. Or it will be. I've seen Rowena's plans. You're lucky to have such a good designer take this on."

"Oh?" His gaze switched to her.

"You don't know her work?" Kent studied him. "Have you been to Toronto lately?"

"Not that I can remember. I drove straight up here from New York."

"You should go back midsummer." He listed three public gardens Rowena had worked on. "She's got real talent."

Then what's she doing here, in the middle of nowhere? Rowena could almost hear the question, though Connor was too polite to ask it.

Just as well. Because she was not going to explain.

"Those clouds are rolling in fast. Guess we'd better get back to work."

"I see they brought the Dumpster," Connor said. "Do you mind if I help you haul the brush to it?"

Rowena almost dropped her saw. "Why?"

He shrugged. "I'm sick of being cooped up inside. I need a break and some exercise. You can use the help, I'm guessing."

She opened her mouth to respond but a half ton pulled onto the grounds near hers. A tall man, younger than Kent but with all his features, climbed out, grabbed a pair of gloves and a climbing harness, then began walking toward them.

"This is my son, Quint," Kent said, introducing them.

"Pleased to meet you, Quint."

"We're just getting back to work. You had lunch?" Kent asked him.

"On the way. I'm used to climbing if you want me to start on the tops of some of those," Quint offered.

"He's like a monkey up there," Kent assured her.

Rowena checked his equipment, nodded. "It would be great to get them down before the wind does any more damage," she agreed. "There are ladders in my truck. Kent, you'll man the safety lines?"

"Sure. Thanks for the coffee, Connor."

"You're welcome."

Father and son walked across the grass, teasing each other good-naturedly. A few moments later the whine of the power saw sliced through the valley and branches began to drift to the ground.

"I might as well start hauling," Connor said, turning away.

"Wait." Rowena frowned. He certainly looked strong enough but she was used to working with an experienced crew. Then there was the whole liability issue. She tried to explain that.

"Look. I'm not going to sue you or my uncles," Connor assured her. "It's my own fault if something happens. Anyway, the trees they're working on aren't near the brush I'll be moving."

"They could be. If the wind picks up—"

"I'll be careful, Mom. Okay?" The grin did her in.

"All right. But you have to wear a hard hat."

He made a face, but donned the hat. "Satisfied?" He looked like a model for designer jeans.

Swallowing, Rowena handed him a pair of gloves. He pulled them on, and sauntered over to the pile she and Kent had assembled. Watching him work was a temptation she couldn't afford, so Rowena concentrated on cutting brush and smaller trees. After a while her arms began to ache so fiercely she had to stop. She quickly joined him picking up the debris.

"It's going to take more than one of these Dumpsters to get rid of this mess," Connor muttered.

"Yes. Some of it we'll cut for firewood for Wingate's fireplaces, if you like. But the elms show signs of disease and I don't want to burn it and risk spreading. I've got some new elm plantings in the nursery that I don't want infected. Most of the boughs will have to go, though."

Connor pitched in happily enough until Chief Bud Neely pulled in.

"Hey, Rowena. Haven't seen you around town much since you moved back."

"I've been kept busy." She waved a hand. "You can see why. This is Connor Wingate, by the way. Great-nephew to the Wingate brothers."

"Pleased to meet you." Connor studied the man.

"These grounds are a mess." Bud whistled at the amount they'd already removed. "Big job to clean this up. I came out here a couple of times after Hank and Henry got in that accident. Heard they're doing better. Too bad I can't say the same about this place. Winter was hard on it."

"Not just winter." She pointed to the chopped trees. "Vandals did that." She turned to Connor. "You didn't notice anything wrong inside, did you? I could look around but I wouldn't be much help. I barely glanced around last fall."

"Everything seems fine." He frowned. "Is there any way to catch whoever did the damage?"

"Likely long gone but I'll keep an eye out for transients." Bud turned to Rowena. "Checked out the mine. You were right. Someone was poking around. Best to get it closed up again."

"I'll do that tonight," she promised, inwardly groaning at her expanding to-do list. "Thanks for checking."

"That's why they pay me the big bucks." His eyes narrowed. "Don't you go getting a soft heart if they're kids trespassing, Rowena. Any problems and you call me immediately," he ordered.

Bud Neely might look like a hick but he had a steel-trap mind and an eye for detail.

"Yes, sir." Rowena stood to attention and saluted.

"Don't give me any of that back talk, girl. I was here when you and those two chums of yours were terrorizing the tourists' kids with your smuggling stories. I know your history."

"Forgive and forget, Bud. That's what the Bible says." Rowena stood on tiptoe and kissed his cheek. "Thanks for looking after us, you old softie."

"Hey. Don't be doing that in public!" He scrubbed his cheek but his eyes sparkled. "Folks on the Bay gotta watch out for each other. That's just part of living here. Say, how's your dad? Is he up here with you?"

"Not yet. I'm hoping I can bring him a little later on, once I've got Wingate on track." If he isn't too depressed, she didn't add.

"You let me know. I've missed him. Nobody else around here can play a decent game of chess. Victor used to give me a run for my money."

"Dad hasn't played in a long time, Bud," she warned. "He hasn't been well."

"Best thing is to get him up here in the fresh air, then. Anyway, playing chess is like riding a bike—the mind never forgets."

Rowena glanced at her watch and waved. "Gotta get back to work. Thanks, Bud."

"You're welcome."

While Connor continued to talk to the sheriff, she hauled brush. A short while later Bud left. Connor looked mad about something.

Because her arms were sore again, Rowena changed jobs, sliding down the wet slope to take a quick look at the first flower bed.

"What do you think? Are you going to meet the deadline?" Connor stood beside her, watching.

"No problem." Rowena quickly schooled her face to hide her doubts that being finished by June 1 was possible.

"What are you doing now?"

"Checking out this soil," she explained, scooping out a handful to get a better look. She leaned against the brick supporting wall to balance herself and dipped her hand into the soil again. The wall shifted.

"Uh-oh." She moved from one terrace to the next, checking for stability. In each terrace, mud oozed through gaps in the corners where the mortar had broken down, in some cases given way completely.

Wingate needed a stonemason before it needed a landscaper and that would cost time and money—neither of which had been calculated into the original project.

"'Uh-oh' means something bad, guessing by your face."

"I need to show you something. Can you handle some mud?"

He favored her with a mocking look, glancing at his filthy

jeans. "I'll try not to fuss too much," he promised as he stepped down, holding out a hand to help her.

Rowena accepted his hand but let go as quickly as she could, her fingers feeling scorched by the contact.

"See here?" She pointed out the defects, forcing her breath to modulate. What was wrong with her? "The mortar isn't holding. The saturated ground is straining the wall. It's oozing out here."

He hunched down beside her, slid his fingers into the gaps she indicated. "Can't you patch it?"

"It's been patched too many times. It needs to be rebuilt."

"Or what?"

"Or it will slide down into the next one. It's unstable. The walls will collapse as soon as I try to work on it." She noticed his eyes were a kind of liquid gold. That made her knees rubbery. She needed space, oxygen—something.

"What's your solution?"

Solution to what? Oh, yeah…

"You'll have to hire a stonemason to install some new bricks." Maybe she shouldn't have had that coffee. Her nerves were way out of control.

"You said *I'll* have to hire. But this is *your* project, Miss Davis."

"I don't do stonework. That was never part of the agreement." She cleared her throat. "I did ask your uncles about the condition of the terraces when I agreed to take on the work. They assured me the masonry was solid. It looked okay under drier conditions. It's not now."

"I see." His face tightened; his eyes grew stormy. "How much?"

"I told you, I don't do masonry. If I had to guess—" She thought for a moment, then offered a figure. Connor's eyes widened. He opened his mouth to protest but Rowena kept talking. "A man in town does excellent work. Whether he'd be able to fit Wingate in is another question. He's always booked fairly heavily."

Connor Wingate glared at her.

"There is no way I'm prepared to authorize such a huge expenditure. You'll have to come up with something else."

"I'm not deliberately trying to cause problems, you know. And there's no other way. Unless you want me to remove the terraces completely?"

He frowned. "But then everything would eventually slip downhill, wouldn't it?"

"As it's doing now, yes." She pulled out a diagram she'd drawn yesterday. "This is Wingate now. This is what I propose." Using her pencil she outlined the small changes. Anger had chased away her case of nerves, thank goodness.

"Cost?"

"It wouldn't cost any more to do it at this stage. We could slip in an underground watering system, make your uncles' lives a lot easier in future drier years."

"It sounds great but the uncles are hoping to retire soon. They haven't got the cash on hand to cover something like what you're talking about. You'll have to come up with something else, Miss Davis, or work with what's already here. That's my decision." He turned to leave.

Why didn't he call her by name? And would it hurt him to unbend just a bit?

"I want it on the record that I feel the terraces are unstable, *Mr. Wingate*." Rowena sighed. "As soaked as they are now, they're dangerous. I can't begin really working with them until they dry out, so my timetable is on hold indefinitely. I'll try a couple of ideas on the lower one, see how it reacts. That's all I can promise."

"June 1. That's the deadline." His bossy tone carried

through the rain. "Remember that everything has to be finished by June 1." He strode across the yard, sprayed his boots off beneath the outside faucet, then climbed the steps without so much as a backward glance.

"I suppose I should have bowed or something," she muttered sourly. "Don't want to get above my station." It was times like this that Rowena wished her work permitted her to wear a power suit that carried weight, to force people like Connor to accept her as a professional and not just some crazy woman mucking about in the mud.

Instead she tromped across the sodden grass in her rubber boots to resume work on the trees. She could forget about the terraces for now, anyway, since there was so much pruning to do.

"Maybe you could send a little sun, Lord," she prayed. "Just so I could figure out how in the world I'm supposed to accomplish this."

That she would accomplish it was beyond question. Completing this job was the only way she had to get the nursery back and she was going to get her father back on that land if it was the last thing she did.

Her two workers had taken a break with a drink in the cab of her truck. She waved them forward.

"Okay, guys. Let's get back to work."

She'd been at it for a week and a half, sawing, cutting, mulching. And all of it done in a steady rain or drizzle. Her crew was good, he'd seen that for himself. But even two skilled men and one tiny woman couldn't make an Eden out of that mess, even though Rowena Davis was a powerhouse.

Connor had come to think of her by her first name in spite of his desire to remain aloof until he got the job done and could leave this place and get on with his future. Whatever that was.

He wasn't here to make friends. He was here to get Wingate Manor up and running, to see it successfully through another season and then hand it over to his uncles, preferably with a tidy profit.

Connor was used to managing. His first job had been supervising a portfolio no one else wanted. His success had led to one management position, then another. Eventually he'd worked his way into his own company and a very hefty client base. His reputation for getting the job done was what Cecile claimed she'd loved most.

Connor deliberately pushed thoughts of her away. The past was finished. He'd assumed he'd be halfway around the world trying to forget his mistake. Instead he was sitting here in Serenity Bay, watching a woman and two men manhandle trees twice their size.

What would he do when his great-uncles came back, when it was time to leave the Bay?

He'd sold the New York condo Cecile chose as quickly as possible after her death. Even his car was new. The only thing that remained from the past was Tobias. Sooner or later he'd find him a good home, too.

Then Connor would start fresh. Somewhere else.

Suddenly aware that the dog hadn't stopped barking for several moments, Connor pushed back a curtain and gritted his teeth. Escaped again. He hoped Tobias hadn't caused worse problems than covering everyone in mud.

Connor strode through the house, shrugged into his slicker and slid his feet into the boots he hadn't yet returned because he hadn't wanted to go into town to buy replacements, preferring not to face the curious stares. He stepped onto the porch, noticed the dog was above him, shielded by the house.

Once he was around the corner Connor saw an orange earthmover perched at the top of the hill. Suddenly he heard a sucking noise. He twisted his head, gasping as a huge pine toppled over. The sopping earth around it immediately pooled into a slick mass that oozed down onto the first terrace. He could see immediately that it was too much for the weakened walls. Before his eyes, the stones loosened, the wall crumbled and the seeping black tide slithered down onto the next terrace, gathering momentum as it broke through that and moved faster downhill.

Someone gave a shout. Connor scanned the area, saw Kent yell at his son, point. He turned to look, watching as the mud slipped over the slick grass to the bottom terrace. Rowena was bent over, hitting a mallet against the rocks around her, earplugs making her totally unaware of the danger above.

"Rowena!" The wind grabbed his warning, tossed it away.

Connor took off, racing downhill as fast as he dared. At the last moment she looked up. Terror filled her eyes as a huge pillow of mud bulged over the edge, capturing her before she could escape. Then she was gone, drowned by the black flood.

She would smother if she didn't get out of there fast!

Connor slid over the edge, reached into the muck, feeling for something, anything, as he prayed.

"Not another death, God. Please, not again."

Back and forth he slid his arms through the mess, grasped an object, pulled it out. A clump of sodden grass. He kept working, heard the pounding footsteps of the other two men.

"Don't jump in," Connor warned. "You could step on her. Stay at the edge and reach in. Pull on anything you find."

Seconds drummed past, his heartbeat thudding in his ear as he searched. Finally his fingers found purchase on a bit of fabric. Connor pulled, but it would not come free.

"One of you, come on this side. Reach here. Now pull." After several tugs, part of her sleeve emerged. "Kent, we'll pull. You scoop it away from her."

They worked feverishly as the words circled round and round Connor's brain.

A few dollars could have prevented this.

If she dies it's my fault.

"No one else dies," he muttered. "Do you hear me, God?"

Finally Rowena's head emerged, covered in mud, her face barely visible. Connor smeared his hands across her cheeks, scooping the mud away from her mouth and nose.

"Get a pail of water, quickly," he ordered.

Quint raced away.

"Is she breathing?" Kent asked.

"I don't know." Using his sleeve, Connor wiped her face clean and pulled on her chin to open her mouth. "Come on, take a breath," he coaxed.

Suddenly they were both doused in icy-cold water. Rowena gasped, opened her eyes. She spit out some mud, then raised her head to glare at Quint.

"I'm not wet enough?" she complained.

"Wet and very dirty," Connor agreed, amazed and utterly relieved by the anger widening her hazel eyes. "We all are. Let's take a break." He boosted her up to Kent, who pulled her the rest of the way out, then slogged out of the muck himself.

Tobias remained some distance away. He'd stopped barking and was now sniffing around the fallen tree.

"We'll rinse off under the tap, then go inside and take hot showers," he told them. "Rowena first."

"I'm too dirty to go inside Wingate," she argued. "I'll go home."

"Forget it. Just do as I say."

"Do you always have to give the orders?" she demanded before ducking her head under the tap.

"Yes." He helped her peel off her coat, took her boots and rinsed them out, sprayed the major portion of soil off her shirt and pants. "Go inside. First floor. Third door to the left. Get in the shower."

"Yes, master." Tossing him a glare that promised later discussion, she complied, shudders racking her body.

"You two next. Come on." Once they'd shed the worst of the mud he showed them the public washrooms at the back of the house. "My uncles had them installed for the cast of the summer stock group that performs. They're on a separate system from the house," he explained. "You won't interfere with Rowena's shower. Take as long as you like. There are towels in the long metal cupboard and some clothes in a box by the door. I was going to give them away."

The two men nodded, removed their filthy boots and moved inside. Connor cleaned himself off. Tobias raced up to him, barking once.

"Yes, I know you sounded the alert. Good boy. You'll get a treat tonight." He reached out to touched the dog's head, saw his own hand tremble and knew exactly why.

She'd come so close to tragedy.

If Rowena Davis had died, he would have been guilty of causing a second death. And for what—a few dollars? He had plenty of those, more than he would ever spend.

So why had he been so cheap? Sure, he wanted to protect the uncles, but underneath there was another motive, one he hadn't wanted to face.

The truth was he needed a barrier between them, a clear line of employer, employee. Why?

Because Rowena Davis was a woman, a very attractive woman whom he'd like to know better.

"Never again," he vowed, an image of Cecile's sad face filling his mind. This time he'd keep his mind on business and not let himself be swayed by feelings he misread. One mistake was more than enough.

Chapter Four

❦

"What's with you?" Rowena pushed her freshly shampooed hair off her face, glaring at Connor. "There's no one to blame here. I told you before that several trees were unstable. Today one fell before we could get to it. That's all."

"If you'd gotten to it any later you might have been killed today," he shot back, his face brimming with anger. "It pushed a pile of the mud onto the terrace. That's what started the whole slide."

"It doesn't really matter now, does it?" She fixed him with a stare that had quelled lesser men. It didn't have much effect on him.

"It matters." Connor turned an accusatory glower on the two men, homed in on Kent. "How long is it going to take to get the rest of those damaged trees down?"

Rowena bit her tongue. She was going to do this job whether Connor Wingate liked it or not. But the way she did it, whether or not she could trust her workers to follow her orders, very much depended on Kent's answer right now.

"You're talking to the wrong person, man." She could have kissed Kent. "Rowena's the boss."

Connor rocked back in his chair, turning his icy glare back on her. "So how long?"

Oh, she longed for those easy jobs in the city where once the client knew the plan, he left you alone to finish it.

"Look, Connor. This isn't an exact science." She cupped the mug of coffee he'd given her and told herself patience was a virtue. "We work as best we can. If we have to stop, adjust the schedule to accommodate a problem, then we do it. But we get the job done. You have to stop pushing so hard."

"I have to push." His face tightened; his hands clenched. "Maybe you should scrap the big fountain idea. That would shave off some time. I mean, you've been at this for almost three weeks and there's hardly anything to show for it."

Quint set his coffee cup down with a thunk, his face dark as a thundercloud about to dump on everyone. "If our clothes are dry, Dad and I should get back to work."

"They're not dry yet so sit down. Everybody just take a deep breath. And you." Rowena turned her attention on Connor. "Listen to what I'm about to say, because I'm not going to repeat it. We are doing this job the way it is supposed to be done. Between the three of us, you've got a lot of experience sitting in this kitchen, and I'm telling you we're making the fastest progress we can, given the circumstances. Maybe it doesn't look like it to you, but you've never gone through this before. Am I right?"

He had the decency to look sheepish. "No."

"I realize you're used to being in control but this time you're just going to have to find someone else to push around while we do our job." Rowena held his gaze.

Tobias sent up a mournful round of howls that rent the tense silence.

"What now?" Connor muttered under his breath. "I'll be back in a minute."

He donned a coat and left. When he returned, he bore a big splotch of mud on one cheek and one knee looked soaked but the howling had stopped.

"He got tied up in a rope."

"Which is why I asked you to keep him penned up. He could get hurt."

"Don't worry. He's back in the pen. I pushed a big stone urn against the place where he'd dug it out." Connor stood in the kitchen under the overhead fixture, his face solemn. The light cast a glow on his hair, illuminating tiny silver droplets that glinted like diamonds.

"As long as he's out of the way. I like dogs. I *don't* like seeing them hurt." She gave him her severest glare.

"I'm sorry I questioned your professionalism," Connor said softly. At least he sounded genuine. "I'm nervous about running this place for the uncles and not running into any hitches. I guess I took it out on you. I apologize. To all of you."

"I think it's the weather. It's getting to all of us." Kent swallowed the last of his coffee. The dryer buzzer broke the awkward silence. He rose. "Our clothes are dry and we've still got work to do. Might as well get back at it. Come on, Quint."

"Do a quick assessment of the worst of them but don't start any more cutting until I'm out there. Got it?" she emphasized when they didn't respond.

"Got it." Kent shared a look with his son, jerked his head toward Rowena. "She's worse than your mother ever was."

Quint burst into laughter, winking at Rowena. "I'll make sure he bundles up and has a clean handkerchief, too. Okay?"

"Very funny. Get back to work," Rowena ordered, hiding her smile. She watched them unload the dryer and return to the basement to change. Then she faced Connor, intent on getting this settled once and for all.

"You look mad. You're going to bawl me out, aren't you?" The corners of his eyes crinkled with his self-mocking smile.

"Yes, I am," she assured him.

"Don't bother. I know I shouldn't have questioned your authority. I won't do it again."

"Uh-huh. Until tomorrow, anyway." How could she stay angry with someone like him? "I'm not kidding about this, Connor. These men work for me. If I went to your staff without talking to you, you wouldn't like it."

"No, I wouldn't. I've already apologized, Rowena."

He'd called her by her first name. Wonder of wonders.

"Yes, you have." That zap of awareness fluttered in her stomach. She ignored it.

"You want me to repeat it?"

"No." She almost smiled at the thought of Connor Wingate apologizing twice for the same misstep—unthinkable!

"Then…"

Rowena settled back in her chair. "What is it about me that's so hard for you to trust? Do I look like a crook or something?"

"Hardly. I'm sure you don't need me to tell you you're a beautiful woman." He leaned his elbows on the counter, watching her.

Beautiful? With mud oozing from every pore of her grimy body? Yeah, right. Gorgeous.

"Now you're being mean."

"Mean?" Confusion darkened his eyes to bronze.

She was so not going to argue about her unbeautiful self.

"Forget it." Rowena rose, stared down at her odd attire. "I think my clothes should be dry by now. I need to get back to work."

He checked her out, a little grin twisting his lips. "That shirt looks better on you than it ever did on my Uncle Henry."

She found his appraisal uncomfortable, and stayed silent.

He chuckled. "As compliments go, I guess that one missed the mark. Let me rephrase."

She shook her head. "Don't bother."

Who wanted to be told she looked better than a sixty-five-year-old balding man with a potbelly? Even if that old gent was a sweetheart? Rowena stepped around Connor, walked to the dryer and lifted out her clothes.

"Mind if I use the bathroom again?"

"Help yourself." Connor remained silent until she was almost out of the kitchen. "Rowena?"

"Yes?" Surprised by his stern tone, she turned, frowned. "Is something wrong?"

"Stay away from the terraces. I'm calling someone in to repair them. Until the work is done, they're off-limits—to all of you."

That rendered her speechless for about ten seconds, long enough for him to leave the room. By then it was too late to say thank you. Connor had disappeared.

"I'm willing to pay whatever it takes." Connor switched the phone to his other ear. "I just want it done as soon as possible. You'll stop by to give an estimate tomorrow? Good. Thanks."

He hung up, paused to study the threesome working outside. Actually, his interest rested primarily on the small woman manhandling brush into some kind of chopper.

How did she do it? She could have died out there this afternoon, yet she picked herself up, cleaned herself up and got on with the job.

Connor knew it would be a long time before the picture of Rowena sucking in that first breath of life was erased from his brain. No way he was going to let anything like that happen again, regardless of the cost. He'd gladly pay to be free of the image of one or both of his uncles one day buried in just such a mess with no one around to help.

"Mr. Wingate?"

Esther Padderson had been his uncles' trusty office assistant for as long as Connor could remember. He couldn't get used to her calling him "Mister."

She stood in the doorway, shorthand tablet in one hand.

"I don't know why you can't call me the same name you've used for years," he complained. "I'm still Connor."

She ignored him. "Yes, Mr. Wingate. Chef Pierre is on the line. He says he's not coming back this year."

Connor jerked upright. "According to his contract, he is. Or else he's going to owe Wingate Manor a lot of money." He translated the look on Esther's face to mean she wasn't going to be the one to tell the temperamental chef what he'd said. "Okay, I'm coming. But while I'm talking to him I'd like you to prepare some advertising copy."

"To replace Pierre, you mean?" She looked scandalized. "But he does this every year."

"Really? And my uncles put up with not knowing whether he'll show or not?" Connor shook his head. "I don't operate like that. Either he's going to be here or we make other plans."

"He won't like it." Esther worried as she followed him to the office.

"Tough. He gets top dollar for his work here, free accommodation, the winters off to spend with his family in France. He's not hurting." Connor accepted the phone, waited till she'd clicked a button on the console. "Hello, Pierre. I understand you're resigning."

Out of the corner of his eye, he watched Esther leave the room, gray head shaking. Connor sat down, tilted back in his chair. He listened for about ten seconds, then cut in.

"You're not sure? Well, I've got an ad waiting to run. I can't wait for you to dither back and forth. I want all my staff in place at the end of April. My uncles are counting on me to have the place in top shape for our first booking and I have no intention of letting them down. So will you be here or do I consider your contractual agreement broken?"

Connor listened, smiled and eventually hung up. One chef hired.

"The meat company is on line two," Esther told him, "complaining about the distance they have to travel to get here. They're talking a major delivery surcharge."

He thought for a moment. "Is there a butcher in town, Esther?"

She blinked. "John Purdy. He and his family own the local grocery store."

"Get me their number, will you, please? And tell the meat people I'll call them back."

"Yes, sir." A glint of humor lit up her round face. "Would you also like the name of a cattle rancher I know who raises his animals organically?"

"Thereby allowing us to advertise that we use only organically raised beef." He followed her line of thought with delight. "Good thinking. Yeah, let's talk to him, too. The uncles' figures from last year will help us estimate how much we'll need. You don't happen to also know a chicken supplier, do you, Esther?"

She shook her head, but her eyes gleamed at the challenge.

"I'll check around, but John might be the best resource for that, too. You wouldn't have to pay shipping fees and he's got tons of freezer space. If he comes across a deal, he could buy ahead."

"Esther, you're a genius!"

Her smile faded. "I wish Henry thought that." She handed him a stack of résumés then padded out of the room.

Connor stared after her. A case of unrequited love for his stodgy old uncle? He shook his head.

"I can fix a lot of things around here, but that isn't one of them," he said to himself.

By the time he emerged from the office it was after five. Rowena and her men were still hard at work, this time on a lower section his uncles called the dale—as in "over hill, over dale." Connor had to admit she'd made amazing progress.

"I'm leaving now." Esther glanced out the window. "They must be tired and half-frozen after the day they've had. It's too bad the old house at the nursery's in such a state. I expect it needs a lot of work after all these years. I'm sure Rowena hasn't got extra money to spend on that."

"Oh?"

"Piper Franklin told me Rowena came back earlier than she'd anticipated because her father isn't well. She thinks it will help if he can get back on the land. He always did love that nursery."

"But he sold it to my uncles."

"Didn't have a choice after a storm nearly wiped him out. I think it almost broke his heart. Hers, too." Esther frowned. "Several of us have invited her for meals just to give her a break. Ida Cranbrook went up there to drop off a pie for the girl. She said the place is practically falling down around her ears. Apparently she can't even use the kitchen, it's so bad. Just a hot plate."

Which meant that she was paying restaurant prices for her meals. That would cut into her nursery's start-up capital.

"Someone ought to do something about that house," Esther said with a dark look in his direction. She snugged her plastic rain bonnet around her permed curls. "It should never have been passed on in that condition. It's a bad reflection on Wingate and I intend to tell Henry so when I see him next. Good night, Mr. Wingate."

Connor didn't even hear her leave. His mind drifted back to his conversation with Pierre and his demand that the freezer be emptied of old stock before his arrival, ready for *zee fresh ingredients.*

There were steaks in that freezer, thick ones that men like those working outside would enjoy—far too many steaks for one great-nephew to consume.

Tobias nudged his nose under Connor's hand, gargling a noise somewhere deep in his throat.

"You want to go for a walk?" Connor translated. The dog woofed his agreement. "You'll get filthy again and I'll have to bathe you again."

Tobias didn't have a problem with that. His tail thumped the floor eagerly.

"Go get your leash, then. I think we're having company for dinner."

"You didn't have to do this," Rowena murmured as she tossed the salad.

"What? Thaw out some meat?" Connor grinned. It changed him from a severe-looking boss to a cohort in this scheme. "Not so hard. But you should know that's all I'm doing because I don't cook. You're totally on your own."

"Not a hardship. It's a dream kitchen," she murmured, glancing at the gleaming stainless steel surrounding them. "A bit intimidating, though."

A burst of laughter from the room across the hall interrupted.

"Sounds like they found a good show to watch."

"It was nice of you to let them. I think it's been a while since they've had much time to just enjoy each other. Kent told me the business they ran together went under. That's hard on a relationship."

"Where are they staying?"

"Above the florist." She shrugged. "It's probably a little cramped but at least they're dry and close to work. Quint told me that when it warms up he wouldn't mind camping out."

"Why?" Connor shuddered. "I camped out once. I remember it vividly."

"Once?" She giggled. "Wow! Mr. Worldly."

He shrugged. "I don't do nature. Numbers are my thing. The stock market's always been my element."

"But you sold your business." Rowena blushed, turning away to study the steaks sizzling on the grill. "Your uncles mentioned it."

"I wish now that I hadn't," he admitted quietly.

"Why?" The potatoes were finished so she switched off the oven. Connor had set places at the kitchen table. Everything was almost ready, and he still hadn't answered.

Too late she remembered his fiancée.

"Oh, I'm sorry. That was too personal."

"No, it's fine. It's just that since Cecile's death, I'm not sure what to do next. I'm in this kind of limbo state. No good for someone like me," he explained with a self-derisive laugh. "I need to be busy."

"I imagine Wingate Manor will take care of that once the season starts."

"I guess. It's the future that I was thinking about."

"Only God knows what comes next for any of us." She smiled to encourage him. "You'll have to talk to Him about it, though I'm not sure He always gives us the whole picture. In my own case all He usually lets me see is into the next day. Sometimes that's enough, don't you think?"

Connor tossed her a veiled look that hid whatever he was thinking. Judging by the downturn of his mouth, they were not happy thoughts.

"Dinner's ready. Will you get the others?"

They made a boisterous group. Father and son teased each other without rancor, setting a light note for the meal. Soon barely a crumb was left, which made Rowena feel good. It had been a long while since she'd cooked, and never in a kitchen as well-appointed as this.

"That was great!" Quint smirked a cheeky grin. "If this landscaping thing doesn't work out for you, Rowena, maybe you could hire on here as a chef."

"I'll take that as a compliment. Thank you."

"What's not to work out?" Kent snorted as he gathered their plates. "She's got degrees in horticulture, has won more than fifteen awards, including some big-name trophy for a rose garden gig she did in England." He turned to glance at Rowena. "Right?"

"The Chelsea Flower Show," she admitted, surprised by his knowledge. "How did you know?"

"My son's the television addict, not me. Serenity Bay has a library and they have a computer linked to the Internet." He shrugged. "I checked you out, wanted to see where else besides Toronto you'd worked."

"Oh." She hid her surprise.

"Dad has a thing for England. My mom was from there. I told my wife we'd spend our twenty-fifth anniversary there. Tell us more about it, Rowena."

"Well, it happens in May when the grounds of the Royal Hospital in Chelsea come alive with the finest collections of flowers in the world." She could close her eyes and smell those heady fragrances even now. Rowena could have so easily stayed in England, continued her work there—if it hadn't been that her father needed her here.

She realized Connor was staring, so she hurried on.

"The show gardens are created by some of the world's leading garden designers."

"Sounds pricey," Connor mumbled.

"Not necessarily." She thought of a daisy garden that had won awards several years earlier and immediately wondered if the idea would work in the roughest terrain here at Wingate. "I came away with memories that still awe me. It's the best place for inspiration."

They sat silent for a moment, then Kent resumed clearing the dishes, assisted by Connor.

"My wife loves flower gardens. Losing the business almost broke her. I hope she gets to see Chelsea one day." Quint's words were so quiet Rowena wasn't sure the others heard.

"I'm sure she will. You seem like a person with a lot of determination."

"So do you. Getting the nursery running—that's a mighty big goal."

"I guess. I'm hoping my dad will move back soon, and be able to help out a little."

Conscious of Connor listening intently to their conversation, Rowena decided to change the subject from her personal life. But Quint wasn't finished.

"The place wasn't kept up very well," he said. "The trees—most of them wouldn't meet retail standards. You're basically starting from scratch."

"I know." There was no point in denying the obvious. Rowena shrugged. "But hard work doesn't scare me."

"Good thing. You're going to have lots of it." He moved to help the others with the dishes.

"You look tired." Connor handed her a cup of coffee, spoke to father and son. "Since we cooked, we're going to watch TV while you guys clean up."

"If you're sure we won't break anything," Kent teased.

"Or take too long," Quint added with a wink at Rowena.

"You do and I'll forget about any more steak dinners."

"Come on, Dad. Work faster."

Connor laughed, leading the way out of the room. Rowena followed. He wanted to talk to her privately—she got that. But about what?

The television lounge looked more like a library. A plasma screen sat above the big marble fireplace but Connor didn't bother to turn it on. Instead he motioned her to one of the red leather wing chairs in front of the fire and sat in the other himself only after pushing the door so it was almost shut.

"I know you don't want to hear this, but I'm really concerned about the time frame of the projects," he said, his face troubled.

"Connor—"

He held up one hand. "Hear me out. You've got the rest of the cutting to do, reworking the grounds, plantings, borders and a whole lot of things I'm sure I don't know about. Putting that fountain on hold until another year only makes sense."

"It doesn't make any sense." Rowena braced herself for the argument. She *had* to do this, had to make this first project in Serenity Bay a showstopper, because it was going to be the showcase for everything that came after.

"That fountain is the grand finale at the bottom of Wingate's gardens. It's the perfect place for a fireworks display on Canada Day or after a big party. In the evening, with the fountain running, it will be a gorgeous backdrop for a wedding ceremony. It's the culmination of all of the rest of our work. And I'm not putting it off until next year."

He studied her for several tense moments, then rose.

"Wait here for a minute." Connor left the room. When he returned he held out a Toronto newspaper. "I'm planning a spread like this for the grand reopening. I've already blocked out coverage and a reporter for the end of May," he told her. "They're sending someone who'll take a ton of pictures, do a write-up and feature the place in their weekend edition. I had to sign a contract. There's no way I can cancel without losing a lot of money. If we're late—"

Rowena took the paper, glanced at it, then set it down. She drew a deep breath. "We're not going to be late, Connor. We're moving along as planned. We'll be in fine shape by the end of May." *I hope.*

"You're sure?" Connor's hard look pierced through her bravado, searching for some indecision.

Rowena refused to show any doubt. "I always make my deadlines," she told him softly.

He heaved a sigh. "You'd better."

"So we have our goal, we have our plan. Now we just need time and no more nasty comments to pull it off." She glanced at Connor. "We've got enough pressure. I don't need you adding to it by constantly reminding us of what has yet to be done. I warn you, when I'm on a deadline I can be very intense. If you don't stop pushing, things are going to get heated between us."

"I'll survive." His dry humor echoed the sloped grin he wore. "Feel free to tell me whenever I'm becoming obsessive."

"I will," Rowena promised. She paused in the doorway, saw that Quint and Kent had left. The kitchen sparkled. "Looks like those two know their way around a kitchen."

"Yeah." But Connor was watching her.

Rowena shifted uncomfortably under that scrutiny, grabbed her ringing cell phone like a lifeline. "Rowena Davis."

"Hey, Row. This is Ash. How are you?"

"I'm fine. Just finished dinner."

"Not at home, because I stopped by ten minutes ago. Where are you?"

"I'm at Wingate. Connor treated Kent and Quint and me to a steak dinner. It was delicious," she added, lifting one eyebrow as she glanced at him.

He bowed from the waist like a well-trained maître d'.

"Oh, good. If he's there with you, you've just saved me a phone call."

"Really?" A wiggle of dread tugged at Rowena. She didn't need Ashley to start matchmaking. "How can I help?"

"Michael and I are making dinner for Piper and Jason tomorrow night. We want you to come. It would be nice if you could bring Connor with you. We'd like to get to know him better."

Rowena stalled, trying to think of a way out.

"Unless of course there's a reason you don't want him to come?" Ashley's voice took on that hint of suspicion that Rowena knew better than to ignore.

"Don't be silly, Ash. If you'll hold on a moment, I'll ask him." She put her hand over the phone. "My friend Ashley and her husband are having some people over for dinner tomorrow night. She'd like to know if you'd be available to join them."

"Tomorrow." He studied her with those intense eyes that didn't miss a thing. "For dinner?"

"Yes. For dinner. It's not a big deal, just them and another couple, I think. Piper and Jason Franklin. I don't know if you've met them."

"No, I haven't. But I've heard about him—he's the mayor, right?"

She nodded.

"Sounds interesting." He nodded. "Sure. I'd be happy to accept. I can drive us both there."

Rowena swallowed her refusal, pulled her hand from the phone and told Ashley, "Connor says he'd like to come. What time?"

She got all the particulars, agreed she wouldn't be late and finally hung up. Connor was frowning. "Is something wrong?"

"No. Just sorting things out." He gazed at her, his forehead pleated in a tiny frown. "You said Masters. Any relation to the florist where your employees are staying?"

"Mrs. Masters is Ashley's mother-in-law," she told him, surprised by the funny smile that suddenly appeared. It made him look far less forbidding. "What?"

"Just thinking about the connections. They say everybody knows everyone else and their history when you live in a small town. I guess it's true."

The odd glint twinkling in his eyes made her nervous. Rowena struggled to maintain her equanimity. "Yes, well, I'd better get on home. I've got some stuff to do tonight."

"You have something going almost every minute of the day, it seems," he mused quietly, an edge to his tone. "Reminds me of someone."

She lifted her freshly washed jacket from the second dryer in Wingate's big laundry room, glad she wouldn't have to go to the town Laundromat tonight.

"Who could I possibly remind you of?" she asked, only half paying attention.

"Me."

That brought her head up. Rowena couldn't read the expression on his face. "Is that a good thing or a bad thing?"

"Definitely bad." His eyes sparked a warning she didn't understand.

Rowena straightened, struggling to understand what he wasn't saying.

"Aren't you the guy Wall Street applauded for never sleeping?" she asked. "A new deal every day?"

Surprise flickered across his face for an instant before he grinned. "The small-town rumor mill?"

She shook her head, chuckling. "Nothing so juicy. The Internet."

"Ah." He nodded. The serious look returned. "Work addicts

don't make for pleasant people, Rowena. Believe me, I know that better than most."

She didn't know how to respond. "If you've got a bag I'll put my coat in it, take yours home with me and wash it. I'll bring it back later, I promise."

"It wouldn't be much of a loss if you didn't," he mumbled but he handed her a plastic bag from a drawer. Rowena stuffed her coat into it, walked to the door. Her filthy boots sat outside, still covered in muck inside and out.

"Can I borrow those rubber boots of Dad's back?" she asked.

"I'll go you one better. These look like a better fit." He handed her a pair that had to belong to one of his uncles. "I'll pick you up at six-thirty tomorrow evening, shall I?"

"I can drive," she told him, refusing to look at his face.

"Yes, but why should you when I'm already driving?"

"Okay. Thanks."

He waited while she pulled on the jacket he'd lent her, gathered up the bag and pulled open the door.

"I won't be around much tomorrow," he said quietly. "Apparently I have to inspect the animals who are to be featured on Wingate's menu."

"Oh." She turned up her nose.

"Exactly my opinion. But it seems the farmer wants to prove I'm getting a very good quality of beef."

"Have fun." She giggled, then pulled open the door.

"Rowena?"

"Yes?" She paused; when he didn't speak she looked at him. All gaiety had leached from his face.

"Stay away from the terraces," he ordered so softly it could have been a whisper.

"I will." Something in his eyes compelled her to add, "Thanks for saving my life."

Before Connor could respond, she scooted down the

stairs and hurried over to her truck, squishing her way through the mud.

In spite of herself, she found herself looking forward to tomorrow evening.

Chapter Five

"**Y**ou look lovely." Connor couldn't stop staring at the gorgeous woman who'd just stepped through the rickety front door.

Tonight Rowena looked like anything but a landscape designer. She wore an exotic skirt in some kind of orange-red-gold pattern that wrapped around her hips and fluttered down to her toes peeking out from flat leather sandals.

Her red top made her hair come alive as it framed her face and accented her big hazel eyes.

"Thank you." She stepped into his car with an easy grace that came not from some past schooling in ballet, but from an ease and lithe comfort with her own body.

He closed the door and got in beside her, grateful that the car's interior gave him a close-up look.

"The seat belt is here." His hand brushed against her skirt as he showed her the catch. "It's a great fabric. Silk?"

"Thai silk. A friend who is a textile designer gave me a few meters when I left Thailand several years ago."

"He's very talented," Connor said, noticing that she didn't correct his assumption that her friend was male. He found himself curious about her past. "Did you spend a lot of time overseas?"

"More than I should have." Her eyes darkened to a deep forest shade. "I went over once on a scholarship and then worked on two fellowships," she admitted quietly.

"Good for you." He was about to ask more when she quickly interrupted him. What didn't she want him to know?

"Is your car new?"

"Yes. When I sold my company, I went a little wild for a couple of days."

"I read that your fiancée died. I'm sorry."

"Thanks." He swallowed, deciding to tell her and forestall the usual questions. "Cecile ran out into the street to save Tobias. His leash had broken and she was afraid he'd be struck by a car. Instead she was."

He saw the shock register with her soft gasp.

"Oh, how terrible. I'm so sorry, Connor."

"Yeah," he muttered, remembering that last look of sad recrimination just before she'd died. "Anyway, I had nothing to hold me in New York. Truthfully, I was sick of it. I wanted to get away. The uncles were still in the hospital after their car accident—it seemed only natural I come here and help them out."

"You know a lot about running a place like Wingate Manor?" she asked, one eyebrow raised.

"Trust me, I'm learning fast," he told her with a twist of his lips. "I don't know all the little details. I have to rely on the staff for a lot of that. But management—yeah, I can do that without any problem."

"Well, good."

She directed him to Ashley and Michael's house. It looked as if it had been there forever, nestled in at the end of a tree-covered lane, its soaring peaks jutting up to the sky.

"It's nothing like you'd expect after coming down that lane."

"They added on after they were married. Ashley never does things halfway. Michael is a wood-carver so there's a big studio at the back. They have a daughter, Tatiana. She's as precocious as they come and as sweet as candy."

Connor undid his seat belt and got out, hurrying around to her side. Rowena emerged gracefully. Her nose tilted up as she lifted her chin to meet his gaze.

"I'll warn you," she said softly. "Piper and Ashley have been my best friends for years. We went to boarding school together, so we're like sisters. Don't be offended if they ask a ton of questions. They think they have to vet everyone I know."

Every *man*, she meant. Uneasiness filled him at the prospect of being grilled. Rowena offered a smile in consolation.

"Don't worry. *Ashley* means 'ash tree meadow' and *Piper* means 'pipe player.' No threat there. If it gets too bad, give me a sign and I'll make an excuse so we can leave. I don't want you to be uncomfortable."

"Thanks." He walked with her to the door.

Rowena Davis kept surprising him. She embraced her two friends eagerly, their husbands, too. Then she introduced him as her boss. "Connor keeps us on schedule," she told them.

"A crack-the-whip kind of guy. Good. We need more of 'em." Michael Masters drew him into the family room.

Connor paused in the act of sitting, focused on a cedar carving of a little girl reaching to catch a butterfly that eluded her.

"That's your daughter," he murmured absently as his brain pulled up a memory of Cecile dragging him to something several years earlier.

"Tati. Yes, it is."

"Michael. Michael Masters." Connor scrounged his memory

for a reason he knew that name. Finally he locked on to it. "I was at a showing of yours in New York." He studied the man, saw a flicker of something wash through his eyes. "You and another artist. The pieces were incredible."

"Mine were very raw."

"'Hidden genius', I think one critic said."

Michael made a face. "I must have missed that one."

"You obviously decided you'd let your genius show. Congratulations."

"Thanks."

Connor glanced at Jason. "And you're the mayor of Serenity Bay."

"With absolutely no creative talent whatsoever," Jason joked. "My life is motors."

"You'd better add me in there, buddy." Piper sat down on the arm of Jason's chair, her fingers interlocking with his. "Don't let him kid you, Connor. He has a big vision for this town. It's something we share."

Jason smiled at her, his adoration obvious. "We sure do."

Piper peered at Connor. "I've been meaning to phone you. The Bay is planning a big publicity campaign for early summer. We'll mail out a tourism book tied to some television advertising. Sound like anything Wingate Manor would be interested in?"

"Absolutely. Send me the details."

"Done."

"Dinner's ready." Ashley introduced herself to him. "Welcome to our home," she said simply then grasped Michael's hand and tugged. "Let's eat while it's hot."

"Ashley's a fantastic cook, Connor." Rowena sat beside him, her face less tense than he'd seen it in days. "You might want to offer her a job once you've sampled what she's prepared."

"I doubt I could equal anything Wingate Manor offers." Ashley smiled, held out her hand to her husband. "Shall we say grace?"

Everyone grasped a hand on either side of them. Connor sensed Rowena's hesitation but he wasn't sure anyone else did. Her fingers curled around his lightly. Her skin felt soft, though he could feel the marks that her work had left on the silken surface.

He kept his head down as Michael offered thanks, then let go of her hand when the others did, though it seemed to him she pulled away a little too quickly.

"So, Connor, what are your interests? Do you like to fish?" Jason asked before tasting his soup.

"I like it," Connor responded. "I'm not very good at it, but I like it."

"What did you do in New York?" Rowena asked, pulling a piece from the roll she'd chosen.

"Racquetball. Sometimes squash."

"Ah, the sport of cutthroats." She grinned. "I thought it might be something connected to power." How had she guessed that?

"We don't have a court here, though in the summer we can use the high school court for tennis," Piper offered.

"You have a lot of other opportunities New York doesn't have," he said quietly. "I imagine snow and waterskiing, sailing, diving—they more than compensate for the lack of a racquetball court."

She smiled at him. "I think so."

"The soup is delicious," he told Ashley. "You can have a job anytime you want."

"Thanks." She smiled. "But the gallery keeps me really busy. You'll have to stop by, see Michael's new collection."

"I'd like to," he told her.

They ate quietly for a few moments. At a nod from his wife,

Michael rose and cleared their bowls, which Ashley replaced with salad. She'd barely set Connor's down when her husband dropped his fork.

"Wait a minute. You said diving. Do you scuba dive?"

"Yes, though I haven't done it in a while. I guess I've let a lot of things slide while I got stuck in the business rut."

"Realizing that is half the battle," Jason said quietly. Connor guessed from the look he and his wife shared that he'd been in the same position once.

"Maybe you can teach Jason and me how to dive." Michael passed out the rest of the dishes, ignoring Ashley's groan. "What? It's good exercise and I've been wanting to check out that old wive's tale about a sunken boat in the bay for years."

"If Connor can't, I could teach you," Rowena offered. "I have my instructor's qualifications."

The entire room fell silent.

Piper blinked at Ashley. "She knows how to scuba dive."

"I heard." Ashley's big gray eyes rested on Rowena. "Just how many more secrets are you keeping, Row?"

"Just enough so you and Pip don't get too cocky."

Her little giggle at their pretended outrage did funny things to Connor's stomach. What was it like to have friends who knew exactly who you were and loved you anyway?

"So you two could teach us four, right?" Michael wasn't about to give up easily.

"Michael, let them eat in peace," his wife ordered.

"I'm an instructor, too," Connor told Rowena.

"Perfect." Michael looked triumphant.

"We'd have to get tanks from somewhere. And wet suits if you intend on going down before the bay warms up."

Rowena didn't sound like she was overjoyed at including him but Connor wasn't surprised. They hadn't exactly been chums up to now.

"Like that's going to happen." Michael snorted. "Serenity Bay never exactly warms up."

"I can probably get all that stuff through my business," Jason offered.

"Where did you learn to scuba?" It was only one of many questions Connor wanted to ask Rowena Davis.

"In Australia. I assisted with some studies about coral on the Great Barrier Reef. Learning to dive was part of the job."

"Tell him about the palace garden." Ashley began carrying steaming serving dishes to the table while Michael removed their salad plates.

"Palace garden? I didn't know Australia had palaces." Connor glanced at her curiously.

"They don't. This was in Bali. Professor Songhi's wife descended from a line of Balinese royalty. He built her a house and wanted to give her a garden suitable for a royal. She was very struck by British royalty so that's where I began."

Bali, Australia, England. This was no backwoods gardener. Rowena Davis was highly trained with a very wide range of experience. If he hadn't quite believed Quint and Kent, here was more proof that she knew her field.

"Roses are very predominant there, aren't they?" Piper asked.

"Yes. Though the Balinese don't treat them quite as we do. The housewives gather flowers for religious ceremonies, which can be as many as nine a year." She glanced around, blushed. "I tend to ramble," she mumbled.

"Tell us about the baths," Ashley ordered, placing a plate with a sizzling filet of perch protected by golden potatoes and glistening carrots in front of her.

Rowena shook her head. "Everyone will be bored."

"It sounds very interesting," Connor said. "I've never been to Bali."

She shrugged. "First, you get a massage with jasmine, almond oil and mint, then you relax in a bath filled with gorgeous exotic flowers. You can't help but relax. Flowers can help the body shed toxins."

"Thank goodness she didn't give us the technical explanation of exactly how that occurs," Piper teased, winking at Rowena. "For that we thank you, Dr. Davis."

"You're a Ph.D.?" Connor asked.

"She has two doctorates. Brains and beauty—that's our Row." Ashley smiled. "When we got up to mischief we always got Rowena to explain. She'd spout some of her scientific jargon from those books she was always reading and sooner or later everybody would stop hassling us."

Rowena shrugged, her attention on her plate. "I'm glad I came in handy for something."

Was there a hint of hurt behind those words? Connor found himself contrasting the three women. Piper was the extrovert, a woman who charged into life full speed. Though all three women were beautiful, Ashley was definitely the glamour queen, her beauty natural and immediately obvious. She was comfortable with herself, appearing open and genuine, but her big gray eyes held shadows from the past that her obviously happy marriage hadn't quite erased.

Rowena was as different from the others as could be. She wasn't quiet but she carried an introspective quality that made her seem more sensitive, more easily hurt. And she was hiding something.

"Is your meal all right, Connor?"

He blinked, glanced around and found everyone's eyes on him. Judging by their almost-empty plates he'd been absent from the conversation a long time.

"It's excellent. Thank you. I'm afraid I got caught up in my thoughts."

"Thinking about Wingate?" Rowena didn't look thrilled by the thought. "I told you we'd be done on time and we will."

"Rowena always keeps her deadlines, Connor," Ashley soothed quietly. "You can stop worrying."

"That's like telling the grass it can stop being green," Rowena muttered, tossing him a dark look.

He opened his mouth to respond, and saw a look flash from Piper to Ashley, who rose and quickly asked, "Anyone interested in chocolate for dessert?"

The tension in the room snapped as Jason and Michael eagerly shot up their hands. Ashley laughed.

"Dumb question. Michael, could you help me bring it in?"

"Jason and I will clear these away." Piper patted his shoulder. "That will give you and Row time to duke it out." She and Jason left bearing dishes.

"I'm sorry." Rowena sighed, met his stare. "I suppose I've ruined everyone's evening now with my crankiness."

"Not mine." Connor inclined his head toward the kitchen. "No one would call them subtle, would they?"

"Not for very long." She giggled. She thrust out a hand toward him. "Truce? Just until after we leave?"

Connor took her hand. "We're adults. You're a doctor. Twice over. I was in business, had to compromise all the time. We should be able to manage more than a mere truce, don't you think?"

She blinked. "Let's not tax ourselves."

When he burst out laughing she withdrew her hand. His laughter faded. "Why didn't you tell me you had a couple of Ph.D.'s?"

"Why would I?"

"Well, for one thing, I wouldn't have been quite as suspicious of your abilities."

She held his gaze, her eyebrow lifting. "Really?"

She saw right through him.

"Point taken." Connor leaned back, studied her face. "I don't think I've ever known anyone like you."

"You don't know me," she said, fiddling with her napkin.

"I know some things. You don't talk about yourself much unless somebody prods you and even then you only allow select bits of information out."

"So I don't go around telling every client my life history. What's odd about that?"

He ignored the challenge, determined to find out what had her protective hackles up.

"By all accounts, your career was on a very big upswing. I can't help wondering why you'd abandon it to come here and resurrect a defunct nursery or take on a project like Wingate when you must have six others begging for your attention, all of them more prestigious and important that this."

"You're going to get lots of publicity for Wingate Manor," she said, chin thrust out. "I'll benefit from that. Besides, maybe I wanted to come back to my roots," she said quietly.

"Why now?" Connor couldn't explain his feeling that her return had very little to do with seeking publicity or homecoming. "Why is it so important to make Davis Nurseries viable again? Wouldn't you have more success in Toronto?"

He waited for her to tell him about her father, about why it was so important to her to get him back here, about why she'd given up everything to do it.

She glared at him but was spared an answer by the return of the others.

"Everything okay?" Ashley asked, glancing at Rowena then him, as if she were ready to do battle for her friend.

"Everything is peachy, Ash." Rowena gave him an arch look. "I was just asking Connor his plans for the future. After Wingate."

The others all looked at him, waiting for a response he didn't have. Connor swallowed, scrambling to find a way to tell them he didn't have a clue how he was supposed to move on once the uncles came back.

"It's a good question," he mumbled, feeling like a schoolboy the teacher had made stand up in class. "I just don't have the answer to it. Yet."

"Well, I suppose you'll be here for a while—till the end of summer, anyway." Michael set a multilayered slice of chocolate cake in front of him. "That's long enough for God to show you the next step."

"I guess." As if God cared what he did with the rest of his life. "I think I'll have my hands full getting Wingate Manor on track. I want my uncles to come back to find the place hasn't suffered with their absence."

"How are they doing?"

The next few minutes were filled with discussion about the uncles and anecdotal memories of the summers he'd come here.

"I wonder why we never met before," Piper mused. "I mean, we were here every summer. We should have at least noticed you. Especially you, Row. The nursery is right on Wingate's doorstep."

"I didn't get here much after I was twelve," he told them, wondering how he was going to sidestep this.

"You didn't like it here?" Jason speared a piece of cake.

"No, I liked it very much. But my mother moved." *To the streets.* "I didn't have much opportunity then." *Or money for the fare to get here.*

"That's too bad. I know your uncles would have loved having you here. They've done a lot over the years to help the youth of the area." Piper glanced at Ashley. "Remember the picnics they sponsored for the youth group every Labor Day weekend? They put so much thought into the activities. We always had a blast."

"I'd forgotten those." Rowena chuckled. "Remember the piñata party?"

The other two women giggled. "I think Hank and Henry got a little more than they expected that time."

"What happened?" Connor asked, curious about the rueful looks the three shared.

"It poured that weekend so all the outside events had to be moved inside. Henry had spent days making this huge piñata. Hank chose every single thing that went inside it so we'd each have a special token. But with the rain, they couldn't hang it outside. They decided the porch would make the perfect spot."

"But it was far from perfect." Rowena's sad look made him curious.

"Why?"

"I remember Mom talking about that." Michael chucked his wife's cheek with a tender grin. "They should have known someone who looked like you couldn't hit the broad side of a barn door."

"That was the problem, Michael." Piper giggled. "Ash hit that hornet's nest dead center."

"Ouch!" Connor grinned. "I'll bet that retreat was quick."

"Except for Row. She was determined to get a better look at the nest." Piper groaned. "I was never so scared in my life."

"Or so loud. You practically screamed your head off," Rowena said.

"Didn't you get stung?" Connor couldn't imagine that beautiful white skin marred by wasp stings.

"Of course." She shrugged that off. "But I also got the best science project for school that year. Cross-section of a wasp's nest. First prize."

"And three weeks of being smothered in gunky pink cream to get rid of the swelling! It's a good thing you didn't go into some kind of allergic shock."

"I'm not the type to go into shock." Rowena calmly tasted her dessert, proclaiming it perfect. "Besides, that lotion created a kind of mystique, don't you think?"

The other two scoffed.

"Oh, yeah. The kind of mystique that turned the guys at school into nasty little creeps." Ashley sounded like she was still outraged for her friend.

"I survived."

Connor watched Rowena, noting the way she ducked her head when Ashley and Piper explained the ribbing she'd taken. He had a hunch she wasn't as impervious to what had happened as she pretended.

Always, she carried her shield of pretended unaffectedness. The question was why.

After the meal, Michael offered to show Connor his studio. It was a huge area with skylights, every tool known to man, and a host of carvings that lined the walls.

"So you still teach shop at the school, even though your carving career has begun to take off?"

Michael shrugged. "I still have bills to pay. Besides, I like the kids. They keep me fresh, give me a new perspective on the world. I always thought I wanted to sculpt full-time and maybe one day I will, but for now my life is pretty good. God's really blessed me."

"God?" Connor didn't want to alienate Michael but he did want to know why the other man was so ready to credit God for his success.

"Sounds hokey, right?" Michael grinned. "But it's true. I'm not saying I have the inside track, though. I think God is right there, waiting to help all of us no matter what we want to achieve. But sometimes our goals aren't what He wants for us and we have to go through some stuff to get our priorities figured out, to start trusting in God and stop thinking we know what's best."

"I'll second that." Jason leaned against the wall. "I came here to escape what I figured was my biggest disaster. Everything I thought I wanted went down the tubes, my life was a mess and I was determined to prove that I was better than the bad rep I got when my best friend betrayed me."

"And did you?"

Jason shook his head, laughed. "I didn't get what I thought I wanted, but I got exactly what I needed. And a lot more besides. I came here with a desire to make Serenity Bay one of the hottest tourist destinations in the area to satisfy my own personal need to prove myself. Don't get me wrong, I still want to do that, but the reasons have changed. Then, too, there are a lot of other things that are way more important, things I never even realized I needed to learn. God had to get me here to teach me those lessons. Serenity Bay was the start of His plan for me, a way to get me moving down the path to learning the things He wanted me to know."

"What kind of things?" Connor found himself curious about the contentment he saw on both men's faces. "You mean you both found your wives here?"

"Well, there's that. Though even that wasn't easy, right, Michael?"

"Don't get me started on the Bayside Trio."

"Who?"

"That's what they call themselves—Rowena, Piper and Ashley." Michael chuckled. "They stick together no matter what. They push themselves into each other's lives to make sure none of them gets hurt and woe betide the guy who tries to tell any of 'em what to do. Those three are not fainthearted women."

"Exactly. So if Rowena says she's going to have Wingate Manor ready in time, my advice to you is to get out of the way and let her do it," Jason said without the hint of a smile.

"I wish I'd met you two several weeks ago," Connor muttered.

"Uh-oh. Sounds like you and Rowena have met head-on." Michael perched on a big stump that sat beside his workbench, sharing a knowing look with his friend. "Wanna tell us about it? We're experts on those three."

"Hardly experts," Jason countered, shaking his head. "But we know enough to tell you to proceed very slowly."

"Why?"

"Our three ladies developed a tight bond because of the difficulties in their youth. We don't know everything about the past—they like their secrets."

"We do know that the bond between them has grown stronger, more durable, because of what they shared years ago," Jason continued.

"And so?"

"We don't know why yet, but getting her father's nursery up and running is very important to Rowena," Michael murmured. "Ashley said she had her pick of lucrative projects in Toronto because of a promotion she just received."

"She turned it down, quit her job, moved back here and began to pour every second she had into that nursery. Piper didn't come right out and say it, but I gather Rowena's risked everything on that place. That's why she's killing herself to get Wingate up and running." Jason kept a bead on him that wouldn't let go. "What Michael and I don't know is why."

"Join the club." Connor decided it was high time he spent a little more time getting to know his beautiful landscape designer.

"He's a hunk, Row."

"He's a client, Ash. A very important client. Success at Wingate could make Davis Nurseries, put us in line for some great contracts."

"And you honestly don't see Connor Wingate as anything more than a client?" Piper asked, her disbelief obvious.

"As you so aptly pointed out earlier, I'm hardly the type men see in a romantic way." Rowena heard the tinge of bitterness in her own voice and fought to expunge it. Her dowdiness wasn't their fault.

"I didn't mean to hurt you by bringing up the wasps, Row. Honestly." Ashley looked ready to burst into tears. "Sometimes I'm so careless. Please say you'll forgive me."

"There is nothing to forgive. You spoke the truth." But Rowena hugged her, anyway, wondering how much the exotic scent Ashley wore cost and then chiding herself for it. Whatever the cost, she couldn't afford it. Besides, it wouldn't go with her usual fragrance, L'Eau de Fertilizer.

Anyway, what did it matter? It was Connor Wingate they were talking about. He was *way* out of her league.

"Listen. I've been thinking about what you said about building a town square, Piper. I thought you might try to make it feel more like a community gathering space."

Ashley shook her head. "Rowena! You're always thinking about work."

Not always, Rowena wanted to say. But she let it go, picking up a piece of paper that Tati had left lying on the counter.

"Look, if you do this, add a small bandstand and block off this one area you'll have the perfect place for farmers' markets, artists' showings…the high school band could play there on Saturdays. You could even host a small children's festival and not worry about vehicles passing through."

"This is great, Row." Piper hunkered down over the paper and began making notes on the side.

But Ashley remained standing to one side, her gray eyes troubled.

"Don't you want more from life than work, Row?" she asked when Piper left to chase down the men for coffee.

"Not right now."

"Because of your dad. Because you're positive that if he comes back, works on the nursery, he'll get better?" She waited for Rowena's nod. "Did you ever consider what could happen if you're wrong, if he never blamed you, if you've sacrificed yourself for nothing?"

Anger bubbled up inside Rowena. She'd thought of it, discarded it and moved on. It didn't help to keep going back over what-ifs. This was the only choice she had and she had to keep pressing on.

"You're the one who's always preaching to me about faith, Ash," she said bitterly. "Why don't you have some in me?"

"Oh, honey. I have all the faith in the world in you and your work."

"But?"

Ashley sighed, but she didn't give up asking the hard question. She never had. "Where does God come into your plans? Are you certain this is the path He wants you on?" Ashley murmured as voices from the end of the house grew nearer.

"I guess I'll know that if I succeed," Rowena said quietly. "God doesn't give me any advance information. Apparently He expects me to push ahead on my own."

How could Ashley possibly understand that God had never spoken to Rowena in that way—that she'd spent most of her life begging Him to tell her what to do and never heard even a whisper? That blind faith described her whole life.

"Maybe you're asking Him the wrong questions," Ashley whispered just before the others entered the room.

Maybe He just wasn't answering.

Chapter Six

"**I** was hoping you'd feel up to coming for a visit soon, Dad." Rowena watched closely for some sign of interest on her father's face.

But his vacant gaze never left the window, where rain spattered in a steady pattern of gray drizzle that never seemed to end.

"I've done a whole new lot of black ash cuttings," she told him, struggling to keep the one-sided conversation going.

"You work too hard."

I'm doing it for you, she wanted to scream. Instead she scrounged for a new topic of discussion.

"Ashley invited me to her house for dinner the other evening. Remember I told you she married Michael Masters?"

Her father blinked, twisted to look at her. "Laura Masters's son?"

"Yes. He has a daughter, did I tell you?"

"So Laura's a grandmother." He smiled, a real smile, the first Rowena had seen in a long time. "I wonder how she likes that."

"She seems to dote on the little girl. They have Friday-night dates and Tatiana sits beside her every Sunday morning in church."

"Laura always did enjoy kids. She should have had ten of them." He fell silent, but his face had lost the bored, hopeless expression it usually wore.

Rowena checked her watch. She'd have to leave soon. The truck had been acting funny on the way into Toronto. She'd prefer to get home before it got too late rather than risk getting into trouble on roads that didn't have much traffic this time of year.

She coaxed him into a couple of games of chess which he won without difficulty, then once again broached the subject uppermost on her mind.

"So do you think you'd be up to coming to the Bay in a week or two? I checked and there's a shuttle you could take that runs every day." He didn't look excited by that. "Or I could take you back with me next time I come in. You could see what I'm doing at Wingate."

"Maybe," he said, as he always did.

"Is there anything you need? Anything I could bring for you?"

"I'm fine, honey. You go ahead and do what you need to. I don't know why you have to have the old place back. It's not worth much now." He shrugged. "But if that's what you've set your mind on, you just do it. Don't worry about me. I'll be fine."

"Right." Swallowing the lump in her throat she leaned down, hugged his frail shoulders tightly. "Think about coming for a visit, will you, Dad? It would do you a world of good to get out of here and smell the spring air. I'm sure Mrs. Masters would love to see you again. And Bud's been asking about a chess game every time I see him."

"I suppose she's still got her flower shop?" Her father smiled, his eyes on some distant memory. "Always loved flowers, Laura did."

"I've got to go. Bye, Dad. I love you. Take care." Rowena hugged him, felt the thin body draw away too soon.

"Bye, honey. I love you, too. Drive safely. Watch out for wildlife on the road."

He said the same thing every time she came, but before Rowena was out the door he'd drifted off into some foggy haze that dimmed the light in his eyes as he became a shell of the father she'd known.

She walked out to the truck, climbed inside and started the engine. While she waited for the defroster to clear the moisture from the screen, she closed her eyes and asked the same question she did every time she came. *Why don't You help him?*

Though she waited, Rowena got no response.

With a weary sigh she shifted into Reverse and backed out of the lot. As she drove home in the spring twilight, the familiar refrain circled round and round in her mind.

Please don't let me have made a mistake in going back. Please help me make Wingate a success. Please help me help Dad.

Connor loved driving.

Something about the smooth roll of the tires against the pavement, the hum of the engine, the whir of the blades against the windshield—it all soothed him into a tranquil state of mind.

But not tonight.

He drove competently through the steady rain, but tonight his brain found no repose in the return journey from his uncles.

"Sometimes you can't force things to go the way you want, son." Uncle Henry's soft chiding had carried a hint of censure. "That's why we call it faith—because it hasn't happened yet but we believe, God willing, it will."

"That's fine, Uncle Henry, but that doesn't stop the rain or get the work done. I know she's competent," Connor had said before his uncles could interject more reassurances. "I get that she's probably overqualified for this job. But that doesn't mean anything if the work isn't getting done."

They'd told him they were praying, that God knew what they were trying to do and He would bless their plans. Nothing they'd said made Connor feel any better, but it had given him perspective on one thing. By renovating the grounds, adding new features and generally making Wingate Manor look like a very profitable enterprise, the uncles were hoping to entice a buyer. That's why they'd been so eager to accept Rowena's trade-off agreement. There would be no huge expenditure on the books but the grounds would look lush and present a pleasing picture to prospective purchasers.

He'd suspected it, of course. What he hadn't expected was that they wanted to retire so badly. Hank was already making plans for a move to Florida to ease his aching arthritis. Henry used his spare recuperative moments to go online and investigate communities with active horticultural societies.

If something happened and a sale didn't go through, Connor knew they'd be devastated. And that put the pressure squarely on his shoulders.

He turned up Hill Road, grateful he'd be home before it was too late. Through the gloomy mist he saw a figure trudging up the side of the road, obviously drenched, head covered by a huge hood. He pulled over, touched a button to roll down the window.

"Need a lift?"

The head ducked down. Hazel eyes peered at him through the dull glow of the car's dashboard lights.

"Connor?"

He blinked. "Rowena? What on earth are you doing out here?"

"Walking," she said drily.

"I meant why."

"Because my truck died about half a mile back and I didn't want to stay in it all night." Rain drizzled down her cheek, dripped off the end of her nose to plop onto the car.

"Get in." He reached over, released the door. "I'll give you a lift. I didn't notice the truck's flashers."

"Because they weren't working." She slid off her coat first, shook it, then slipped into the seat.

"Give me that." He put her coat on the backseat. "I'll turn the heat up. You must be frozen."

"I'm w-way past that." Her teeth chattered so hard she had to stop speaking.

Connor flicked the switch to high, directed the vents toward her. "Surely you weren't working today?"

"No." She held her fingers over one vent, sighing as the heat washed over them. "I went to the city."

"Toronto? But I was there, too. I would have given you a ride if I'd known."

"How are Henry and Hank?"

"Doing quite well. Uncle Henry's left cast should come off in a couple of weeks. Then he'll do more rehab. Uncle Hank will be incapacitated a little longer. His hip isn't healing all that well."

"I'm sorry." She ran her fingers through her hair, fluffed it up around her face. It seemed to be the only thing that wasn't wet.

Connor waited for her to explain her visit. When she didn't offer any further information, he decided to ask. "Were you visiting someone, too?"

"My dad. He's in a convalescent home."

"I'm sorry. Is he ill?" He remembered she'd said something about it that day the sheriff had visited her at Wingate Manor.

She sighed, glanced at him and frowned. "Dad's recovering from a major depression. At least, the doctors say he's recovering."

"You don't see it that way?" A pang of empathy washed over him as her face tightened and she shook her head.

"He doesn't seem to care about anything. He's dragged himself down into the past and I don't see him making any effort to dig himself out. I've tried everything I know to pique his interest but nothing seems to work."

"Someone once told me coming out of depression means taking two steps forward and one step back." His mother's doctor had said that, only his mother had never broken free of it.

"I guess." She stared through the windshield, giving a funny laugh. "I'm starting to feel awful myself. This weather is horrible."

"It has me worried," he admitted, wondering even as he said it if this was a good time to echo his concerns. "You've done a lot, but if things don't dry out soon, I'm going to have to consider canceling some of the bookings I've taken."

"I've told you a hundred times that we will be finished before the deadline," she grated, eyes flashing with anger.

"I'm not doubting you. Really. My uncles are very insistent that you'll get the job done."

"Then what's the problem?" She tilted her head, looking at him like a curious sparrow.

"I was talking about engagements I've accepted. This isn't for public information," he warned. She nodded. "I've only just realized how much they're counting on me to show a solid profit this year. I wish I'd never told them my plans now because the uncles are hoping this season will make a big splash. They think that with the added publicity about the gardens and the other changes I'm instituting, they can attract a buyer."

"They mentioned selling when I met with them last fall," Rowena murmured thoughtfully. "But I thought it was a distant goal. I didn't realize they meant immediately." She frowned. "This means we have to get it right with no room for error. A buyer will home in on problems and cut the asking price without a second thought."

"Yes." He felt a measure of peace that at last they'd found some common ground to meet on though it meant the pressure intensified for both of them.

Silence stretched between them. Then Rowena asked, "Where's Tobias today?"

"I left him in his pen. There's no way he could come and he's safe there. I got a doghouse put in so he could stay dry," he added, hoping to appease the challenge he saw rising in her eyes.

"Good. It's important to take care of pets."

He's not my pet, Connor was going to say. But that wasn't strictly true. He'd taken over care and feeding of the dog after Cecile's death. Technically Tobias was his until he found him another home. For some reason he wasn't quite ready to do that yet.

Connor pulled into her yard, slowing to a stop in front of the house. There were no lights on, but even in the mist and gloom he could see that the roof needed work. "Are you sure that house is safe to live in? Esther seems to think it needs an overhaul."

Rowena leaned back to gather her jacket. She pretended nonchalance.

"It's not Wingate, but it'll do," she told him. "I closed off parts of it that need the most work, but the area I live in is fine. I'm not there much, anyway."

Good thing. From what he could see the porch sagged, the windows needed caulking and paint and the door looked as if the big, bad wolf could blow it in with a cough.

Feeling her scrutiny, he wished he hadn't stared quite so long.

"I'll get to it, Connor," she told him quietly. "But not till Wingate's finished."

He nodded, but in the back of his mind he wondered how she could finance Wingate's restoration, pay her laborers and keep the greenhouse going while still finding enough cash to fund the kind of bills restructuring this place would amass. A prickle of guilt rushed in when he recalled Esther's comment about passing on an unfit structure in return for work.

"I could get someone in to take a look if you want."

"Not necessary. Thanks for the lift," she said before climbing out.

"What about your truck?"

"I'll call the garage in the morning. Good night."

Rowena slammed the door shut before he could ask how she'd get to work without it.

Connor waited until she'd unlocked the door and disappeared inside. A moment later a light flickered on. He took that as a sign that everything was okay and shifted into gear, driving down the road to Wingate Manor. His conscience tugged at him as he walked through the thick oak door into the gorgeous interior complete with chandeliers, velvet couches, broadloom and a host of other comforts he took for granted.

A mental image of Rowena crouched in front of a fire trying to dry her clothes while all around her pots and buckets caught a steady drip from the ceiling sent him stalking into the kitchen to prepare a cup of hot chocolate. She'd said it was fine. It wasn't his business to question her.

Suddenly the phone rang.

"I'm glad you got home safely, son."

"I'm fine."

"I meant to ask earlier and forgot—you did check on that house at the nursery, didn't you, Connor?" Uncle Henry's quiet voice still had the power to make him pay attention.

"As a matter of fact, I—"

"I spoke to Esther this evening. She reminded me that it was in disrepair for many years. There could be problems with the roof or mice inside. Anything, really. I don't want Rowena to have to live in slum conditions. It's not fair when she's working so hard for us. You'll take care of it, won't you, son?"

"I gave her a ride home tonight. Her truck broke down coming back from seeing her father. I asked about the place. Rowena said she'd closed off part of it but that the rest was fine. I think she'll do some work on it after she's finished Wingate Manor."

"If you say it's all right for her to live in, I'm okay with that. I trust your judgment, Connor. I know you'll do your best to make sure she's safe there." Henry paused; when he spoke again his voice was brimming with sadness. "Poor Victor. He was always such a happy, contented soul. Perhaps when we get a little more mobile, we'll go to see him. I imagine he could use a visitor or two."

"Rowena said he's suffering from depression," Connor said.

"Yes, though I'm not sure her plan is going to make the difference she thinks. All we can do is pray and let God work it out."

"Her plan?" Connor didn't understand.

"I have to go, son. That nice nurse is here to give me my pill. Take care, now."

"Bye, Uncle Henry."

Connor hung up the phone, made his hot chocolate and took it to the sitting room in the rear where he lit a fire and chose an armchair in front of it to curl up in. After a moment he rose, moved to the window to check on Tobias, who was sound asleep in his house, with only his nose poking through the opening. No neglect there.

Back in his chair, Connor stared into the flames thinking of the daughter who'd gone all the way into Toronto in that tired truck to see her father. Uncle Henry's words came back to him.

Let God work it out.

As far as Connor was concerned, God wasn't working out

a whole lot of anything for Rowena at the moment. Or him. Thoughts of the future pressed on his mind like a weight. What came next?

He didn't want to be one of those people with no goal, no ambition; he couldn't imagine not having a dream to pursue. Yes, he had money. Plenty of it. So what? Cecile had been right about one thing—money didn't make him feel any less alone.

The old Wingate family Bible lay open on the table at his elbow. He picked it up, glanced at the yellowed pages of onionskin that were probably close to a hundred years old.

Casting all your cares on Him for He careth for you.

Connor wanted to believe that God was up there, lobbing the possibilities back and forth, waiting for just the right one to send his way. He longed to be able to relax and accept each day as it came—but he couldn't.

His mother had done that. She'd said God would look after them. And look how her life had turned out. She'd lost her home, her job, even him. Eventually she'd lost the will to keep fighting.

God cared for him? How? Cecile had died because of him, because he wasn't able to love her the way a man needed to love the woman he promised to cherish for eternity. How was her death an act of caring by a God who loved him? Connor knew he should have been the one to die. His useless life should have been snuffed out. No one would have cared, except maybe the uncles. Cecile had been the one with the mountains of friends. She walked into a room and a party started.

She'd tried so hard to be what he wanted, to ignore his frequent lateness, to pretend she didn't care when he changed their plans without consulting her. Their relationship, he now realized, was on his terms. She'd let him dictate the length of their engagement, choose the date of their wedding and the style.

He didn't deserve her. Fortunately he'd figured that out in time, though telling her that had cost her life.

The phone rang, breaking into his reverie.

"Connor?"

"Rowena? Is something wrong? It sounds like you're in the middle of a tornado."

"Um, it sort of feels like it, too. A tree fell on the house."

He jumped to his feet. "A tree! Are you all right?"

"Yes, yes. I'm fine."

He heard the hesitation in her voice. "I'll come and pick you up, take you wherever you want to go."

She laughed but a hint of nervousness lay beneath. "Thanks anyway, but I'm staying here."

"Do you think it's safe?"

"It's fine. The thing is—Connor, Tobias is here. I guess you'd say he warned me out of harm's way."

"What?" He rose, pushed the drapes out of the way and peered out the window. The pen was empty. A small pile of dirt lay inside the fence. The dratted dog had dug his way out again. "Is he all right?"

"He seems ravenous, but otherwise fine."

"Rowena, he's always ravenous."

"He must really be hungry tonight." She giggled. "He's eating my leftover bean sprouts."

"I'll come get him."

"No, don't go out again. He's fine. I just wanted you to be aware that he'd escaped but that he's all right."

"Okay," he said softly, feeling oddly rebuffed that she hadn't told him to come over, invited him for coffee. Something. "You're sure you're okay?"

"Yes. Thinking I should perhaps have chosen another career, maybe."

"You know you're doing exactly what you love doing and

wouldn't change for the world." He had a mental picture of her surrounded by flowers.

"Oh, wouldn't I?" she asked softly.

"No." Connor didn't know why he was so certain of that but he was. It seemed odd, speaking to her like this, and yet easier somehow. As if they could be more honest, more open without the usual Wingate argument getting in the way.

"I guess you're right. I'm a sucker for gardens. Always have been." She was silent a moment. "What do you love to do, Connor?"

"Change things. Make them work more efficiently.'

"Is that what you'll do when you leave here?"

"I don't know. My future is uncertain right now."

"And that bothers you." She said it confidently, as if she knew him.

"I'm not much for leaving things to chance. I like to chart my course and follow it pretty closely."

Rowena's tiny gasp turned into a laugh. "Does your life actually turn out like that? I mean, sure, it would be nice. But I don't think anyone gets to live exactly the life they planned. Even if you did, it would probably be pretty boring and it wouldn't leave much room for God to get our attention."

"You think that's how He does it? By changing our plans?"

"Sometimes. I mean, think about it. You're going along, living your life, then wham! Life hands you a great big lemon. So you work at it, struggle with what to do with it, and eventually you realize you've got a chance to do something you couldn't have done before—make lemonade."

"Whether or not you like the stuff," he grumbled.

Rowena chuckled. "You remind of when I was a kid. I went to Piper's for dinner one night. Her Gran made broccoli. Dad had always grown broccoli and we ate it often. Truth to tell, I liked it. Piper didn't. I'm not sure she'd ever tasted it before, but she'd heard other kids talking about horrible old broccoli and she'd made up her mind it was bad."

"You think I should eat more broccoli?" he asked, anticipating that quick little giggle he knew she'd give. "I'm on Piper's side. Yuck."

"It's an analogy, Connor."

"Yeah, okay. Sorry. You were saying?"

"So there Piper is with this broccoli tree on her plate—"

"Figures you'd call it a tree," he interjected with a smile.

"Anyway," she said slowly, drawing out the vowels. "She had to eat it or we couldn't go biking after supper—and we really wanted to go biking. There was a bike-a-thon planned. After it, all the kids were meeting at Mrs. Masters's. It was a special youth night."

"So Piper was faced with her great big lemon—er, broccoli."

"You're making fun of me.'

"No, just trying to keep the fruits and vegetables straight. Go on. I know there's a point here somewhere."

"If you keep interrupting me, we'll never get there."

"My lips are sealed."

"Ha. Anyway, Piper dithered and dawdled, begged her grandmother to throw it out, pretended it made her sick. Every trick every kid has ever tried, Piper used. It didn't work. The broccoli got cold but it still sat there and Ash and I were losing patience. We really wanted to go see Mrs. Masters."

"Michael's mother."

"Yes. She threw the most fantastic parties. Anyway, finally Ash and I threatened to leave if Pip didn't get that green thing into her mouth and swallow it. We walked to the door. At the last minute she shoved it in her mouth, chewed once and swallowed. When we got to Mrs. Masters's later that night she had trays of food set out for all of us. There was a game involving broccoli."

"I'm beginning to see the light."

"Yes, Piper learned that even she can eat broccoli if it means there's a chance you'll win a cute little stereo system for your room."

Connor squinted at the phone. "That's it? That's your moral? Eat broccoli, or make lemonade out of the big lemon life hands you, and you'll win a stereo?"

"Well, you interrupted so many times I had to shorten it. But the main gist was that turnarounds in life can often lead to new opportunities we would have never otherwise experienced."

"But not necessarily good things," he countered.

"Are you always so negative?"

"I'm realistic. I like to face the issues head-on, with an appreciation for what could happen."

"That's what I said—a pessimist."

He let that go, debated whether or not to ask her the question uppermost on his mind. Connor decided to go for it.

"Was coming here, revamping Wingate's grounds, rebuilding the nursery—was that a lemon?"

Rowena was silent for several minutes, making Connor wish he hadn't been so personal.

"You don't have to answer that. It's none of my business."

"It isn't, but I'll tell you, anyway." He heard her inhale. "Losing the nursery was a lemon for my father that I thought I could turn around by getting it up and running again."

"And now you're having second thoughts?"

"No. It's just…harder than I thought, I guess. The weather's kind of got me down. Besides that, there's the truck." She sighed. "I'm tired, I guess. I should go to bed instead of sitting here talking to you."

"Yes. It's getting late." He saw that the rain had finally stopped. "Maybe tonight the clouds will clear. I'm sure that's what you're praying for."

"Actually it isn't." She sighed, the sound of her breath like the soft brush of a spring breeze against his ear. "What are you praying for?"

It had been a very long time since Connor had prayed, so he couldn't answer that.

"Good night, Rowena. Thanks for telling me about Tobias. Send him back whenever you want."

"By the look of him, he's staying all night. Good night, Connor."

She didn't hang up right away, making him wonder if there was something else she wanted to say. But the moment he opened his mouth to ask her, the click of the phone being set down told him he'd waited too long.

"If you're not praying for better weather, what are you praying for, Rowena Davis?"

"Three days of sunshine and warmer temperatures sure make a difference." Piper handed Rowena a soda and a chicken sandwich. "Connor seems to have mellowed."

"No kidding. When he told us where you were working, he also said we should feel free to have our picnic here. It almost sounded like he wanted to join us." Seated in the lawn chair that was always tucked into the trunk of her car, Ashley looked ready should a photographer appear to snap her picture for a magazine.

Piper, too, was elegantly garbed in black silk pants, a red camisole and a jacket in a pattern so vibrant only she could pull it off. Beside them, Rowena knew she came off looking like a grub. She stifled the feelings of inferiority and concentrated on relishing the sunshine as she enjoyed her lunch break.

"Are you finding him easier to work with?"

"Connor?" Rowena glanced at the house, shrugged. "I've only seen him for a few minutes these past few days. It seems as if everything's happening at once up there. Hordes of people have been coming and going."

"Not to mention the painters finishing that gazebo. It's going to look so romantic with the vines climbing up."

"It'll take a couple of weeks to get them going, Pip. Then you'll really notice how perfect it is there."

"I gather that means Connor had other preferences for its placement?"

"We came to a compromise." Rowena simply smiled at their demands for more information.

"And the fountain? Has he come around on that?"

"He thinks we're spending too much time preparing the fountain bed. He'd prefer it if we got everything else ready and worked on it last, if we have time."

"Which you're not going to do," Ashley guessed with a grin.

"I can't." Frustrated that no one could seem to understand her vision, Rowena tried to explain. "Everything in the landscape plan directs the viewer to take another step down the garden path. Literally. How would you feel if you followed it all the way down only to have your anticipation shattered when you arrive at a big patch of yellow tape with a sign that says, 'Sorry. We couldn't finish in time. Come back in a month.'?"

"I'd feel cheated." Pip nodded. "Do it. You deserve the opportunity to show all of your skills when Wingate Manor opens again. If there's anything we can do, you have to let us help."

"I agree." Ashley rose, brushing off her silk skirt. "Just name it. I know everyone thinks I'm useless but I'm willing to do anything to help you get this off the ground. I'll—" She glanced around. "I'll wash out the cement buckets if you want."

Tears pooled in here eyes at the determination filling their pretty faces. Friends like these were worth more than all the money in the world.

"You've already done more than enough," she told them,

dashing the wetness from her cheeks. "Anyway, we don't have any cement buckets. Coming here today, this lunch, your encouragement—they're exactly what I needed to get me back on track. Thank you."

"For chicken salad?" Ashley scoffed. "I can do that with one hand tied. That's not helping."

"It's your thoughtfulness I appreciate, Ash. But the chicken salad was delicious, too. The dill was perfect."

"I knew you'd like it. Pip thought I was nuts but I remember those jars of dill pickles you used to hide at school."

"That's what curled my hair so well." Rowena preened like a model on a catwalk.

"Your hair is straighter than straw," Pip scoffed as she began gathering up their trash. "And Ash puts dill in everything. You're both cuckoo. I've got to get back to work."

With a full heart, Rowena watched them leave. Then she turned back to the excavation work to remove the thin, patchy grass once known as Wingate's lawn. A huge load of sod would be the first step to making the place look lush, but she had to get it down before it dried out.

"Party over?" Connor stood ten feet above her, watching as she unrolled the short sections of Kentucky blue grass, snugged the edges and trimmed excess bits.

"Hardly a party. But yes, we all had to go back to work." She tilted back on her heels to study him. "Why didn't you join us? Ashley made a ton of sandwiches. Chicken salad."

"My favorite. I wish I had." He held her gaze unblinkingly. "I had to share one of Tobias's bones."

Rowena froze in shocked surprise, searched his face. "You made a joke."

"Imagine that."

Heat flooded her cheeks at his dry tone. She decided to shut up and concentrate on her work.

"I don't know how you managed it but this grass makes a whale of a difference. Once it's down, can I let Tobias out of that pen? He's really missing you guys."

"Are you crazy?" Rowena surged to her feet, her short temper fraying beyond her control. "Do you know what I had to do to get this stuff?"

"Rowena, I was teasing—"

"It's not funny. I'm doing everything I can to get this job back on schedule but so help me, if you let that dog walk on this grass before it's taken, I will—"

His silence stopped her. She lifted her head, took a second look at his face. He was laughing. At her.

"Get off my site," she snarled. Embarrassment, shame, stupidity—they climbed on top of each other, heaping condemnation on her. Why couldn't he just leave her alone?

"Look, I'm sorry. I didn't mean—"

"Just leave," she said, refusing to look at him.

After a moment's pause, Connor turned and walked away. Rowena's heart squeezed tight. She'd never felt more alone.

Chapter Seven

"They arrived before nine and have been going hard at it ever since. They're making a world of difference. I can't thank you enough, Oren."

Connor froze beside the hydrangea grove as Rowena ended her call. Who was Oren?

"Three days at the most, I think, though if they keep up this pace they'll finish in two. It was sweet of them to volunteer their Saturdays so you wouldn't lose time on your project. I don't know how I'll repay them. Thanks again."

He watched her pocket the cell phone, her face cloud-free for the first time in ages. Undoubtedly the week of sunshine had made the difference. Rowena had remained distant ever since his little joke had fallen flat. Not that he blamed her. She was under a lot of pressure and he'd been an idiot to say what he had. But when this crew had arrived this morning she'd cheered up immensely.

"Connor? Did you need to see me?"

She'd come upon him unawares and now he found himself at a loss to explain his presence here.

"Not really. Just looking around. These men really know how to work."

She nodded and called out to Kent to leave the sod off a wide enough spot for the transport vehicles to move through.

"We have to bring in the trees and the shrubs, not to mention the plumbing stuff," she reminded him. Rowena turned back, shook her head at Connor. "Sorry. What was I—oh, yes. We've got most of the terraces ready to fill and plant. The fountains are ahead of schedule and the watering systems for the hanging baskets are almost finished. It's just a matter of keeping everything and everyone moving."

"Looks like you're doing that very well." He glanced at the oval dug into the ground about two feet deep. "I don't remember discussing this. What is it?"

She grinned. "Since the kids' playground is going to be right behind this area, shielded by a row of cypresses, I thought we'd put in a little trout pond in front. Kent's going to make several benches out of those giant cedars we had to cut. They'll weather well, won't need paint, and folks can sit and visit, watch the kids fish, or whatever."

She did it over and over, sneaked in a little pond here, added a vista there. Connor was amazed at the details and how each one seemed a natural part of the original plan.

"And over there?"

"That's going to be the maze we talked about. Boxwood. It hasn't arrived yet or we'd have it planted. I had to move it a bit to allow for the picnic area. The tables are cement, the benches, too. No maintenance."

"Then we'll need garbage containers."

She pointed to one almost totally hidden by the plantings around it. "They're there, but discreetly placed."

"It's almost the end of April. When will the flowers go in?"

"Not for a couple of weeks at the earliest." She tilted her

head up to meet his gaze. "I want to make sure the frost is past before I plant any of the annuals. The perennials we'll start placing as soon as the other work is done but we'll do it area by area. Before that I'll need you to come up to the greenhouse and approve my selection."

"Okay."

One of the men working on the lower fountain called out something. Rowena twisted her head, nodded. "I've got to go see what's wrong."

"I'll come, too. I'd like to watch," he added, just in case she thought he was spying on her.

Connor matched his step to hers as they tramped over the still-muddy slope. "Why are the steps gone?"

"I'm removing them all."

"Whoa!" He reached out and grabbed her arm. "You never told me that. It's going to delay us even more."

Rowena sighed impatiently, pulled her arm out of his grasp. "When are you going to start trusting me, Connor?"

"I do, but—" He was missing something, he could read it on her face. "Okay, explain."

"There's a camp for disabled kids near here. They often come for rides on Jason's houseboats. They might book Wingate for some events, too, but not if there are steps. The place would have to be completely wheelchair accessible— not just the upper levels. So we're making it wheelchair accessible. I'm going to reuse the old brick from your planters to pave the paths."

"But the house itself isn't—" Connor caught her drift. "You think I should have some ramps installed on Wingate Manor."

"Discreet ones, yes. I've got a couple of drawings I could show you," she said, distracted by the commotion in the fountain pit. "But not now. I've got to get this fixed first." She strode forward, jumped down. "What's the problem, Ed?"

"The system you chose for this fountain means we need at least four feet clearance."

Rowena whipped a tape measure out of her pocket and gauged the distance. "Which you've got."

"For the pipes, yes. But we have to compensate for the lowered water when the fountain is operational. We need another six inches."

"Then dig it."

"Can't do it fast enough. There's a lot of clay down here. It will take us days to dig by hand. We'll have to bring a backhoe in. It's going to make a big mess, Rowena."

Connor watched the frustration fill her face. She'd worked so hard. It didn't seem fair that she'd have to redo so much. Better leave her alone to work it out.

He tromped back up the slope, noticed the underground sprinklers had gone in. Quint was beginning to lay the upper paths with the old bricks. A glimmer of hope flickered inside. Maybe, just maybe, they'd be ready in time for guests?

"You look cranky. Got time for a coffee break?" Michael Masters stood at the side of the house, holding Tobias's collar in one hand.

"Sure." Connor glanced at Cecile's dog. "What did he do now?"

Michael pointed at the big clay pot that had crashed off Wingate's back patio and fractured into a thousand pieces. "I believe that's his work."

"I suppose he dug himself out of his pen again. The dog's name should be Houdini." Connor put Tobias back inside, laid several big stumps over the area he'd dug through and told the animal what would happen if he left again. "Come on inside, Michael. I think Esther just made a fresh pot."

Indeed she had and told one of the kitchen assistants to make some muffins, as well. They carried their cups and food to the back patio, away from the main noise of Rowena's helpers.

"This place is a beehive today. How come?"

"I'm not really sure. All I know is that Rowena was speaking to someone called Oren on the phone."

"Her former boss." Michael nodded. "Ashley said she called in a couple of favors he owed her. You're lucky she's got connections with one of the largest landscape firms in Toronto." He took a sip from his steaming mug, chewed thoughtfully on a piece of muffin. "How are you doing? Is getting this place up and running driving you into the ground?"

"This will probably shock you, but I'm actually enjoying myself. Some of the uncles' former staff have returned and insist on giving the place a total shakedown. It needs it. I overheard a couple of them talking over coffee break this morning. Apparently the hardwood floors require sanding and refinishing. I doubt the uncles would have tackled it if they were here. They don't like their routine upset, but I've hired a company to come in and redo the entire place, top to bottom."

"That's going to cost some bucks."

"The money isn't important," Connor told him. "I just want to make sure that when they come back, they can walk in the door and not feel like there's a whole to-do list waiting."

"You've grown pretty fond of the old coots, haven't you?" Michael asked quietly.

"I was always fond of them. I feel badly that I didn't come up as often as I should have in recent years. I let myself get too busy with my own life, cut myself off from them. They tried—invited me for Christmas, weekends, stuff like that. I just never made the effort. I wish I would have. They're really nice men who took me in when a lot of relatives would have said no."

"Problem child, were you?"

Connor debated whether it was a good idea to discuss his past. He'd always been a loner, kept to himself. Which was how he'd landed here in the first place. He chucked caution to the wind.

"My father went to the first Gulf War. When I was ten, he came home in a body bag. My mother found it very hard to deal with. There were a lot of debts and very little income. She was proud and didn't want Henry and Hank to know how bad off we were, but when she got sick one summer, she had to ask them to let me come and stay. It was a real turning point in my life."

"How so?"

Connor smiled at the memory. "Uncle Henry has this saying. Whatever happened doesn't matter. What you do next does."

"Okay." Michael sprawled out in his chair, eyebrows raised.

"I was drifting through school, angry at God for letting my dad die, too aware of my mom's problems, not focused enough on what I had to do. My grades were lousy and I'd found a bad group of kids to hang with. At first I didn't want to come here and I made sure the uncles knew it."

"I can see Hank dealing with that."

"Patience personified," Connor agreed. "He just kept asking me to help out with the mowing, pull weeds, help those little old horticultural society ladies with their teas. And every so often he'd take me fishing."

"Ah, the bait."

"No, we used hooks." Connor grinned at Michael's groan. "Anyway, he'd start off rambling about something or other and in spite of myself, I'd end up listening. I never even noticed when it turned to stuff about integrity and honesty and following your own road. When I had to go back home at the end of the summer, they'd make sure I had decent clothes to go back to school with, a few bucks in my pocket that they called my 'wages' and a whole lot of homework that I had to write them about every week."

"Good for them."

"It was ingenious. Even if I was tempted to stray, a letter would arrive every Friday morning, two pages from each of them. Sunday night I had to call them collect. If I missed even one week I risked losing the whole next summer with them and there was no way I was going to do that. I was the envy of every kid in my school."

"I can imagine." Michael held his gaze. "And your mom?"

"In a way, I think the uncles taking over kind of left her anchorless. My dad was everything to her. When he died, she had no reason to keep hanging on, fighting back. Gradually she just let the craziness take over."

"Craziness?"

"She saw things, heard things. Eventually she was institutionalized and I went in foster care. It took the uncles a while to find me. We lost touch. When my mother died they were notified and we met at her funeral."

"But you didn't come back."

Connor shook his head.

"By then I'd won a scholarship to business school and was focused on escaping the bad memories of the past few years. I couldn't leave, couldn't come back here no matter how much I wanted. I was too afraid that what she'd had was hereditary, that if I stopped pushing I'd start to hear what she heard, lose my way."

"Must have been a lonely time," Michael said quietly.

"I never really thought of it that way until Cecile said much the same thing."

"Cecile?"

Why did he feel that he could talk to this man? Something

about Michael's quiet questions and unspoken empathy told him he'd faced his own share of ogres.

"I was engaged to her. She was beautiful, talented, sweet, funny. Everybody was Cecile's friend."

"Sounds like you cared about her a lot."

"I did care about her. But I didn't love her. Unfortunately I only realized that two weeks before we were supposed to be married."

Had Michael really not heard about the whole tawdry thing? The papers had covered every aspect of it, especially when he'd sold the business. Surely someone in town would have spread the gossip about him.

Or was it that Michael chose to ignore it all? Connor couldn't tell if he was bluffing or if he really didn't know the truth.

"At least you realized in time."

"I guess. I told her I was calling the wedding off the night her parents held a big, fancy party for us at a ritzy hotel a couple of weeks before the wedding. That's why she died." The baldness of that truth stung but Connor let it bite deep, welcoming the pain, hoping it would cauterize the guilt.

"I doubt that."

"What?" He sat up straight, glared at the other man. "Are you saying I'm lying?"

"Oh, you might believe that. You've probably been telling it to yourself ever since it happened." Michael leaned forward, elbows on his knees as he looked straight at Connor. "But I don't think it's true."

"I see." Anger had him clenching his lips together.

Michael wasn't put off by his silence.

"Women are intuitive, Connor. That's the way God designed them—probably to counter our stubbornness." He smiled ruefully. "And I have that information firsthand. Anyway, I'm pretty certain Cecile recognized that you didn't love her the way she needed you to. Maybe she didn't say anything, maybe she kept hoping things would change. But I think, deep down, she knew."

With crystal clarity Connor remembered her words.

"You're a coward, Con. You're afraid to let go and just love. You want guarantees and there aren't any. I feel sorry for you because you've made yourself into an island. You won't let me inside. You'll be all alone, Connor. But that's because you choose loneliness over me. Over anyone who tries to love you. One day it isn't going to be enough."

"Maybe you're right," he admitted quietly. "Maybe she did know. But I didn't have to do it that way. I could have waited, chosen a better time."

"In my humble opinion, there is no good time for that particular announcement. And I should know." Michael gave him a quick sketch of his past, of a marriage that hadn't worked and a child he'd only recently learned he'd fathered. "There's no way you can be prepared for everything life is going to throw at you. That's why we need to keep trusting God, to ask Him to lead us. Then when we get lemons—"

"We can eat our broccoli."

Michael's expression altered to confusion. "Huh?"

Connor chuckled. "Something Rowena said the other night. You just put it more clearly."

"Ah." Michael checked his watch. "Anyway, I'm no expert on life, but anytime you want to talk, I'm around."

"Thanks."

"No prob. I came over to invite you to our Bible study. There's one tonight, actually. At our place. You're more than welcome to join us."

Connor hesitated. Bible study? How was that going to help him figure out his future?

"I'm not sure tonight is possible, but I will think about it.

Thanks for asking." He looked at his own watch. "How is it you escaped school this afternoon?"

Michael grinned. "My class got canceled. Seems the football team needs an extra hour to get to their out-of-town game. What could I do but sacrifice my class?"

"Tax dollars at work."

"You betcha."

Michael's grin offered a sense of fun Connor hadn't shared in a very long time. What a fool he'd been.

"I'm planning to hold a barbecue the day before we reopen. You and Ashley will be invited. I hope you'll come."

"Name the time and we'll be here. And seriously, if you want to talk, just give me a call. That's what friends are for."

A friend? Was that what Michael was?

Connor watched him walk away. He didn't feel intimidated as he often had at work when someone had offered to befriend him. Why was that?

Because there's nothing Michael wants from you. He's not trying to score points or get a bonus or match wits. He's just a guy who loves his wife and daughter, teaches kids and sculpts wood. His life is full.

"And mine isn't."

Connor didn't realize he'd said it aloud until Esther's head poked out the door. "Did you say something to me?"

"No." He rose. Rowena and two men were conferring over a plan. That fountain was going to be the death of them, if he let it. He decided he'd go up to her place tonight—sort of wander over while walking Tobias. He'd take a look at her plants, approve whatever she chose and stress the fact that time was running out.

As if she'd heard his thoughts, her auburn head lifted and she returned his stare. Of course, they were too far apart for him to read her eyes and figure out what she was thinking, but he had a hunch Rowena anticipated his plan and that it wouldn't make one iota of difference to her intent to have that fountain in working order before Wingate Manor reopened.

Sighing, Connor went inside to check on the painters in his uncle's rooms. A little voice reminded him that the time limit extended to his own work and it wasn't progressing as fast as he wanted, either.

Sometimes being a know-it-all really sucked.

Chapter Eight

Rowena loaded the last of the bedding-plant flats onto her truck bed, slid the cap over the back with Quint's help and secured it.

"That should protect them from the wind. Thanks. If you can take those flowering bulbs over to Wingate and get started planting them as we discussed, I should be back to help in about an hour. Just remember the color sequences."

"Got it." He loped off across the yard to back up his truck into her spot as soon as she pulled away.

Rowena drove at a steady rate down the hill into town. Mrs. Masters had asked for bedding-plant stock to fill her customers' requests over a week ago. If she didn't get them delivered soon, the order would be canceled. This opening after lunch was the least-busy spot she'd found to do it.

She ignored the to-do list thrumming through her brain and thought about the assortment she'd chosen. Most of the flats were four or six packs of familiar bedding plants would-be gardeners used across the country to bring life and beauty to their gardens: asters, marigolds, petunias, pansies. Rowena had included a few hanging baskets as requested, but she hoped to keep the majority of those to sell from the greenhouse on Mother's Day. People paid well for showy hanging baskets and she needed the sales to generate some much-needed income. The house roof was leaking everywhere now. If she didn't do something soon, the entire interior would be ruined.

"I'm trying, God. But I could sure use some help. Maybe you could give Dad a boost?"

No voice reassured her that help was on the way so Rowena shifted gears and focused on the changes in town. The biggest difference in Serenity Bay, besides the creation of Piper's town square, had to be the expansion of the florist shop. In spite of the larger space inside, it spilled out of the small false-fronted building and onto the sidewalk, attracting the attention of anyone who walked the street.

Laura Masters was a creative woman who didn't mind trying the bold or the exotic. Today she'd placed old-fashioned cream cans on the sidewalk and filled them with an assortment of fresh-cut and dried flowers around a small water fountain. There was a little wrought iron table and two chairs set to one side of the door with a couple of poppy-red mugs strategically placed on top as if waiting to be filled. Laura might not have a college degree but she had marketing down to a science. Odd she hadn't finished the end of the display.

Rowena climbed out of the truck and walked through the open door, inhaling the heady fragrance of exotic flowers as she glanced around for the owner. Voices from the back room whispered toward her.

"Mrs. Masters?"

"Hi, Rowena. We were just talking about you." Laura walked forward to embrace her, then stepped back. "Look who came to visit."

"Dad?" She couldn't believe it was the same man she'd visited in the home a few short days before.

Victor Davis looked happier than she'd seen him in years. His eyes shone, his smile quirked up the corners of his mouth in the funny little grin he used to wear when she was a girl and they'd made their quota of cuttings for the day. He reached out and hugged her.

"Hi, honey. How are you?"

"Busy. I didn't know you were planning to visit," she muttered, confused by his buoyant attitude. "When did you get here? Why didn't you let me know you were coming?"

"Victor decided to come down for a visit on the spur of the moment," Laura told her. "He caught the bus this morning. I was working on the display outside and noticed him getting off so I invited him for coffee. It's been ever so long since we've seen each other."

"I see." A flicker of hurt pricked Rowena's heart, vying with a flash of anger. He hadn't bothered to call, to tell his own daughter he was coming. He felt well enough to make the long trip by bus but he hadn't offered to help at the nursery even though he knew she was struggling.

"Are you all right, dear?"

She felt Laura's scrutiny and dredged up a smile.

"Of course." She turned to her father. "Just surprised. I'm glad you came, Dad. It's beautiful up here right now."

"Yes." His gaze rested on the flower shop owner.

At a loss to know what to say next, Rowena did what came naturally and concentrated on business.

"I have those bedding plants you asked about, Laura. Where would you like them?"

"I have an empty wire display rack I got with a pottery order last year. It has wheels, so I thought it might be good to use. That way I can roll the plants in at night and water them without hurting anything. Do you think this will work?" She motioned toward a rack sitting in the middle of the floor.

"Looks fine," Rowena agreed, wondering if her father had already seen and approved the setup.

"Victor suggested we put it on the south end. The plants will get lots of sun there and it's protected from the wind a little more."

So he'd had time to discuss where to put Laura's bedding plants, but no time to call and tell her he was in town.

"That looks fine. If you'll place it exactly where you want it, I'll start unloading. I'd stop to chat but I've got a lot going on at Wingate Manor today and I've got to get back."

"It was kind of you to take the time to bring them down," Laura said quietly as she moved the rack into position. "I know how busy you are. Everyone in town is talking about how wonderful it's going to look up there when you're finished."

The whole town knew Rowena was spending every waking hour between Wingate and the nursery. Everyone but her father. Well, he knew but he hadn't said a word about it. He didn't even seem to care. In fact, he seemed totally and utterly obsessed with staring at Mrs. Masters.

Rowena couldn't just walk away.

"I don't know what your plans are, Dad. But if you want to call me, I could pick you up later, show you what I've done at the nursery. And you can look around Wingate Manor, too. I know Connor would like to meet you."

She struggled to suppress her expectations, though everything in her yearned for him to spend a few hours at the old place, see the difference she'd made. Maybe then he'd see that here in the Bay, doing what he loved was possible again.

"If you want to show me, honey, I guess I could go."

Hardly an eager response. She caught her breath at the sting of hurt, fought to smile as Laura handed her a check to cover the cost of the bedding plants.

"Of course he wants to see. If you're busy, I could drive him."

"Thanks, Laura. But it's not a problem. So we'll meet up later, Dad?" He gave a half nod. "Great! You have my cell number. So does Laura. Just give me a call and I'll pick you up whenever you're ready. I'd better get back to work now. Thanks a lot, Laura. Let me know if you need more plants."

"I'll do that, dear. And thank you for bringing them."

"No problem." She gave her father one last searching glance, wondering if she should ask him if he wanted to come with her now. But Victor seemed perfectly happy to remain in the flower store, his hands cupped around a mug of coffee.

"Bye, honey." Her father waggled his fingers, his attention homing back to Laura as if he were a lost ship and she his beacon light.

"See you later." Rowena closed the tailgate, waved once then climbed back into the cab and headed back up Hill Road, turning off at Wingate.

He'd come on the bus—which meant he'd had to arrange for someone to take him from the home to the bus depot. As far as she knew, there was no returning bus until tomorrow night and that meant he'd have to stay over. The question was where?

Rowena pulled into Wingate, switched off the motor and tried to think. The house was a mess; there was no way she could get a room fixed up for him in time, not with the arrival of cement trucks scheduled to start pouring the koi pond in two hours. Since Laura already had the apartment over her store rented to Kent and his son, that was out.

Maybe she could get the motel to rent him a room in return for some landscaping work. Goodness knew their flower beds could use some work, though her time frame to get everything she'd promised completed was getting tighter and tighter.

"Problems?" Connor leaned against the truck door, peering at her with that inquisitive, golden gaze that missed nothing.

"Not really."

One sculpted brow arched as if to contradict her.

"It's just my dad."

"He's sick?"

She shook her head. "He's in town."

"That's a bad thing?" He opened the door, held it while she stepped out.

"No. It's just—he didn't call me to tell me he was coming," she murmured, wishing she could understand what made Connor seem so approachable one minute and so aloof the next.

"Maybe it was a last-minute decision."

"That's what he said."

"You don't believe that?" Connor studied her. "Why not?"

"For months, almost a year, he's never stepped foot outside the home he's been staying in unless I insisted. He never seemed interested in anything or anyone. I've been telling him about the restoration at the nursery for ages now, every time I see him, in fact. Not once did he even mention wanting to see it. But suddenly he's here. Why? It doesn't make sense."

She'd come on too strong, let her frustration show. Connor looked surprised. Pretty soon he'd guess she was hurt. Rowena faked a smile, tried to pretend it didn't matter.

"Never mind." She turned to walk away but his hand on her arm stopped her. He was frowning.

"Wait a minute. You're not really upset that he came to Serenity Bay," he guessed, his gaze intense.

She shook her head. "No, of course not. I've been asking him to come for a visit."

"But he's here now—and you're not happy." His grip didn't weaken though she pulled back. "What's really wrong, Rowena?"

"It doesn't matter," she mumbled, her chin tucked against her chest. "Forget about it. I have work to do."

"You're always working. It seems as if everything in your

life takes a backseat to your work." He frowned. "You know the world won't fall apart if you take five minutes to talk to me."

She blinked, lifted her head and stared at him. "This from the 'Deadline Man'?"

"I've been assured *you* always make *your* deadlines," he murmured, a hint of steel wrapped in his velvet tone. "Besides, I'm trying to change my ways. Now stop stalling and tell me the truth."

Rowena wanted to confide in him—in someone—so badly. Ash and Pip wouldn't understand how desperately tired she was of managing, of scraping through the day. They couldn't possibly know what it cost to drag herself back to work after a slapped-together meal, to force herself to complete just one more thing so she'd be that much closer to achieving her goals for the nursery, wouldn't miss the June 1 deadline, wouldn't forfeit her name, her reputation or any of her meager funds.

They certainly wouldn't understand how horrible it was to look in the mirror and know you'd never looked worse. Rowena was positive neither of them had ever tried to cut their own hair. They certainly didn't mend their jeans patch upon patch or spend eons trying to get the topsoil out from under their nails.

And even if they could understand how ugly she felt, there was nothing they could do about it but feel sorry for her and she did *not* want anyone's pity.

Suddenly everything just seemed too much. A rush of tears swelled into her eyes and she turned away to hide them, but moved too quickly. A burst of dizziness made the world tilt several inches too far to the left.

"Rowena?" Connor had bent and was now peering into her face. "You've gone very pale. Did you have breakfast this morning?"

"Of course." He was still holding her arm. She drew it away. "I'm fine, Connor."

"Really?" His fingers closed around the protruding bones of her wrist. He looked as if he might argue but after a pause he inclined his head and simply said, "Then you won't mind having coffee with me. I have a few questions that need answering."

"Now?" she asked, darting around him to get a better look at Quint's work with the bulbs. She'd forced them for three months just to make sure the blooms would appear on time to achieve exactly the color combinations she wanted. If he messed up, there wouldn't be a second chance.

"Right now," Connor insisted. "As you've told me before, you have excellent employees. So I'm sure they can handle whatever needs to be done while you take a break. Come on. Let's go."

Since Connor sounded more amenable than he had in days, and because she was more tired than she'd been in years, Rowena decided to go along, answer his questions and update him on the big fountain's progress—or lack thereof. While everything else was moving ahead full steam, that one item was giving her migraines.

Connor led her into the kitchen, poured two big mugs from the silver carafe on the counter and grabbed two of the cinnamon buns cooling on a rack. Rowena recognized Pierre, the chef, who'd been there last fall when she'd spoken to the brothers about Wingate Manor's revamp. She grinned when he turned just in time to see his baking disappear. He exchanged glares with Connor.

"The profits run down the drain once more," Pierre mourned as Connor added a handful of strawberries.

"We'll survive. Besides, Rowena's got hanging baskets that will be oozing strawberries under the kitchen arches. You'll soon have too many."

Pierre huffed his response, but winked at her before turning his back on his boss.

"Come on, Rowena. It's nice out. We'll sit on the back

deck. Then you can keep an eye on your workers, though we both know they don't need it."

Rowena sat, sipped the coffee he'd poured and then sampled the steamy roll. It was soft and light, the cinnamon fragrance enticing. The sweet, tart flavor of the strawberries tasted like nectar.

"This is good. How come Pierre's baking today?"

"He's trying to train one of the kitchen helpers to prepare Sunday brunch." Connor made a face. "Le Chef usually takes Sunday morning off but when Piper told him about a contest Serenity Bay holds with another town for most patrons at Sunday brunch, he insisted on participating. I could hardly deny him the pleasure."

The look of smug satisfaction washing across his face and the intensifying glint in his topaz eyes made her shake her head. So that's what Piper had been doing here last week.

"Having you and my friends join forces to scheme together is really scary," she told him. "I feel like I should warn Pierre."

"Mind your own business," he said good-naturedly. "And tell me what's going on with your dad."

"Maybe you should apply your advice to yourself," she suggested softly, watching him.

Connor didn't take offense, but Rowena knew he hadn't given up, either. He took a long, deep drink of the rich, dark coffee then leaned back in his chair, crossed his ankles and waited.

"What?" she demanded when she could stand the silence no longer.

"I know I'm a crank and a nag about this place and that you'd like to sock me in the nose ten times a day," he said, amusement lurking in his deep tones. "But I can see you're bothered about something, and I'd like to help if I can."

Rowena closed her eyes, tried to swallow the hurt, but it sat there like a huge, painful lump. She blinked, caught Connor's steady gaze on her and realized she was trapped.

He also saw her predicament and softly murmured, "I'm not going anywhere so you might as well spill it. Take your time."

"Time's the one thing I don't have. Anyway, it's not really your business."

"No, it isn't."

Ignoring him was useless. She sighed, crossed her arms over her chest and sought the simplest way to get this over with.

There wasn't one.

"I thought he'd be interested in the nursery," she said baldly.

"In what you've done, the work you've accomplished." Connor nodded. His hard face tightened as he grimaced. "I take it he isn't?"

"For months now my father hasn't seemed the least bit interested in anything. Yet today when I walked into Mrs. Masters's store he barely noticed I was there." It hurt to say it. They'd been each other's support for so many years—at least Rowena thought they had. "His focus was totally on her. He was reluctant to agree that he'd even come and take a look. If she hadn't encouraged it, I'm not sure he would have agreed."

Connor remained silent for several moments. Finally he spoke. Rowena had the sense he chose his words very carefully.

"Don't think your friends have talked about you behind your back or given away any secrets, because they haven't. Piper and Ashley are two of the staunchest supporters I've ever seen. You're lucky to have friends like them."

"But?" Her nerves tensed as she waited for the caveat.

"I happened to have overheard them talking about the nursery." He leaned forward, peered into her face. "I know you used to live there with your father, that you hoped to finish school and come back to work with him. But something happened and that wasn't possible."

"He lost it. Your uncles bought it for pennies on the dollar," she said bitterly.

"And you blame them."

She shook her head. "Of course not. It wasn't their fault. It was mine. Dad needed the money for my schooling and thanks to them, he got it. If they hadn't made an offer, he might have had to declare bankruptcy. As it was, he paid off what he owed and walked away."

"But he had nothing to walk away to?" Was that sympathy lurking in his eyes?

"No. He was injured the winter before. They said he was fine, but he'd lost the agility he had and couldn't do his job. That's why he had no chance of getting the nursery going again." She bit her lip. "Not without help."

"You think you should have been there."

"I *know* I should have. If I hadn't insisted on just a few more months, he wouldn't have needed to work those extra hours. He took a pay raise, accepted a more dangerous job because he needed the money to pay for my schooling."

"So you're blaming yourself." He said it in a dull, hard tone, as if she'd chosen one of several options.

"It's my fault, Connor. Every other year he was back at the nursery by that time. But that year he couldn't be. Because of me. Because my expenses were drowning him."

"You're sure of this?"

She nodded. "I got most of the facts from your uncles. It wasn't hard to piece together the rest."

He frowned, his forehead furrowed in lines of confusion. "I didn't realize they knew so much about your father's situation."

"It's a small town," she reminded. "Everybody knows

everyone's information. I'm sure the state of Davis Nurseries' finances was well-known."

"Maybe." He studied her. "So you decided to get the land back, to get your father back on it. Why?"

"Why?" She couldn't believe he didn't understand. "Because he loved this nursery. There's nothing that could have kept him from working it." Realizing her raised voice was drawing attention, Rowena forced herself to calm down. "Leaving the nursery has left my father like a zombie."

"Until today," he reminded her.

"Yes. But that's because he's back in the Bay."

"Are you sure?"

Something in his voice caught her attention, an unspoken warning. Or maybe it was a suggestion to look more closely at the situation. But Rowena had gone over it in her mind a hundred times. Nothing else made sense.

"I don't know what you're suggesting." She bristled. "I know my father. I know how much of himself he poured into the nursery and what it cost him to walk away."

"All of that may be true, Rowena." He leaned forward, his face less forbidding than she'd ever seen it. "But he's had a lot of time to get over it, a lot of time to find new interests."

"Dad never was one for hobbies." She studied his hands, the long, muscular length of fingers that so ably held the reins of Wingate, hands that could hold on like steel or support you with a kind firmness meant to help. She quickly looked away. "I know you're trying to say something, Connor, but I don't understand what it is. I'm not good at guessing games."

"I'm not playing them." He kept watching her, his face altering slightly, softening. "I don't want to hurt you, Rowena."

"Don't worry about it. I'm tough."

"You pretend to be." He held up a hand at her protest, a smile flickering over his lips. "I know you don't want to hear this, but is it possible that your father got over the loss of the nursery a long time ago?"

She shook her head vehemently. "No."

"Why?"

"Because it was everything to him."

Connor smiled. "I think you were probably that. You're his daughter. I'm sure he wanted you to go to school. I suspect he wanted you to get all the training you could, to be as prepared for life as it was possible for you to be."

"You're saying he didn't begrudge me the extra studies," she said, finally realizing what he'd been hinting at.

"I think he would have given you more, if he could have."

She thought about it, nodded. "Look, I know my father loves me. You don't have to reassure me about that. It's just—"

"He didn't react the way you expected. Why do you think that is?"

"I don't know."

He looked as if he knew something she didn't. That made Rowena uneasy.

"I think it's something to think about. Maybe coming back, getting the nursery going again—maybe you wanted to do that for *you,* not for him."

She almost laughed. The ratty living quarters, backbreaking work, pouring every dime she owned into one project—

"Connor, do you know what I gave up to come here, to do this?" She glanced around the grounds, felt a rush of pride that her vision was finally coming to fruition. She returned her focus to him. "Do you understand what it cost me to walk away at a time when my career was reaching its peak?"

"No, I don't know. I only know what you've told me."

Rowena pushed the cup and plate away, pulled her gloves from her pocket and rose.

"I loved what I was doing," she whispered, trying to

suppress the well of emotions that rose too easily these days. "Nothing could have persuaded me to give up work that filled my soul, made my days happy and gave me so much pleasure. Nothing," she said fiercely, holding his gaze with her own, "except the fact that I love my father and I'd do anything to help him heal."

She turned away and trod down the steps onto the sod she'd only just ordered laid.

"Rowena?"

It took every ounce of control she could muster to pause, stand there and wait to hear whatever he wanted to say.

"I never doubted you love your father. But sometimes love clouds the truth."

His footsteps died away, leaving her alone.

He thinks I made a mistake in coming back here. But oh, God, I haven't, have I? You led me here, You opened the doors for me to get the nursery back. I've followed in Your path. Help me to be content with the life You've chosen for me.

Rowena lifted her head, thrust back her shoulders and strode toward Quint. Time to get back to work.

Chapter Nine

"Come on, Tobias. You and I need to visit a certain lady."

Connor kept the dog on the leash until they reached the edge of the Davis property, then released him. Tobias licked his hand gratefully, then bounded across the acres like a prisoner set free.

At least he'd stopped seeing Cecile's face whenever he looked at the dog. That was progress.

But as he walked, Connor was troubled by another more recent memory—Rowena's face. This afternoon she'd climbed out of that decrepit old truck looking like one of her flowers that had been cruelly crushed and all he'd wanted to do was make it better.

Which was really stupid. He'd made a vow to himself not to get involved. Love was something he wasn't capable of. If he'd learned anything from Cecile, it was that he couldn't open himself up for that kind of vulnerability. He was too selfish, too determined to have his own way.

But Rowena had tried so hard. That was the difficult part. She'd worked herself into a frazzle trying to meet his deadline and make her father proud. How could the man not even take an interest?

A tiny flame of anger burned inside, surprising him with its intensity. Why was he so keen to ease Rowena's pain?

Thankfully Connor didn't have to answer that as her house came into view. He heard a noise but couldn't see her.

"Rowena? Are you here?"

"Up here."

He looked up, saw her standing at the edge of the roof, a hammer dangling from her fingers.

"What are you doing?"

"Nailing in some new shingles. The leaks were beginning to get the best of me. But I'm done now." She disappeared. A few moments later she walked toward him, hammer gone. "Out slumming?" she asked, a crooked smile twisting her lovely mouth.

"You said I should come check out the plants," he reminded. "Is this a bad time?"

"No. It's perfect. We're going to start placing some perennials tomorrow." She shoved a length of hair out of her eyes. "Come on to the greenhouse and we'll take a look. Sorry I look so bad but I wanted to get that roof fixed."

Fixed? From what Connor could see she'd barely made a dent. The tree lay where it had fallen. His uncle's reminder to make sure her home was habitable came back to haunt him and he took a good look at the place in the full shine of daylight.

He'd been so busy with Wingate he hadn't bothered to check out the house and he should have. It didn't look livable. It looked like it might tumble down the hillside it sat upon.

"Connor?" She frowned, followed his gaze. Her cheeks flushed a deep rose and she bit her bottom lip.

Something grabbed his heart and squeezed it. In that moment he envisioned her as a little girl, eager for attention, doing everything she could possibly think of to gain her father's attention and praise.

"Is something wrong?" She lifted one hand to touch a ragged corner of her hair. "Is my face dirty?"

"No. I was just thinking about something else." He saw the disbelief in her eyes. "I let Tobias off his leash and he hasn't come back."

"Oh." Her color returned to normal. "I'm sure he's just chasing squirrels. He'll be back soon. So should we look at the plants or not?"

"Yes, of course." He followed her to the glass structure, noticed that though her jeans were tattered and worn, they were clean. How did she have time to do laundry, and was she using the same old appliances that had been there when she was a child?

The difficulties Rowena must have to deal with on a daily basis filled his mind like a checklist of problems. He listened to her speak about her intentions for the flowers but his brain was busy trying to make the glory of what she created mesh with the hovel she was forced to live in.

"So what do you think?"

"I think you'll do a wonderful job. Whatever you choose is fine with me."

"Such agreement." She frowned, studied him. "Are you really that worried about Tobias?"

"He's my respons—" Connor stopped when Rowena held up her hand.

"Did you hear that?"

He shook his head. But a moment later he did hear it. It was the dog.

"That's not a bark, that's a whine. Do you think there's something wrong?" he asked her.

Rowena's lips tightened as she jerked her head once in a nod. "There's an abandoned mine shaft on this property," she explained. "I've boarded it up several times but the local kids think it's a great spot to play in and they keep removing the boards. Tobias might be stuck in there. Many of the boards are rotten and it's not safe."

"Can you show me?"

"Yes, but it's dark down there. We'll need flashlights. I've got a couple in the house."

Connor followed her and stood waiting on the doorstep while she hurried inside. One glimpse showed him an assortment of pails and pots dotted around the kitchen. Obviously the place was in worse condition than he'd ever imagined.

"Okay, I've got them." She closed the door quickly, grabbed a rope from the back of her truck and surveyed him, one eyebrow raised. "Ready?"

He nodded.

They tramped across the nursery fields until they came to the trees surrounding the far side of her property where it bordered the government forest land. She stopped at the top of a ravine, listened. Connor pursed his lips at the mournful sound—Tobias's whine for help was getting fainter.

"It's really rough going down here. I'm used to it but you might want to wait at the top," she told him.

"I'm not a wimp, you know. I won't wilt just because I have to do a little climbing." He felt compelled to defend himself as he clamped his hands around the rope. "I've done a fair bit of climbing. I can rappel with the best of them."

"Okay." She tied off the rope, wrapped it around her waist. "I'll go first since I'm familiar. I'll yell when I get down and you can pull up the rope, tie yourself to it. Watch out about halfway down. There are some jagged bits."

She surveyed his khaki pants and the light cotton shirt he wore.

"Rowena, I'll be fine. Go ahead."

She nodded once, then let herself over the edge, testing her footing first then easing the extra rope around her waist as she disappeared over the rim.

The rope moved methodically—tightening, slacking. It jerked once, then nothing happened.

The bitter gall of fear rose in his throat. Connor grasped the rope more tightly.

"Rowena? Are you all right?"

No answer.

"Rowena!"

He moved closer to the edge, watched a few pebbles dislodge and trickle over the hedge. He hesitated to go too close in case the entire cliff gave way.

"Don't come down!" Her voice floated up.

"What's wrong?"

"Tobias is here but he's slipped into a hole. His leg is caught. I have to work him free."

Connor could hear the dog's soft whimper followed by Rowena's softly reassuring voice. He waited several minutes, trying to find the words that would make an acceptable prayer. "Please help them," didn't begin to express what he was feeling.

Somehow over the past weeks, he and Tobias had bonded. It had nothing to do having to care for the animal, it had to do with the dog's unflagging determination to stay with him. Sure, he ran off occasionally, but Tobias always came back, always ready to lick his hand, trot by his side or just sit at his feet.

Somehow, in spite of his best intentions, Tobias had become his dog. Connor was responsible for feeding him, walking him, making sure nothing happened to him. It was a scary thought to realize someone else depended on him.

On the heels of that thought came the realization that Rowena had become his friend.

Connor didn't know how it had happened. He hadn't wanted a friend, or even company. But she'd planted her tiny feet on the ground, dug in and stayed her course and somehow she'd worked her way into his life so completely that he couldn't imagine Wingate without her.

That thought scared him so much he had to do something.

"This is taking too long. It's going to be dark in half an hour. I'm coming down." He ignored her protest, eased himself over the edge and rappelled down to the protest of muscles left idle too long.

"I thought I asked you to wait."

He ignored that, untied the rope and walked over to where she knelt on the ground. "What can I do?"

"We have to move this boulder. But it can only go to the left. If it shifts right it will crush his paw." She stared at him from beneath her incredibly long lashes as if she was assessing his reliability. Worry creased her tanned forehead into a pleat. "Can you do it?"

Connor smiled, smoothed away the wrinkles.

"It's okay," he soothed. "We'll get him out."

She studied him for a moment, then smiled. It was like watching the sun appear from behind the clouds.

"Well, old boy, looks like you got yourself into a fix this time." He knelt beside her, slid his fingers next to hers, seeking some purchase on the smooth stone. "All right, I'm going to heave it up and you move him. Okay?"

She nodded. He flexed his fingers in the small space, got a grip and lifted as hard as he could. "Now!"

Rowena's fingers worked next to his as she slid the furry paw free, holding Tobias's body still against her side with her other arm.

"He's out," she said, just when he thought he couldn't hold on a moment longer. "Let it go."

When he'd made sure her hands were out of harm's way, Connor let go of the stone and sat back with a huff.

Tobias licked his paw for a few moments, swiped his tongue over Rowena's face then bounded over the stone and up the cliff face using a different route than the one they'd taken.

"That's thanks for you." Connor stood, held out his hand to help her up.

Holding his gaze, Rowena slid her tiny hand into his, gripped her fingers around his hand and let him draw her upright so that she was standing just a few inches from him.

"Are you all right?" he asked quietly, not wanting to let go.

"I'm fine. I banged my shin on the way down but I'll be okay." She turned his hand over, studied his bloodied knuckles. "You need some antiseptic and a bandage."

Her fingertips gentled over his broken skin but Connor didn't feel a thing.

"We'd better get back up before the sun sinks completely," she whispered.

"Uh-huh." But he couldn't move. Something private, special, secretive, fluttered through the night air and held him captive.

Her big green eyes were wide, forest shadows hiding at the back. He lifted his free hand, cupped her chin, his thumb brushing against the delicately smooth skin that covered her sculptured face.

"You know, you're very beautiful," he murmured, sliding his hand past her chin to her neck and slipping back to cup her slim nape in his palm. "Like a flower hidden deep in the Amazon."

"Connor." Her breathy whisper caught on the night breeze and fluttered into nothingness as he bent his head and touched his mouth to hers in a kiss as soft as eiderdown.

She froze, her tiny form stilling as he placed his other hand on her waist and drew her closer to taste the sweetness of her lips once more. One tentative fingertip touched his chest, darted upward to brush against his jaw as she returned his kiss in the solemn silence of the forest glade.

"What are you doing?" she asked when at last he lifted his head.

"It's called kissing." He did it again, to be sure she understood.

"Yes, but why?"

He smoothed the arch of her brow, traced it down to her cheekbone, to the soft up-tilt of her nose.

"Because I wanted to." She frowned at that so he tried again, using humor this time. "Because it's a shame to waste this twilight."

Her face altered and for a moment he wondered if he'd hurt her. Connor decided to go for honesty—well, partial honesty.

"Because you're kind and generous and you helped my dog and I wanted to say thank you."

"You didn't have to." She turned away.

He reached out, grasped her arm, forced her to look at him.

"Rowena, you more than anyone should know that I don't *have* to do anything," he said softly.

After a moment she nodded. The beginnings of a smile toyed with the corners of her generous mouth. A shaft of light spun her hair a ruby gold, turned her skin to alabaster.

"Yes, I do know that," she said quietly. Then, after a moment, "Okay. You're welcome. Come on. It's time to go. I'll make you a cup of hot chocolate."

She was nervous.

Connor said nothing as she grabbed the rope and began her ascent. Perhaps she needed a few moments to collect herself. That was fine with him. He had no idea why he'd embraced her, kissed her. But he didn't regret it. Not for an instant.

Rowena Davis was a constant surprise and that kiss had done funny things to his brain and his stomach. Connor sat down on a nearby stone to think about it while he waited for his turn on the rope.

After a while a soft swishing got his attention. The frayed end wavered back and forth in front of him.

"Is it too dark down there, Connor? Can't you see the rope?" she called from above.

He realized she'd already gained the top and had been waiting for him. "Yeah, okay, I've got it."

The effort of climbing back up required his full attention. By the time Connor levered himself over the edge, Rowena was untying the other end of the rope from the tree and forming it into big loops.

"I'll have to get it covered with something else," she mumbled, her face tucked into her neck like a shy turtle. "I don't want anything or anybody to get hurt. There." She slid the coils over one shoulder, glanced at him. "Ready for that hot chocolate and a bandage?"

"The first. Don't need the second." He walked with her to the house, pausing on the deck when she grasped the doorknob. "I'll sit out here and wait for Tobias to come back."

"Okay. The inside's a mess, anyway." She slung the rope over a nail then disappeared into the house.

Tobias returned, limping a little but otherwise none the worse for wear. Connor's reaction to the experience was entirely different. He could pretend nonchalance as well as Rowena, but he hadn't yet wrapped his brain around what had happened out there. He wasted a few moments trying to puzzle it out but when no flash of lightning dawned he bent over to scratch the dog's ear.

Tobias left long enough to sniff the entire deck, moving lightly over the areas that creaked beneath him, completely avoiding the edges where the railing looked as if it would crumble into sawdust. Finally Tobias returned to flop down across his feet.

"Ah, I see the prodigal has returned." Rowena handed Connor a big, steaming mug and sank down in a chair on the opposite side of the table. The yard light clicked on, lending a soft glow to the area as the last rays of sun dimmed the daylight to dusk.

"The prodigal?" he asked, curious to know the connection between the story and the dog.

"Don't you remember the Bible story? The prodigal son left home, squandered his wealth, lost everything. Finally he decided to go home. The father forgave him, welcomed him back with open arms as if he'd never left."

While inside Rowena had shed her work boots. Now her feet were bare. One small toe poked the dog's fur. Tobias obligingly licked her digit then put his head back down and closed his eyes with a soft rumble of contentment. Rowena giggled, tossed him a marshmallow from her cup.

"Here we are welcoming this runaway back without even a little lecture. You're a big wuss, Tobias."

Tobias didn't seem to mind the denigration. He swallowed the marshmallow with one swipe of his pink tongue and went back to his nap.

She giggled. "At least he doesn't seem the worse for wear."

"No, he doesn't." Connor needed to come up with a way to talk about renovations. If Uncle Henry got a good look at the condition of this deck, Connor would get a severe lecture.

"Is something wrong?" She was peering at him, her face puzzled but also apprehensive.

"No. Yes."

She laughed. "Has anyone ever told you that you have a problem with decisions?"

He met her gaze, refused to look away. "I never had a problem before," he said.

"So it's just me." She sighed. "Well, I may look like something the cat dragged in, especially after that jaunt over the hill, but I assure you, I won't do anything really nasty. You can tell me what the problem is."

"It's the house."

"The house. Wingate Manor?"

He shook his head, glanced around.

"My house?"

"Yes." Connor felt like a schoolboy confessing to pulling pigtails.

"What about it?"

He drew in a lungful of courage. "I was supposed to get it fixed."

Rowena didn't say anything, just looked at him.

"Uncle Henry made me promise that I'd make sure the place was livable, that whatever repairs needed to be done would happen so you wouldn't have to live with years of neglect. I didn't do it. The truth is, I forgot."

She shrugged. "No biggie. I'm not here a lot and when I am I mostly just use the kitchen, the bathroom and the bedroom. I fixed the roof so it's not leaking in those parts."

"Yes, but—"

Her face tightened. "Look, I know their money is tight, that they need a nest egg for when they sell the place. I don't expect them to waste a bunch of money on this house. That wasn't part of the deal."

"Waste?" He frowned. "Rowena, I know you're trying to be nice and I appreciate it, but this house should never have been turned over to you before an inspector went through and made sure it was all right."

"Well, I've been living here for almost five months and I'm still okay." Her chin had jutted out—ready for battle.

But Connor would not back down. Maybe she was prepared to do some self-sacrifice thing here, but he wasn't. She wanted to have her father come and stay, help out with things when he was able. And Connor wanted her to have that dream.

"Tomorrow I'm going to have some people come over, take a look and starting putting things to right." He ignored her swift intake of breath. "I have to, Rowena. I promised my uncles. I already feel awful about letting it go this long. The last time I was in the city Uncle Henry reminded me and I should have taken action long ago. It's agony to have to sit through one of their monologues about duty," he told her, trying to lighten the mood.

"I'm sure you quake in your boots when those two kindly old men reprove you," she scoffed.

Connor grimaced. "Henry has guilt down to a science. They never had to punish me, you know. I always confessed long before they found out I'd broken a vase or poured salt in the sugar bowl. Guilt is a terrible tool."

"You're faking," she said, studying him.

"Ha! That only proves you've never had Hank remind you that God hates sin, that He can't even look at it." Connor pointed to his chest, enjoying this more than he'd expected. "I've been through those lectures. The one about lying is the worst and I'm not having that on my conscience any longer. Tomorrow morning some men will be here and you'd better let them in or I'll sic the uncles on you."

She smiled. "Fine. If you want to waste money, who am I to complain? But I'd rather spend it on Wingate's grounds."

He shook his head. "This is in a special account. If I pretended I'd used it for here and spent it on Wingate I'd be worse than pond scum."

Rowena leaned back in her chair, her eyes dancing. "It's good to know those lessons on integrity that you learned at your uncles' knees have stuck so well."

She had no idea.

"I suppose you'd say no if I asked to take a look around, just to get an idea of the kind of workers that will be needed. Day after tomorrow I'm going to the city and I'll have to give a detailed report to the old duffers. It would be easier if I had the facts and figures at hand."

"You're going on Sunday?"

"Yes. Why?" He studied her face, trying to decipher the odd tone in her voice. "Did you have something planned for me?"

"Not me. Michael said you'd agreed to go with us for a first scuba lesson."

He groaned, slapped a hand to his head. "I completely forgot. Do you think he'd mind changing it to tomorrow afternoon instead? I promised the uncles I'd be there on Sunday and I don't like to disappoint them—why are you shaking your head?"

"Tomorrow's cleanup day in Serenity Bay. Michael's in charge of the kids' group. We all pitch in to make sure the main streets are free of debris. Crews will come to pick up those enormous baskets I planted and place them on the corners downtown. We'll plant Piper's town square, put up new flags, hang a welcome banner. You know, a general workday."

"You're going to help?" he asked, surprised that she'd volunteer when she was already overburdened with work.

"Of course. It's really a fun time with the community. You should come."

"I wouldn't know what to do," he prevaricated, knowing he'd feel like a misfit.

"There are crew leaders for every aspect but if you want, you could work with me," she offered. "Why don't you come up here around eight? You can help me load up the flowers we'll use to make a maple leaf on the hill coming into town. We could go together if you want."

Rowena made it sound fun, and suddenly he longed to be part of the community, to give something back.

"You'll need to bring lunch, though. We all gather together at noon, eat our lunches, then finish after that. Then there's a big barbecue at the mayor's in the evening."

"Okay, I'll come. I'll bring lunch for both of us."

"And a little bit extra," she said with a grin. "Just in case someone else forgets."

"Sure."

She was curled up in her chair like a cat, her big green eyes wide and expressive, the shadows gone. Was she thinking about their kiss, too? All at once, Tobias rose, taking off across the yard as if he'd spotted breakfast.

"He knows when we've overstayed our welcome," Connor joked, noting the yawn she tried to conceal. "I'd better get going, too, though I'd like to take a look inside first," he said, hating to ask her to move when she was clearly worn-out.

"If you must. Though I still think—"

"Rowena?"

Connor turned, saw a tall lean man standing at the corner of the house, Tobias by his side.

"Dad! How on earth did you get here?" Rowena asked, jumping up.

"Walked. It did me good."

"If you'd called me, I'd have picked you up."

Connor thought she'd looked lovely moments earlier, but now, with her face lit up from the inside, she was stunning. Her eyes glowed with love.

"I'm so glad you came." She hugged him briefly, then stepped back. "This is Connor Wingate, great-nephew of Henry and Hank. Connor, this is my dad, Victor Davis."

"Please to meet you, sir." Connor shook hands with him, feeling the frailty in the slight grip. He grinned at Rowena. "Aren't you going to tell me the meaning?"

"Of what?" she asked, the skin between her brows furrowed.

"Of his name. As I recall, it's a habit of yours."

"Oh." She blushed. "*Victor* means 'conqueror.'"

"A misnomer, if ever there was one," her father explained, a hint of amusement embedded in the words. "I'm about as meek as you'll ever meet, Connor. Rowena has no trouble keeping me in line."

"You make me sound like some kind of militant," Rowena protested, her cheeks fiery red. "And it's not true."

"About landscaping it is," Connor contradicted, delighted to see her so flustered. He turned to Victor. "I'm glad you could come and see what she's been doing here. You're more than welcome to visit Wingate Manor, as well. I don't think you'll recognize the grounds."

"My daughter is very good at what she does," he agreed, his pride obvious. He touched Rowena's shaggy hair, his smile gentle. "I apologize for waiting so long to come and see what you've done, honey. Mrs. Masters and I had lunch and time sort of got away from me. I thought I'd stay with you tonight and then tomorrow you could show me what you've been doing. Maybe I could even help."

"That's not necessary, Dad. You need to regain your strength."

Something in the way she said it made Connor realize Rowena was panicked. And he knew why. Victor couldn't stay in the house, not in that condition, and he had a hunch she didn't want him to see the mess.

"Rowena probably forgot to tell you she's in the middle of renovations on the house," Connor interjected. "But I have lots of room at Wingate Manor. Would you come and stay with me? There are more bedrooms than I need and our chef is back, so I can offer you some pretty good meals."

Rowena never said a word but the look in her eyes was thanks enough.

"That's very kind of you, though I don't mind bunking down here." Victor shrugged. "I don't need much, you know."

"You need a bed and I happen to know your daughter's short on those at the moment. Please come. It would mean a lot to be able to tell the uncles you stayed."

"All right. Thank you."

"It's my pleasure." Connor scrambled for a reason to get into the house. If he let her put it off, Rowena could quite easily change her mind and he wasn't going to let that happen. She deserved a decent place to live. "Rowena, maybe you want to show your dad inside the greenhouse tonight. I've got to get those measurements we talked about, remember?"

She caught on immediately but it was clear she was having second thoughts. "You have to do that tonight?"

"Yes. I think the workmen should get started as soon as possible." He held her gaze, refusing to back down.

She sighed. "Fine. Do you want to see the greenhouse, Dad?"

"Of course."

"It's a good time," she said, leading him away. "Community workday is tomorrow and a lot of the plants will be moved out."

Connor waited until she was a good distance away. Then he ordered Tobias to sit and wait before pushing open the damaged door and stepping inside.

It was a horror.

The house was a ranch style with no upper story, the damage from rain evident on the stained ceilings. Pails were everywhere. She'd blocked off the living room and three other bedrooms. No wonder. He saw evidence of mice and who knew what else. He thought it might have to be gutted.

Connor felt slightly sick as he caught his first glimpse of her bedroom. He'd seen street people who lived better than this. He quickly shut the door, moved to the kitchen. The cabinets were old and cheap, made of some particle board that could not be saved. The big picture window with its showstopping view of the valley had leaked and rotted the wood. The appliances were obviously not working, because she had a hot plate and a small bar fridge tucked into one corner.

He'd never seen anything more spartan in his life. Uncle Hank would slap him upside the head if he saw this.

Connor turned to leave. His attention caught on the old oak rocking chair tucked into a corner and the Bible that lay open on a tiny table beside it. He couldn't help but read the verse she'd underlined.

So humble yourselves under the mighty power of God, and in His good time He will honor you. Give all your worries and cares to God, for He cares about what happens to you. 1 Peter 5:6-7

Humble herself?

This was as humble an existence as he could imagine. How did she keep her spirit alive, keep slaving away when she had only this to look forward to at the end of a long day? How could God allow a woman like Rowena to endure conditions like these?

Connor quietly closed the door behind him. After checking to be sure father and daughter were still in the greenhouse, he pulled out his cell phone and dialed.

"Esther? It's Connor. I'm so sorry to call you at home but I need some help and I need it fast."

His unflappable assistant listened, then promised to find him the people he needed.

"It's going to cost you a lot to have it done so fast," she said softly.

Connor grimaced. "Money isn't the issue here, Esther. I can pay whatever it costs."

The blasted money he'd thought would be his ticket to happiness was little more than a millstone, blindsiding him to what was really important in life—people. He could make more money. That was simple. Helping Rowena without injuring her pride was going to be much more difficult.

"If they can be at Wingate at seven, I'll add a bonus," he told her. "I want this done fast and well."

"Yes, sir." He could tell Esther was smiling.

There was just one more call to make.

"Uncle Henry, I need you to back me up on something. The nursery house is a disaster and I'm insisting on having it repaired. Rowena balked a little so I told her there was money specially set aside to get the place livable."

"But we don't have—"

"I do, Uncle Henry. And I never said it was your money, just that it had to be used on this house."

"You sound appalled by the place. Are conditions really that bad?"

"Worse. I should have checked it out when I first got here as you asked me to." But he'd been too busy wallowing in his own selfishness to consider someone else. "I'd like to get her completely out of there while they work but I doubt that will happen. Anyway, I just wanted to be sure you'd back me up."

"I won't lie, Connor."

"I don't want you to. If she asks, just tell her there's plenty of money to do the repairs without impinging on Wingate's renovation."

Silence greeted his words, then he heard whispers in the background.

"All right, son. If anyone asks, that's what we'll say. Is everything else all right? How are you doing—feeling better now?"

He was talking about Cecile. Connor winced, realizing it

had been days since he'd even thought about her. Selfish didn't begin to describe him.

"I'm fine, Uncle Henry. Looking forward to the opening here."

"We were right about hiring Rowena, weren't we?"

A certain timbre in Uncle Henry's voice made him pause before answering. The old boy knew a lot more than he pretended.

"Yes, you were quite right. She's making a big difference. You won't recognize the place when you come back." And then I'll leave here and try to figure out what I'm supposed to do next.

The idea of starting over, making new friends, fitting in somewhere he didn't belong—the thought held little appeal.

Connor said goodbye and closed his phone. He felt Tobias brush against his leg. For once he didn't mind the dog's affection.

"Don't ever let anyone tell you you're not a lifesaver, Tobias," he whispered as he ruffled the thick chocolate coat. "You might dash in where others fear to tread, but your heart's in the right place. If it wasn't for you tonight, I'd never have known it was so bad."

Tobias swiped his tongue across Connor's face then took off to greet the couple emerging from the glass enclosure. Connor followed at a more leisurely pace, busy with his own thoughts.

In a way Tobias was exactly like Rowena. They both rushed in to make a difference in whatever way they could without counting the cost to themselves.

But after listening to her speak of her father, seeing her yearning for his approval, after hearing Victor's reason for not arriving sooner, Connor felt a hint of trepidation steal through his heart.

Though Connor was no expert on fatherly reactions, Victor

didn't act the part of a man delighted to be back on his land, anxious to dig his hands into the soil and create beauty. Yet that's exactly who Rowena wanted him to be.

Sooner or later the two of them would have to talk about their futures and Connor had a nagging feeling that one of them was going to be terribly hurt. He stumbled on the path as the stark realization hit him like a sledgehammer.

Connor desperately wanted to spare Rowena that pain.

Chapter Ten

"You see, it's not as bad as you thought, is it?" Rowena waited for Connor's admission that the town workday was actually kind of fun. "People around here are really nice if you give them a chance to get to know you."

"Which I haven't done," he admitted. "I guess I lived in New York too long. I've gotten used to ignoring people when I walk down the street."

"It's nothing you can't change," she said, tucking another petunia into the massive bed they'd begun more than two hours ago. "Are you sick of this yet?"

"Digging holes?" He inclined his head as he considered the job she'd given him. "It's actually rather relaxing, though a bit hard on the knees."

She grumbled a not-so-nice comment about would-be gardeners and he laughed.

"Okay, I suppose relaxing isn't exactly the word a landscaper would use."

"Not about Wingate Manor, anyway."

They'd worked out a system. Connor dug the hole for the plant and poured in a ladle of water; she followed behind, set the plant in place, then pushed the dirt around to be sure it was secure. So far they'd made a good team.

Rowena tucked in the last red petunia, then changed to finish the section with white flowers, hoping he had no idea that butterflies were dancing the first movement of a Cinderella ballet in her stomach and had been ever since he'd arrived this morning. Having Connor so near for so long was unnerving.

Besides, crouching next to him on the ground in the dirt wasn't exactly the way the magazines advised to impress a man. She ignored the snide little voice inside that demanded to know why she was trying to impress a man like him. Memories of his kiss, the way he'd held her so tenderly—her face burned.

"You said you're nearing the end of the work the uncles authorized you to do. It can't be all that bad, can it?"

"No, it's not bad," she agreed. "We'll start putting in the annuals next week if it stays as nice as it has been. Then it's on to the finishing details, making sure everything will work as I'd planned, adding the final touches."

"So what's the problem?" Having reached the end of the planting bed, he leaned back on his haunches and frowned.

"The problem is that big fountain," she admitted. It was quickly becoming her nemesis. "I wish I could figure out what is wrong with the thing. No matter what we try, it just won't do what I want."

"Maybe you expect too much," he muttered, repeating the same argument he always used. "It's a fountain. It's supposed to spray water. It doesn't really matter if it goes through all those different spurts and stops, does it?"

This time she sat back and shot him a glare meant to quell.

"Are you kidding me?" she demanded, exasperated that he refused to understand. "Buying those little 'spurts and stops,' as you call them, drained what was left of the budget. What little there was after the speakers for the sound system arrived, that is. They're buried in those columns around the terrace to provide the ambience because the water is choreographed to move in patterns, according to the music we choose. If it doesn't work—"

"It's just a fountain, Rowena."

She clenched her hands, reined in her temper with difficulty.

"Calm down." He touched her arm, his eyes molten gold, his voice gentle. "All I meant is that it's only one part of a fantastic plan. If the fountain doesn't work properly right off the bat, that's only to be expected. Every project has glitches and kinks that have to be worked out."

"I do not have *glitches* on opening day," she snapped, stabbing the last flower into its spot. She smoothed the soil and rose, tired of the heat, the bugs and the feeling that her jeans and T-shirt came out the worse for wear against his spotless chinos and blue checked shirt.

Didn't the man ever get dirty?

"Are you in a bad humor because you're tired, Rowena? Or are you angry at me because the men started tearing apart your house this morning?" He was more shrewd than she'd given him credit for.

She jerked around, ready to tell him what he could do with his men. But a certain glint in his eyes told her he was trying to restore the camaraderie they'd shared last night. And, in fact, the chip on her shoulder had nothing to do with him.

Rowena gulped down the wash of shame that wouldn't go away.

"They're tearing out the cabinets, the ceilings, everything. I don't need a lot of fancy stuff, Connor. I don't *want* a lot of fancy stuff. I'm not used to it. I'm a plain person. I just need a place to sleep and eat."

"The contractors need to know that what they build on is solid and safe. You wouldn't go ahead with the terraces at

Wingate when you knew the foundations were unsafe—it's the same thing with them." He grinned. "I think you can rest assured that you're not going to end up with gilt ceilings and Romanesque murals on the wall. It's not going to be Buckingham Palace."

He was teasing her, trying to get her to let go of her fears.

"I know it sounds ungrateful," she told him, feeling just that. "But I liked not having to worry about ruining anything if I dashed inside for a cup of tea or to pick up my keys."

"Did you like the roof leaking constantly?" he asked, then held up a hand. "Okay, I'm sorry. That was uncalled-for and if I'd done what I was supposed to do in the first place, you wouldn't have had that problem."

He was sweet, but Rowena couldn't shake the feeling that living in the kind of house the builders were discussing was going to intimidate her.

"I'll have to take my shoes off at the door for fear the Italian-marble floor will be ruined."

"There will be no Italian-marble floors, so relax." Connor stood, stared down at her. "Why do you do that?" he asked after a long silence had passed.

"Do what?"

"Pretend that you don't like beautiful things."

"I don't do that."

He nodded. "Yes, Rowena, you do. And it's odd because you go out of your way to create beauty. But outside of gorgeous landscapes, it's as if you can't allow yourself to enjoy something just because it's lovely."

"I enjoy beautiful things. I just don't need them."

"Everybody needs beauty in their lives. There's nothing inherently wrong with the nice things, you know."

"I realize that." *But I can't afford them and I don't want to end up bitter and jealous of everyone who has them.*

She turned her back, began loading the tiny shovel, water pail and ladle they'd been using into the back of her truck.

"There's more to life than fancy stuff."

"Of course there is. But sometimes that 'fancy stuff' helps us enjoy life. Isn't that why God created us?" He hesitated, his gaze unblinking. "Maybe I shouldn't say this, but when I was looking in your house I noticed your Bible sitting on a side table."

"So?" she said defensively, feeling exposed, as if her private space had been invaded, torn open so the world could see how pathetic she was.

"It's a beautiful Bible. The cover looked like top-notch leather and the pages were the finest onionskin. There was even a touch of gilt along the edges. I can understand why you like to hold it, to read it."

"I don't read it because it's pretty," she said, sniffing. "I read it to learn more about God. Anyway, I didn't choose it. It was a gift from Piper and Ash the year I got my second doctorate." She shrugged. "They have good taste."

"So do you, Rowena. When you let yourself." There was something odd in the way he looked at her, as if he could see beyond the barrier of nonchalance she'd erected. "The fabric in that skirt you wore to Ashley's dinner party—that was very exotic silk. Why not admit you enjoyed the feel of it against your skin?"

"It was all I had," she admitted. "I'm not saying I don't like nice things, Connor. It's just that I can't afford to choose beauty over function."

"Which is, of course, why you chose landscaping. Flowers and fountains are all about function, aren't they?" A crooked smile curved the corners of his mouth. "I'm not buying it. Why are you so afraid of the house changing, Rowena? Is it because you're afraid you'll get used to it, start wanting more than you have in your life?"

If he only knew how much she wanted.

A beautiful home was only the beginning. She wanted children who would play through the house, discover the wonders of God's creation in nature, as she had. She wanted her friends gathered round, laughing, praying, cheering each other on. She wanted to be the hostess instead of always being the guest. She wanted her father happy, doing work he loved, reunited with the friends he'd left behind.

But most of all she wanted someone who saw beyond the dirt she dug in, beyond the mess she was. It didn't matter what they lived in. What she craved was someone who would always be there, who would tell her she was the loveliest thing in his world even when she wasn't, who would make her part of a circle of love that only grew stronger with time or distance or circumstances.

She wanted to be rooted, grounded in one place where she could nurture and be nurtured. She wanted to come home—not to a house, but a life. His kiss had only fanned the flames of that dream.

Rowena kept her head bent, concentrating on making sure the area was cleared and no tools had been left behind.

"Have I offended you?" Somehow Connor had soundlessly moved behind her. His hands slid over her shoulders, curved around them, warm, comforting. "I didn't mean to hurt you, Rowena, but I don't want you to have to live in a place you hate, either."

He turned her so she faced him.

"Talk to the men, tell them what you like, what you don't. Change whatever you need to so that it's your place. Otherwise their work will be for nothing." His thumb brushed her chin. "If you don't want something, say so. It's your decision."

"But so much renovating—it's terribly expensive," she

countered worriedly, remembering the cost estimate sheets she'd glimpsed.

"The money is there, waiting to be used."

She shook her head. "You don't understand. For most of my life I've struggled to learn how to be content with what I have. This seems like such an extravagance. Once Dad gets established, I'll leave and—" She didn't want to think about that.

"You'll deal with that when the time comes. For now, just accept it. As a gift, if you like. Though I hardly think necessary property improvements qualify." His fingers slipped into her hair, rubbing the strands as if he was polishing them.

She could rest there. Given the opportunity she could have relaxed against him, found contentment in letting the world pass by.

But that wasn't how it was going to be. Connor wasn't staying. He'd be moving on after the summer, when the uncles came back. She'd do well to remember that.

"You work so hard making things lovely for others." He leaned in, murmuring in her ear. "Let this be something someone does for you, that you can enjoy."

"I'll try," she promised as she drew away from him. A short siren burst through the air. "That's the call for lunch. Shall we join the others?"

Connor didn't say anything, simply followed her to the truck, sat silently as she drove to the town square. The other workers were seated on the grass, which was lush and green after so much rain.

He took out the picnic cooler he'd brought, waited for her to choose a spot. When they were seated between Ashley's and Piper's blankets, Connor responded to Michael's teasing about calloused hands with less than his usual acerbic wit and Rowena knew something she'd said bothered him.

She'd said too much, let him see too deeply inside. It was something she'd always tried not to do, but with Connor she found it more difficult to keep her barriers in place.

"What's for lunch?" she asked.

"A surprise." He lifted out a clear glass dish, removed the lid and told her to sniff.

"Shrimp salad?"

"Pierre's secret recipe. Along with fresh croissants, lemonade and coffee, and fudge brownies for dessert." He lifted out a container. "Ta da!"

"Shh…" Rowena glanced at the two men whose heads had perked up at the mention of fudge. She leaned forward. "Remember what I said about a little extra? If you don't have it, you'd better start eating your dessert now. Those two never met a brownie they didn't like."

"Not to mention Tati," Ashley chimed in. "I'll just take one for her, shall I?" She lifted a corner of the lid, snatched one dark square and "accidentally" smeared her finger with icing. Which meant she had to lick it off. "Ooh. Yummy."

"You wouldn't believe this is the same woman who always tells our daughter to finish her meal before dessert, would you?" Without a pause, Michael stole the brownie from her fingers, took a bite and groaned. "If these go on the menu at Wingate Manor I'll be living there this summer. Hey!"

Jason seized the remaining piece and ate it without a glimmer of remorse, then added his praise.

"Now they won't eat my plain old chicken sandwiches," Piper mourned. She made a face at Connor. "Thanks a lot!"

Connor wisely ignored that to dish up two plates for himself and Rowena. He then offered the rest of the salad to the others.

"This is by way of a peace offering," he explained. "Rowena reminded me that we were supposed to have our first scuba lesson on Sunday. I'm afraid we'll have to put it off because I have to go to Toronto to see the uncles."

"Very clever," Rowena whispered as the men made only the weakest protest, too busy enjoying their expanded lunch to kick up much of a fuss, especially after the cover "fell" off the brownies. "I'll bet you were a real manipulator in your old job."

"Hey, I'm not manipulating. Just improvising as I go," he joked, leaning toward her to whisper sotto voce, his amber eyes glinting in the warm sun. "It does help to have a secret weapon, though." He tapped the top of a second brownie container.

"Manipulating." She took another bite of her salad and decided to let the matter go. The salad was scrumptious. If the brownies were as good…

For a time everyone munched away happily.

"I heard your dad dropped by for a visit. How did he like the nursery?"

"It was pretty late when he came by last night," Rowena murmured. By now the whole town had probably heard. "He seemed to enjoy the greenhouse but this morning there wasn't much time for him to look around before we had to come to town for this."

"Where is he now?" Piper asked.

"He stayed overnight with Connor because the house is getting some improvements." Rowena glanced around, searching for the woman her father could hardly wait to see again. "There he is now. Sharing lunch with Mrs. Masters."

"They seem to enjoy each other's company," Michael said nonchalantly.

The men were busy trying to entice Connor with the possibilities of fishing, so Ashley and Piper moved closer.

"Is there something going on there?"

"Where?" Rowena jerked around, stared at her father's

laughing face and gulped. "You mean between Dad and Mrs. Masters?"

"Of course." Ashley handed her stepdaughter, Tatiana, a cookie, smiled as she flopped on the grass to eat. "The summer I came back to sell my dad's house they certainly spent a lot of time together. You were overseas so you wouldn't have noticed, Row."

"But—" She couldn't imagine it, had never even considered her father dating again, much less—

"They're probably just good friends," Piper soothed. "After all, they have both lived in the Bay for years. They have a lot in common."

"Dad has a lot in common with Bud Neely, too, but I don't see them lunching together."

The other two quickly changed the subject to the barbecue at Piper's house that night.

"Will everyone be dressed up?" Rowena couldn't imagine how she could find anything to wear in the mess her house was in.

"Hardly. It's more of a luau than a barbecue. We're doing the Hawaiian thing. Jason and Michael got a whole pig from the butcher, who showed them how to make a fire pit to roast it. My dear hubby was up about every half hour last night making sure the fire was hot enough. Michael appeared before dawn to make sure Jason was doing it right." Piper shook her head at Jason, her adoration obvious. "We'll be eating ham for the next year if a lot of people don't show up tonight."

"It'll be gone before the night's out." Jason's chest puffed out. "To think some people implied Mick and I don't know how to cook." He sneered, glaring at Ashley.

"Yeah," Michael chimed in, his grin splitting his face. "Some people!"

"The proof is in the tasting, hot shot," Ash told him. She

winked at Rowena, then opened her eyes to a wide, innocent look. "You do have a backup plan if the pig doesn't work out, don't you, honey?"

Jason looked crestfallen. "A backup plan?"

"As if we'll need it!" Michael ruffled his wife's too-perfect hair. "Ignore her, Jason. And you better be prepared to eat your words, *honey*. I'll want a full retraction when you taste our creation."

"Hmm." Ashley's low chuckle was meant for him alone. "I think I can come up with a suitable apology if necessary."

Rowena's heart squeezed at the obvious affection the couples shared. What would it be like to be loved like that? She happened to glance up and found Connor staring at her. Heat rushed over her cheeks and she quickly looked away.

"That might be something you can try at Wingate," Jason enthused. Having gained Connor's attention, the men launched into an in-depth description of the process of roasting a pig outside.

Pip leaned closer to Rowena and whispered, "If there is something going on, at least it might mean your dad will be staying around."

"Maybe." She shrugged as if she didn't care one way or the other, but the thought of her father and Mrs. Masters wouldn't be dismissed. Before lunchtime was over she made it a point to go over to the couple. "Hi, Mrs. Masters. I guess you have someone in the shop today covering for you."

"Yes. I usually take Saturdays off unless we have a wedding or a special event. Tatiana and I have a standing grandmother-granddaughter date on Friday nights and I need the extra rest." She laughed.

She didn't looked tired. She looked pretty, flushed and smiling as she peeked at Victor.

"Are you going to the barbecue at Piper's tonight? I was just wondering because I thought maybe Dad and I could spend some time at the nursery." Rowena caught the quick shared look between Laura and her father and wondered what it meant.

"Oh, I am sorry, dear. I asked your father to go with me. I thought it might be fun for him to meet up with some of his old friends while he's here."

"Yes, I'm sure it would."

"You're going, aren't you, honey?" her father asked. "I mean, you three girls have always done everything together. I just assumed—"

"She's going with me." Connor's voice came from behind Rowena's left shoulder. When had he started sneaking up on people? "Do you want to ride over with us, Victor?"

"No, thanks. Laura's promised to pick me up."

"Well, there's the siren. I guess it's time to get back to work." Rowena dug in her pocket, pulled out the list she'd been handed a few minutes ago. "Looks like I'm on beach duty this afternoon. That shouldn't be too tough. I can dip my toes in the water if I get too hot. See you later." She waggled her fingers, turned away, swallowing her disappointment at her father's disinterest.

"Is anything wrong?" Connor followed her back to the truck, picnic basket in hand. He set it in the back, got into the truck and rode with her to the beach. "Rowena?"

"I don't get it," she blurted out.

"What? Your father's attraction to Mrs. Masters? She's a lovely woman."

"Of course she is." She glared at him. "She's been a lovely woman for as long as we've known her, which is over thirty years. So?"

Connor turned his head, but not quickly enough. She saw the smile he tried to hide.

"This isn't funny."

"It is, actually. You're making no sense. It's bad that Mrs. Masters is nice?" He threw her a look that begged "please help me understand."

Rowena chuffed out a breath of air, ruffling the bangs on her damp and hot forehead. Why couldn't the stupid air-conditioning work in this truck? Who wanted to be all sweaty and hot when they were seated next to a handsome, coolly composed man?

"Look, forget it." She dredged up a smile. "I guess I'm just a little disappointed that Dad hasn't spent more time at the nursery this weekend, but that will come. I know it will. He loves the work, loves that land. Once he gets back in the swing of life here I'm sure he'll be telling me I've got the spruce crooked or put the flowering plum in the wrong place." She shook her head in rueful apology. "I guess you were right. I am cranky today."

"If I had to stop leaks after all the rain we've had, I'd be cranky, too."

She flashed him a grateful smile and drove to the beach. Once there, they found paint cans and brushes for the benches and picnic tables that were strategically placed for anyone who wanted to sit and eat or just talk.

"Do you want to paint the benches or those boards the kids hide behind?" She pointed to the sheets of plywood that had pictures drawn on and cutouts for posing. A child could stand behind, insert his face and become a pirate, a sea captain, a sailor on a yardarm or a variety of other simulations.

"I suppose you're an artist, too?"

Rowena laughed. "Hardly. I like gardens but I'm lousy with perspective when it comes to flat surfaces. They should have asked Ash. She's the artist. But she's already creating some kind of mural on the front of the recreation center. So if you're better than me, and you have to be, you're elected."

"Actually I did take a painting class." He made a face at

her astonished expression. "Cecile wanted us to spend more time together so I agreed. I thought she meant seeing a Broadway show or taking a trip."

"But she chose painting."

"I'll have you know, the instructor said I showed potential." He puffed out his chest. "I'll take the boards. It's more or less paint by number."

"A comedown for a talent like yours," she teased. "But this is only Serenity Bay. If you want fame and fortune you'll have to go back to New York."

"I will, eventually," he said quietly, blending yellow and red to get the orange shade he needed. "This is only a temporary stay for me."

Rowena began work on the benches. "What will you do when you return?"

"I don't know. I'm not even sure if I'll go back there." He glanced at her. "I came to help the uncles but also because I needed a change. I'm kind of enjoying the lack of noise and the space."

"But not enough to stay?"

"What would I do here?' he asked, gazing across the water.

"Well, what did you do in New York?" she asked, knowing the answer but hoping he'd talk more about himself.

"Stocks, bonds, trading. It was fun and I enjoyed it, but it ties you down. You have to be constantly watching the markets to make your trades at the appropriate time. There's more to life than a computer," he murmured in a tone that made her wonder if that was something Cecile had said to him.

"You're lucky you realized that soon enough to do something about it." Rowena moved to the back of the bench and began to apply the paint in smooth, even strokes. She paused when Connor didn't respond.

"I didn't," he said softly, staring at her. "Realize it in time, I mean."

"I'm sorry." She didn't know what else to say. He was talking about the woman he'd loved who had died.

"Yeah. So am I."

They worked silently for a while, each concentrating on their own task until a group of teens approached.

"Hi, Rowena."

"Trish." Rowena laid the brush across the can and rose. "Shauna. Greg. How are you?"

"Great. We really enjoyed that field trip to the nursery last month."

"I'm glad. I hope I didn't bore you."

"More like inspired us. We've got this, like, major project for biology. We're hoping you can help."

"I can try."

"That would be great." The other two waited for Trish to continue.

"We chose to do a paper on grafting for our major project. We've done all the research." Trish glanced at Connor, smiled, then continued. "But we thought we could really boost our marks if we could actually demonstrate the technique in class, maybe show some samples of grafting we've done."

"That's where you come in." Greg stepped forward, shoved his glasses up his nose. "We were wondering if you would show us how to do it."

"I could," Rowena agreed with a frown. "But I'm not doing any grafting. Primarily I'm doing cuttings to get new stock going. It's quite different than grafting."

"Oh." Their crestfallen faces forced her to explain further.

"You see, I don't have the stock to graft. I won't be handling fruit trees for a couple of years and I'm bringing in the roses for Wingate's gardens."

"You're changing the uncles' prize rose bed?" Connor interrupted, a frown marring his good looks. "Why?"

"Because it needs it." She tossed him a glare meant to remind him that he'd said he wouldn't argue with her decisions anymore, then turned back to the group who'd now been joined by another half dozen kids. "I'm sorry, but—"

"There's a crab apple tree by the back door at Wingate Manor," Connor interrupted. "Would that help?"

"You need something to graft it to," she explained. "And there's no guarantee that the graft would take, anyway."

"Isn't there a hawthorne bush at the end of your greenhouse?" he asked, lifting one imperious eyebrow when she sighed.

"Could we use that?" Shauna asked, eyes huge in her pretty face.

"Yes, you could graft a crab apple to a hawthorne," Rowena admitted.

"Would you show us?"

"When is your assignment due?"

"Not for a couple of weeks. That's why we thought if we practiced first—"

They stood there, looking at her with the same soulful stare Tobias used when he wanted a snack and wasn't allowed to beg. Rowena couldn't help but grin.

"Okay, how about next Wednesday evening?"

"Great! What time?"

Arrangements made, the group paused long enough to offer a critique of Connor's work, giggling when he dared them, on penalty of having their faces painted, to do any better. The girls twittered; the boys backed up when he aimed his brush in their direction. They left, charging across the beach to meet up with some friends, madly chattering, one voice on top of another.

"You don't mind showing them how to graft?" he asked, an odd look on his face.

Rowena shook her head, took one last swipe that finished the bench.

"Actually I'll enjoy it. I get too used to working alone in the greenhouse. It's nice to have company sometimes. And I like kids. I grew up asking questions. If someone hadn't taken the time to answer them, who knows where I'd be now."

"Ashley told me you're taking a group of girls out boating in the summer."

She nodded, wondering what else her friends had said. "Yes. I like to be involved in the community."

He went back to his painting, but judging from the look on his face, he was thinking about what she'd said. She finished before him so walked over to his cutout and added some blue for the captain's hat and painted in the last sail.

"No fair. You chose the easy parts."

"Of course. I'm not dumb." She tamped the lids on the paints, wrapped the brushes in plastic and placed everything in the little work shed that would be locked up later. "I think we're finished."

"Just enough time for a shower before the barbecue," he agreed, checking his watch. "Look, your father's headed this way."

Rowena turned, watched him stride toward them. His energy had certainly returned.

"I came to ask if you're going back to Wingate," he said when he'd complimented their work. "I want to shower and change clothes before Laura comes. I'll probably take the bus back tomorrow. It will be too crowded and stuffy tonight."

"I'm going in tomorrow," Connor said. "You could ride with me. It would take a lot less time and I'd have someone to talk to."

"You wouldn't mind?"

"I'd enjoy it."

The decision made, the three of them climbed into the truck and Rowena drove toward Wingate with Connor's shoulder bumping hers every time she hit a pothole.

There were a lot of potholes.

When the two men finally got out, her pulse was racing and she felt hot. Connor must have noticed. He leaned in through her open window, brushed her cheek.

"You worked too hard and I think the sun got your face. It's quite pink." He frowned. "At least the water's still working at your house. Go ahead and soak out all the kinks, but be ready in an hour. I'll pick you up."

"I don't think I'll go." She hesitated, worried by the prospect of an evening where she was totally out of her element.

He gave her one hard stare that burned through all her excuses.

"You're going. I'll see you in an hour." Then he followed her father into the house.

"Some men are so bossy," she muttered as she ground the gears before finding First. But as the old truck lumbered up the hill she couldn't help humming the words to Amy Grant's song "Simple Things."

The house was a wreck but the old claw-foot tub was intact and as she took the first bubble bath she'd had in years, Rowena decided that simple things were the best.

Home, friends, family.

Love.

If only she could have them all.

Chapter Eleven

Victor Davis was a quiet man. But he became loquacious once started on his favorite topic. Today that seemed to be Laura Masters.

After more than half an hour of listening to him rave in the car about the florist's remarkable capabilities, Connor decided to change the focus of the conversation.

"You seemed to enjoy the barbecue last night," he said at the first opening.

"I have some happy memories of Cathcart House—Piper's home," he explained. "Her grandparents introduced me to my wife. We were married there. It's a beautiful place."

"Yes, it is." Connor waited a moment before uttering his next comment. "I'm not sure Rowena enjoyed herself, though. She seemed…uncomfortable."

"Well, I don't know why. She spent enough time there every summer. Cathcart House was like her second home."

"Maybe it was all the people, then. The whole town must have shown up."

"It was always like that after a town workday." Victor

scowled. "Come to think of it, I did go looking for her before I left. I couldn't find her."

"I did, too. But I think she must have left early. Maybe she was tired from all the work."

"Rowena's not the type to get tired." Victor's voice dropped. "She's not much for big parties, though. I think they intimidate her."

"Why?" Connor couldn't quite imagine the tiny landscaper intimidated.

"Rowena's always been a bit sensitive about herself." Victor sighed. "Maybe it was my fault, maybe I didn't tell her how pretty she is enough times. I don't know. I'm not the flowery type. She should have had her mother for that."

"What do you mean—sensitive?" Connor asked.

"Give her a landscape and her confidence is right where it should be. But put her in a crowd of fancy dresses and she feels like she can't compete."

"But she's a beautiful woman!"

Victor gave him a sideways look. "Maybe you should tell her so. My words don't seem to have any effect."

They rode in silence while Connor digested that.

"You must be very proud of her," he said, hoping to learn more about the woman who occupied most of his thoughts these days.

"It's easy to be proud of Rowena. She takes on challenges a lot of other women wouldn't even think about and she always triumphs. She's a very determined girl."

It wasn't exactly what he was hoping for. Connor tried again.

"What did you think of the nursery?"

Victor grimaced. "It needs a lot of work. Left untended too long. But she'll turn it around. She doesn't give up once she's set her mind to something."

Connor was familiar with her steely determination.

"I'd think it would be difficult to handle a place like that—for one person, I mean."

"Difficult isn't something that gets in the way of what my daughter decides to accomplish." He smiled. "You must have noticed that in her other work."

"Actually, I haven't seen it. I wonder…" Connor paused, let the idea mushroom for a moment before he voiced it. "Would it take too much of your time to show me some of her work?"

Victor cast him a sideways glance, his brown eyes curious. "I thought you said you came to visit your uncles?"

"Yes. But I can spare a couple of hours. We left so early this morning that there was barely any traffic and I won't drive back until tomorrow so I have some extra time today. If you don't mind," he added.

"Don't mind at all."

Victor directed him to the appropriate route and soon Connor found himself driving past one of Toronto's most well-known landmarks, a castle that sat high above a bank of stairs.

"Those gardens and the fountain, they're her design," Victor told him proudly, pointing to a parking spot. They got out, walked around the perfectly presented landscape. "Spectacular, isn't it?"

Stunned by the intricacy of the project, Connor could only nod.

"I'll show you something completely different now." Rowena's father directed him to a commercial part of the city, quiet on this Sunday morning. "The gardens are public. Rowena suggested they put the security fence behind, hidden by those trees so people on lunch breaks or families still living in the area and needing a picnic site could use it outside of regular office hours. The company won a lot of community support for this. My daughter won two international awards."

Victor seemed keen to show him every nook and cranny

and Connor followed, amazed by the skill and talent required to take so many needs for a space into consideration. He was beginning to recognize her special touches. Unexpected bursts of color, a play space protected from the street by boulders and a waterfall, a bronze statue of a child.

Back in the car Connor was more confused than ever and he made no effort to hide it.

"I don't understand why she would leave all this success behind to return to Serenity Bay and start over. It's obvious she's well-known and highly sought after here. I'm sure she can ask whatever fee she wants." He glanced at Victor, hoping he'd have the answer.

But her father merely shrugged.

"Rowena's always had a thing about that nursery," he said. "Even years after it was gone she'd talk about the times we had there, ask me if I didn't want to get back on it, make it like it was. She and those other girls always loved the Bay. Maybe it's her way of recapturing the memories or something."

"Maybe. But it's an awfully big challenge for one woman alone."

"That's what I told her. But she didn't hear me. She'd already made up her mind to make a deal with your uncles and there was no swaying her. We turn here."

Connor drove into the circular driveway of the address where Victor lived. The convalescent home wasn't swanky, but it wasn't horrible, either. There were plenty of older people sitting outside, some in wheelchairs, talking with family or friends. The lawns were neat, the flower beds bright, if ordinary.

"You must miss having her nearby," Connor said with sudden insight. "It has to be hard for her to visit often, especially with all the work she's taken on."

"Rowena has her own life. I don't expect her to be here nursing me all day. I wouldn't want it, either." A nostalgic smile softened his face. "One thing I always taught her was to reach for what she wanted and count on God to help her. She's doing both real well." Victor got out, waited till his case was freed from the trunk. "Thank you for bringing me back, Connor. And for having me at Wingate Manor. Your uncles will be proud of the work you're doing there."

"I'm sure they'd be delighted to see you, if you wanted a visit."

"I tried a couple of times, but it's a long way from here to where they're staying and the bus service isn't that great. That's why I like the Bay so much. You can walk almost anywhere you want to go." He chuckled. "Laura and I nearly wore ourselves to a frazzle checking out all the old walkways. Truth to tell, I'm a little stiff this morning."

"I'm sorry."

"I'll heal." Victor's laugh reminded Connor of a schoolboy. "Most of those paths are still there. Need a little repair maybe, but still there."

For a moment his face had dulled, lost its excitement, but at the mention of the florist his eyes flared and sparkled once more.

"I might just come up again," he said.

"I'm sure Rowena would love to see you. And I know she'd love to have your expertise. She's told me a bit about how knowledgeable you are." He waited to see how that went over.

"She knows ten times what I ever did," Victor murmured. "I don't think she needs me to give her advice."

No, she needs you to be there, to help her. Connor swallowed the words. And smiled.

"I know she'd love you to come again. And until her place is finished, you're always welcome at Wingate."

"Well, thank you. I appreciate that." Victor studied him, his brown eyes intense in their scrutiny. "What will you do when your uncles return to Wingate?"

Good question. He asked himself that almost every day. "I'm not sure yet."

"You should think about staying," the older man suggested. "Serenity Bay might be a small town miles from the city but it's a good place to live, to raise a family. A good community to be part of."

Having said his piece, Victor thrust out his hand.

"Goodbye, Connor. Drive safely. Tell your uncles hello from me." Victor nodded, then strode inside.

Watching him leave, Connor had a hunch his gait was quite different than the day he'd left. Obviously that's why Rowena wanted her father back in the town he knew so well. There, he didn't seem like a man stuck in a depression. There, he seemed happy and interested and trying to get on with life.

But as he drove away, Connor felt the same sense of disquiet that had plagued him since the night Victor had arrived at the nursery. Something wasn't right.

It was clear father and daughter loved one another, but Victor hadn't displayed the yen to return to his former land that Rowena had led him to expect.

Why was that?

"Pull a little more, Kent," Rowena called after checking the roots. Removing these roses was taking a lot more effort than she'd expected or wanted. "Nothing new about that."

"Is that good, boss?" Quint asked.

"Perfect," she said. "You know, I like the way you fit that together so well. If you need a reference, I'll be glad to give you one."

"Am I going to be looking for work soon?" he asked, his brows drawn together. "I thought you had a lot more to do at the nursery. We haven't even begun to get the weeding under control. And there are a lot of cuttings to be done."

"I know. And I really appreciate everything you and your father have done," she told him sincerely. "But I'm not sure I'll be able to keep paying you all summer. This project took more than I'd estimated. Way more."

"It's worth it, though, isn't it?" Kent moved beside her, surveyed the grounds from their vantage point. "Your work is going to draw some visitors, I'd say."

"Good. That's what we want. And it's your work, too. I couldn't have done it without both of you. You've gone above and beyond what I asked of you."

"Okay, we're all heroes." Kent snorted. "Now let's get back to work before the day's over."

It took about three more hours to remove all the bushes. By then it was way past six o'clock.

"That's it for today. Tomorrow we'll replace the soil, add some nutrients and start planting the new bushes." Even though they wanted to keep working, Rowena ordered them to go get their dinner. "Get some rest," she told them. "You deserve it."

"So do you. But I suppose you're going to hang around and tinker with that fountain some more." Kent's comment wasn't a question. "Why don't you just call the company and tell them to get out here and fix it?"

"Because if it's my fault, if there was a problem with the installation, or a mistake, I'll have to pay mileage and labor and I can't afford it," she confessed. "I'm sure I can figure it out if I can just spend some time on it."

Once her crew had left, Rowena walked down the hill to stare at the one thing that threatened to ruin her entire project.

"If you could just shed a little light, Lord," she murmured, as she removed the cover to the assembly, took out the directions and began tracing the system. "Just a little to help me fix this."

She struggled until it was too dark to see. She was putting

in the last screw when she heard someone behind her. Wheeling around, Rowena saw Connor's tall form.

"Hi," she said, aware of the lilt in her voice. "How was the city?"

"You're fired," he said as he stepped into a patch of moonlight.

"What?" She frowned. "What are you talking about?"

"I said you're fired. Get off this land and don't come back." He wheeled around, stormed up the hill.

"Wait a minute!" She raced after him, grabbed his arm to stop him. "We had a deal. I'm almost finished. You can't stop me now."

"I can and I am. I don't want you or your crew here anymore."

The landscaping lights switched on and she got a good look at him. He was furious.

"What's wrong now?" She sighed.

"That." He pointed to the pile of uprooted rosebushes. "Who authorized you to dig those up?"

"Your uncles did. Remove any diseased or unsuitable plants, they said. It was part of the deal. Why?"

"Do you have any idea what you've done? Those roses were my uncles' pride and joy. They've spent over thirty years nurturing them, grafting them. They prize the blooms for their horticultural show. And in one day you've managed to decimate everything they've worked for all their lives."

"Connor, the bushes—"

He held up a hand. His eyes, hard shards of topaz, pierced her explanations with no mercy.

"There isn't any excuse, Rowena. I know they told you how much those roses meant to them. I know I asked you to be careful when working the bed. You deliberately ignored me and went ahead and tore them out. But then you've done that with most of this project, haven't you?'

"I don't know what you mean." She deliberately reined in her temper, trying to understand what had brought this on.

"I told you to ignore that fountain, get the rest of the place finished, yet here you are, fiddling with it till all hours. What else got done around here today?" He scanned the area. "Nothing that I can see."

"Maybe that's because you're blind." She was fed up with trying to explain herself. "You came here determined to show us all what a hotshot you are, big city boy visiting Hicksville, showing us the way things should be done. You've never really accepted that I knew what I was talking about, that I had a plan for this place. All you've ever seen was the destruction."

Chagrin washed over his face. "I never—"

"Just shut up, okay, Connor?"

He stared at her in shock. She'd never spoken to him so harshly.

"You want me out of here, I'm gone," Rowena promised. "But I'm going to tell you something first. I didn't do anything here that I wouldn't have done for any other project I worked on." She swallowed the tears that threatened, clenched her fists at her side to help her focus.

"Your uncles relied on me to make this place a showstopper and I think I've done that. I've given this place the very best I could. I'm sorry if that isn't enough for you. But then you never really trusted me, did you? Is that because you've never really seen me as a capable designer who actually knows what she's doing or is it because you've got so little going on in your own life, you have to try to control everyone else's?"

He tried to say something but she ignored it.

"It doesn't matter. I'm sick of being second-guessed, questioned, taken to task for pouring every waking moment into making your deadline. You sit in that house and you demand we all acquiesce to your supreme power, no matter what. And you treat me like a silly girl who has to have your input before a single decision can be made. Well, not anymore." She glared at him. "You're so smart, Connor, *you* finish the grounds. Wield your power and get the peons to finish this project the way you want. I'm outta here."

Rowena stomped up the hill, climbed into her truck and drove home. On the way she phoned her crew.

"Change of plan, guys. We're working at the nursery tomorrow," she told them. "Eight sharp." Then she hung up.

Connor Wingate was a pain in the—

Forget him. It's time to focus on getting the nursery up to speed so your father can take over. Then you can leave Serenity Bay.

So why didn't the thought of leaving make her happy?

"You're positive?" Connor listened to the assurances as dismay filled him. "All right, thank you. I appreciate your swift response."

He set down the phone, stared out the window at the heap of dying rosebushes that sat exactly where Rowena had left them.

"She's been gone for two days now. Time to eat crow, isn't it?" Esther stood in the doorway, a frown on her usually cheerful face.

"You heard?"

"I hear everything," she assured him smugly. "Seems to me it's time you fixed things."

"How?" Connor raked a hand through his hair. "I tore her apart, criticized her expertise, fired her. What can I possibly say to fix that?"

"Maybe 'I'm sorry'?" Esther grinned. "It's good for a person to eat humble pie once in a while, Connor. It's probably been years since you've had a taste of it. I expect it will do you a world of good."

"Saying I'm sorry isn't going to get Rowena Davis back here to finish what she started."

"You have some other option?"

"Esther, you're a harsh woman." He groaned. "I feel like a fool. Offering an apology is hardly enough."

"So you start by groveling, sweet-talking her. Bribe her if you have to."

"Bribe her. Good idea. With what?"

Esther thought for a moment. "With most women I'd say offer flowers and a fancy dinner but Rowena isn't like most women. She's got enough flowers of her own and fancy doesn't seem her style."

"Which leaves?"

"Abject apology? And maybe offering to help her get ready for her big Mother's Day sale this weekend." Esther flicked his arm with her fingertip, her tone scathing. "You're a big, strong man. Those arms of yours ought to be useful for hauling pots and baskets. Or maybe you could run the cash register. I don't know. You're supposed to be the brain who's going to bring us fame. You've handled New York City's power tycoons. Surely a wonder boy like you can think of something."

"Thanks for your support." Connor was beginning to wish no one had ever found out about his past. They all thought he was a snob.

"No problem. I've got work to do." Esther left and the room's silence seemed as if it would suffocate him.

The truth sank in.

"Okay, God, I'm a jerk. I got too focused on myself and my problems. Same old story." Cecile's comment from that day echoed in his brain but he shut it off, rose from the desk. "If You could just get her to listen to me, that's all I ask."

He stepped through the door, reconsidered.

"On second thought, maybe You could get her to listen *and*

help me figure out what I'm supposed to do with the rest of my life," Connor added. "Because if You've been sending me hints about that, they're not getting through."

"You are talking to someone?" Pierre asked, his face perplexed as he glanced around.

"Yes, I am. Can I help you with something?"

"*Oui.* I am come to ask your permission."

"For what?" The man had more ideas than Edison. Some were great but many made Connor wonder if he couldn't persuade the uncles to come back early, casts and all. They had experience handling this guy.

"I want to do something special for *la petite* Rowena. She has made for me the so wonderful herb garden. It is my great—how do you say—triumph?" He waited for Connor's nod, obviously pleased that he'd mastered this new word. "*Bon.* Sunday is her big day to sell the flowers to the mothers, yes?"

"Yes, it is." Yet another reminder that Wingate Manor wasn't Rowena's all-consuming passion, that she had a nursery she was trying to revive.

"So I think perhaps she would like also to give some of Pierre's very delicious cookies to her customers. Maybe some coffee. I will pay for all myself but I must need to use the ovens here. For this I seek the permissions. Is okay?"

Everybody, it seemed, loved Rowena. Connor felt like a grinch withholding treats as the chef waited for his approval. Was he really so horrible?

"Of course, use the ovens. And our ingredients. It's the least we can do to help her after all she's done." Pierre's grin of delight made Connor feel a little better. "I'm headed over there now. Shall I tell her?"

"You go to apologize?"

The severe glare warned Connor that suggesting the chef

butt out of other people's business wouldn't go over well. Was nothing around here private?

"Yes, Pierre." He sighed. "I'll apologize."

"Is good." A grin split the pointed face. "Then you can tell her Pierre will send his best cookies to wish her many of the success." That matter settled to his satisfaction, the Frenchman turned on his heel and headed back toward the domain he adored, humming a tune that sounded vaguely operatic.

"You don't make holding on to pride easy, do You, Lord?" With a sigh Connor dragged open the door and stepped outside. "All right, I'm going."

Tobias yelped a greeting from the pen that confined him. Connor blinked.

Rowena liked Tobias. She snuck him snacks, took him for long walks when she thought no one noticed, sometimes even groomed him. Maybe Tobias could smooth his path to humility.

"Come on, you," he said, unlocking the gate. "We're going for a walk. And this time I expect you to earn your keep."

The dog woofed his agreement, barely holding still long enough to allow his leash to be attached.

The heat of the day was oppressive as he walked uphill. When Connor had prayed for the rain to stop, he'd never expected it to be followed by day after day of unrelenting heat that threatened to scorch everything.

At least the outside of Rowena's hilltop house looked great, an asset to her nursery instead of a detraction. Except for the Dumpster that sat by the workmen's trucks. But he'd make sure that was moved before Sunday.

Connor paused to assess the change. Freshly painted white siding complemented the dark brown roof and trim. Window boxes spilled flowers everywhere. The deck had been redone, only this time it was made out of paving stones that wouldn't deteriorate. Here, too, pots of flowers and shrubs made an attractive, inviting scene. He could imagine her sitting out here at night, curled up on one of those hand-fashioned willow chairs, inhaling the sweet fragrance of those blooms as she stared at the stars.

He let himself admire the built-in barbecue he'd insisted be installed. It was perfect, meant for gatherings where everyone could relax and enjoy their friends. In his mind he could almost hear the twilight laughter echo over the hills. He could certainly imagine Rowena there, giggling with her friends.

Connor yearned to know how the renovation was faring but no way would he go inside without an invitation. He decided instead to phone the contractor and make sure nothing was being held up.

The nursery looked better, too. Not as lush as it should, perhaps, but then hadn't she said something about having yet to replace much of the irrigation system? Watering such a large area would be backbreaking.

He could see Quint weeding between the rows of cuttings he'd heard them talking about planting just two weeks ago. A scratching sound emerged from inside the greenhouse. Tobias took that as an invitation and bounded toward the building.

"Tobias! Come back here." Connor broke into a run. If the dog went into the greenhouse he'd decimate her flowers.

As Tobias reached the doorway, Rowena emerged. She wore a washed-out chambray shirt and a pair of shorts that showed off her tanned, shapely legs. Her hair was pushed back off her red face but she laughed as she bent and ruffled the dog's fur, allowing him to swipe her face in affection.

"Hello, Tobias. Where did you come from?"

"Me."

She froze for an instant, then straightened. She glared at him, her green eyes shooting darts. "What do you want, Connor?"

"To talk to you." He watched Kent move to the back of the greenhouse to give them privacy. Suddenly he glimpsed the Edenlike world she'd created inside the glass building. He whistled. "Wow! This is amazing."

The interior was a riot of color; there was something to see everywhere. A tiny, trickling waterfall surrounded by roses; a pyramid of begonias, each side color coded; hanging baskets; row upon row of bedding plants, urns, tubs—she'd thought of everything.

"You've done a great job."

"Thanks." Rowena's face didn't change as she waited for him to continue.

Connor didn't have to look very hard to find the glint of hurt in those almond-shaped eyes. A prickle of shame suffused him.

Don't let me mess this up, God, he prayed silently.

"Look, I'm busy. If there's—"

"I came to apologize, Rowena. I should never have doubted you or even suggested that you would remove the roses without a very good reason. I'm really sorry."

The ice maiden showed no signs of a thaw. "Are you?"

"Yes. I sent a sample to the university test lab. They told me the disease on the bushes meant they had to be removed or they would infect anything added."

"And you didn't think I knew that." She didn't hide her bitterness. "As usual you couldn't accept that I possess the knowledge and experience to know my job enough to be trusted with even your uncles' roses. Why is that?"

"Actually it wasn't you," Connor admitted. "I wasn't really reacting to what you'd done."

"Was it the full moon? Or perhaps you were tired from your long drive."

Connor sighed. Revealing his personal feelings, opening himself up—it wasn't something he'd ever done well. Cecile had told him that a hundred times. Coming to Serenity Bay had put the spotlight on his difficulty with community and people who got too close.

"Was there something else?" She shifted from one foot to the other, clearly impatient to get back to work.

"Yes," he snapped, irritated by her snarky manner.

"Then would you please go ahead and say it. I have things to do."

"It isn't easy," he muttered.

"You may not have learned this yet, Connor, but a lot of things in life aren't easy. The best thing is to grit your teeth and get it over with. So you've apologized. Great. You can feel better now. And I can get back to work. Okay?" Rowena whirled around.

Connor let her take one step before the words blurted out.

"One of those bushes was mine."

She turned and frowned at him.

"It was a memorial bush, for my dad. I planted it one summer—the first summer I came here. I was here for two weeks before they told my mom he'd gone missing in Iraq. She phoned one afternoon, said he was dead, killed in an explosion. There wasn't any body. He was just…gone."

"I'm sorry."

"Thanks." Connor dredged up a half smile. "He was younger than the uncles. But that day, when I looked at them, I couldn't see him, couldn't remember what he looked like. Uncle Hank suggested we have a memorial service—look through old photo albums, talk about happy times."

Suddenly he could see the past clearly.

"We came up here and bought a rosebush from your father. It was a deep, dark red. Hardy, your dad said, strong enough to take the freezing-cold winters, outlast droughts and come back every spring just as beautiful as ever. I liked it because its freckles reminded me of my father." He blinked, surprised by the clarity of that day. "I'd forgotten that."

"Morden Ruby."

Connor frowned. "What?"

"Morden Ruby. It's the name of a rose variety Dad particularly favored. The blooms repeat and are long-lasting. He thought any rose worth planting should be able to hold its own against whatever the Bay climate threw at it." She motioned to the stack of pots of young roses which she'd arranged. "I have several of them."

"Will you plant one in the new Wingate rose garden?" he asked softly. "For my dad?"

She began nodding her head but Connor ignored that, took her small, capable hands in his and held them as he looked into her eyes.

"I'm not good with memories, Rowena. I prefer to stuff them away, concentrate on something else."

"Preferably something you can control."

"Yes. When I saw my father's bush hacked up and lying on the ground it was like I was ten again and reliving the day they told me he was never coming back, that I couldn't see him again, talk to him. Something inside me snapped and I lashed out at you. I truly am sorry."

She stood mum, simply watching him.

"Wingate Manor is your baby, Rowena. Nobody but you can pull it all together, complete the vision, make your dream a reality. Please say you'll come back and finish the job."

She remained silent.

Since his appeal didn't seem to be working, Connor upped the ante. "Pierre wants you to finish putting in the fruit trees. He's going to create a new Wingate Manor jelly in your honor."

She rolled her eyes.

"Esther is mad at me and Tobias whines all the time.

Besides, *I* need you there. I need you to help me make a splash for Wingate—so the uncles can finally retire." He swallowed, prayed for inspiration. "Pierre's even sending you cookies for your Mother's Day event."

"You don't have to buy me off with your chef's cooking." She laughed, but her voice cracked as she said it. A fat, glossy tear rolled down her cheek. "I was ready to come back after you told me about your father."

Relief swelled, shocking him with its intensity. When had having Rowena at Wingate come to mean so much?

Connor pulled her hands until she was close enough for him to wrap his arms around her and breathe the fresh citrus tang of her shampoo, close enough to feel the warmth of her face pressed against his chest.

"Thank you," he whispered, meaning it with every fiber of his being. "I promise I won't get in your way again."

He felt laughter shake her small body.

"Right. Until tomorrow."

It felt perfectly natural to hold her, to let her lean against him while he soothed the tension from her shoulders and absorbed her nearness. So right, Connor had to force himself not to reach out and grab her when she stepped away as a horn sounded.

He turned, glared at the carload of teens emptying from a vehicle that had definitely seen better days.

He felt a faint rush of anger that they should take her time, especially when he wanted her to himself.

"Whose idea was it for those kids to come here today?"

Rowena chuckled at his frown. "You wanted me to show them how to graft, remember?"

"Why in the world did you listen? You already know I'm an idiot."

"I'm going to remind you of that. Many, many times." She

winked then herded the teens down to the cutting shed where she had several potted crab apple trees waiting.

"Yes, I dug up part of yours," she told Connor before he could ask. "Students, say thank you to Mr. Wingate for generously donating the plant material."

They singsonged their thanks then returned their attention to Rowena, who showed them the proper way to prepare to graft. They all wanted to try. Connor remained at the back, content to watch the master gardener painstakingly teach until each one held a viable bit of graft material.

"Now we'll attach these to my hawthorne bushes." They all trailed behind her outside, impatient to get close enough to see exactly what she did.

She had an easy, relaxed way of dealing with them. In fact, Rowena had a knack with old men, students, employees—anyone who came into her sphere of influence. She was a beautiful woman who'd taken on a huge burden for the love of her father, but that didn't stop her from extending a hand to others.

Connor thought he was beginning to understand this business of community, of looking out for each other, of seeing other people's faults and letting them see yours and helping them anyway.

Unfortunately, he was afraid he would never be able to learn how to love.

Chapter Twelve

With the new grafts complete, the teens looked to Rowena. She checked each one's work, then smiled.

"Grafting is not easy but you've done very well. Congratulations. I think you'll get top marks if you do the same in class."

Their chests expanded with pride at her praise.

This isn't what you do in that shed, though, is it?"

Rowena smiled at the garrulous Trish. She, Greg and Shauna seemed to be the ringleaders and their curiosity knew no bounds.

"No. This is actually the cutting shed. We cut parts of the trees here. They go into rooting powder and when the roots are the right size, we plant them. After two years they're ready to sell."

She demonstrated, conscious of Connor watching every move.

"You're going to plant all these?" Greg asked, his eyes round.

"This is about a quarter of what I hope to prepare for planting."

"A quarter?" He blinked, but undaunted, grinned. "Can I learn how?"

"Sure." She showed them and five minutes later the entire troop was busy making cuttings. Rowena moved beside Connor, grinning. "The Lord works in mysterious ways."

"Hmm?" He was too busy staring at her gorgeous eyes to hear what came out of her lovely mouth.

"I wasn't sure I'd get enough cuttings done, but these guys are like an assembly line. At this rate—" She paused as Greg high-fived Trish. "What now?"

"Rowena, you've been working really hard to make the town look good and helping us and stuff. That probably made you behind here. Maybe we could help out and well, we were wondering—would you be willing to hire us to make these cuttings? We'd donate our wages for an orphanage we sponsor in Haiti. We haven't sent much this year. But if we worked for you—"

Connor caught the momentary flicker of dismay before she masked it, but he knew immediately what had caused it. Rowena was tapped out, down to her last nickel. She couldn't afford to pay them wages.

"I'm—"

"Wait." Connor laid a hand on her arm to stop her, and interrupted. "Good for you for wanting to earn the money, but you guys are novices and she already has some top-notch people who do this work."

Their faces fell. "Yeah, I guess so."

"But I might have another idea." Their faces perked up. "Maybe there's a way you could help Rowena and earn some money for the orphanage. Why don't you hold a cut-a-thon."

"A what?"

"Well, people have walkathons. Why don't you get sponsors from the community who will pay for each cutting you do—maybe a penny each?"

"A penny?" They looked scandalized.

"Okay, a nickel. Whatever. The point is you should be able

to do a whole pile of cuttings in an hour or two—if you practice. And you have the potential to earn more than a few bucks an hour, if you get a number of sponsors."

Up to now Trish had remained silent, which Connor thought was unusual for the garrulous girl. Maybe she didn't like the idea.

"Hmm. Interesting." Greg glanced at Rowena. "Would that be all right with you?"

"I guess. We can't do it this weekend, though. It's Mother's Day and I'm expecting a lot of buyers for the baskets."

"What about next weekend?" Trish grinned at Shauna. "On Saturday. We could put up posters around town—Come and Watch the Cut-A-Thon at Davis Nurseries. We might bring a few more customers for Rowena, too, and it would definitely give people a better idea of what you're doing up here."

"I guess so." Rowena looked stunned by the teens' quick planning. "I'd like to know a little more about how you think it should work." She checked her watch. "Maybe we should turn this into a dinner meeting. We could grill some burgers— I have a brand-new barbecue that needs breaking in."

"Great!" Several voices vying for supremacy drew Quint and Kent's attention.

Connor let out a shrill whistle. "If we're having a barbecue, Rowena and I need to do some planning. Maybe you guys can practice your cutting skills while we talk. Okay?"

"If they're very careful. You'll have to do it in teams— maybe four each?" Rowena glanced at the bench. "There's not enough space for more than that."

"Hey, teams! That's good. We'll have a competition between teams to see who'll raise the most money." Shauna was clearly focused on the fund-raising aspect. "People will come to cheer on a team."

Connor left them to it, drawing Rowena outside. "This

isn't going to upset your work too much, will it? They won't be in the way?"

She shook her head, her lips spreading wide in a smile. "They'll do fine. I've already got a couple of ideas for complicating the competition so no one has an edge. I'm sure Quint and Kent will be judges."

"You're devious," he teased.

"Absolutely."

There she was—drawing everyone into the action again. By the time this thing was over, the whole of Serenity Bay would probably be up here.

"Unless you've got several dozen burgers in your freezer," Connor said, thinking aloud, "I'll make a quick trip into town. What else should I get?"

They decided on sodas, chips, all the necessary condiments. Dessert was left up to Connor.

"Can I be the one who uses the barbecue?" he asked, feeling like a kid desperate to try a friend's new toy.

"Ah. That's what this is really about, isn't it? Big he-man just wants to play with the barbecue."

He grinned. "Absolutely."

She burst out laughing. "Well, since I've never really grilled anything successfully, you're on."

He patted her shoulder. "Leave it to a pro. I'll be back in an hour or so. Don't touch it before then."

"Yes, sir, Connor."

He hurried away before his red face made her laugh again.

"What's going on?" Kent asked as he approached Rowena and Connor.

"The kids are planning a cut-a-thon. You're invited for supper if you like grilled burgers and chips."

"Love 'em." He huffed a sigh of relief. "I was wondering how we were going to get enough stock into the rooting cellar before the season got too late. This will really help Rowena out."

"Yeah, it will." Connor didn't mention the idea was his. Instead he whistled for Tobias, who refused to leave the adoring teens. Shrugging, he jogged back to Wingate Manor, climbed in his car and headed for town, but first he invited his entire staff to the grill party. If Rowena could involve the community, so could he.

"That's a lot of burgers." Jason Franklin's eyes widened as Connor loaded the last box into his car. "Pierre's into fast food now?"

"Hardly." Connor gave him a brief explanation. "You guys are welcome if you want to help out. Maybe you could let Michael and Ashley know, as well."

"Sure." Jason followed him into the grocery store, hefted a case of sodas in each hand and followed him out. "Got time for a coffee?" he asked as he loaded them into the trunk.

"If it's quick."

They got two coffees and carried them to the benches by the beach.

"You and Rowena make up?" Jason asked after taking a sip.

"I apologized. She forgave me." Did the whole town know about their private squabble?

"Good. She needs to finish that job, Connor. And she needs the publicity that goes along with it. Piper says she's killing herself with work. I'll be glad if this cut-a-thon thing gives her a break."

"Actually I was hoping it might bring in some more clients for her. You know—family and friends buy a basket or a tree while they're there?"

Jason studied him. "You care about her a lot, don't you?"

Connor so did not want to discuss this in the middle of town.

"Rowena's made a big difference at Wingate Manor, gone

way beyond what I ever expected. I'd like to return the favor, help her out if I can."

"And that's all it is? Helping her out?"

"What do you mean?" Connor knew exactly where this was going. It was time to stop it. "Jason, I don't know what you've heard about my past, but I was engaged."

The other man only nodded.

"Cecile was everything a man would want but somehow that wasn't enough for me. I couldn't love her. I told her so just before she was killed."

"So?"

"So I like Rowena a lot, but I'm not the type who can love someone. I don't think I have it in me, if you want the truth."

"That's ridiculous."

"No, it's a fact. Why are you shaking your head?"

"With the exception of maybe a psychopath, all people are capable of love. It might come in varying degrees, but it's still love." He leaned back, crossed his ankles. "Tell me about your fiancée."

"She was beautiful. Everyone loved her."

"I got that. Now tell me why you loved—okay, liked—her."

"I don't know." He frowned, scoured his brain. "She was sweet."

Jason made a face. "Connor, I'm sure you've met lots of 'sweet' women."

"Fine." He glared. "She was easygoing."

"Meaning?"

"She didn't throw a fit if I had to work late or got stuck in a meeting."

"Did you do that a lot?"

"Yeah. I was pretty focused on business."

"Would you have cared if she told you she was in love with someone else?"

"I would have hoped they'd be happy."

Jason smiled, took another sip. "What do you think about Rowena?"

"She's determined. Nothing gets past her. She doesn't cut you any slack. If she thinks you're wrong, she says so." He couldn't suppress his smile. "Besides Pierre, I've never seen anyone with so many ideas. I thought Wingate's renovations would be fairly straightforward but every time I turn around she's come up with another way to make it better, to make it sing, as Uncle Henry would say."

Jason kept smiling in that know-it-all way that irritated him. "Now, let me ask you this—what if you found out she was getting married?"

"To whom? I never heard her say a word about anyone. In fact, she's alone, working most nights. What kind of a fiancé—" He stopped. "Oh."

"Oh, indeed." Jason tossed his cup into the garbage. "You see, Connor, you care. That's what love is. Caring. And trust me, you have it in you. All you have to decide is what to do with it."

The other man rose, clapped a hand on his shoulder.

"I've got to go. I'll tell Piper about the cut-a-thon and dinner tonight—if it still stands?"

"Yeah, of course." He glimpsed understanding in the other man's eyes.

"We can talk about this again, if you want. Anytime."

"Thanks."

"No problem." Jason sauntered away, whistling as he went.

Connor thought about what he'd said. He did care about Rowena. Cared that she achieved her goal, cared that she didn't kill herself trying to reach it, cared that she wouldn't be too hurt if her father didn't come back.

Did that mean he loved her?

He couldn't love her. He hadn't even gotten the next step

figured out for his own life. How could he possibly—it hadn't been long enough since Cecile.

That was a stupid excuse and he knew it. This wasn't about Cecile. It was about him, about these funny, spritzlike bubbles that danced around inside him whenever he thought of Rowena.

But love? That was a whole other question. Love hurt. He must have loved his mother but she'd sent him away. He thought he'd loved his father but that was so long ago and he couldn't really remember much. The uncles? Well, sure, he cared about them, a lot. But loved? He searched his heart but couldn't find that mind-boggling overpowering rush of emotion the movies always portrayed.

What was love?

"I could use a little help here, God."

He'd been trying to figure this out for so long. The pastor preached that we were supposed to ask for God's guidance in important matters. Okay, he'd asked and asked. Where was the answer?

"Connor?"

He jerked out of his own thoughts, found Victor peering down at him.

"Are you all right, son?"

"Victor! What are you doing here? I mean—" He didn't know what to say, how to ask why he'd come back. Worse, he was afraid to hear the answer.

"I couldn't stay away. Is your offer still open?" Victor waited a moment. "You know, to stay at Wingate Manor?"

"Yes, certainly. Of course." He stumbled to his feet.

"I thought I'd stop by the nursery. I remembered Rowena has a big event planned for Mother's Day. Maybe she could use some help."

"I'm sure she could. Actually I'm on my way there now.

She's got a bunch of teens there. She's going to grill some burgers. They're planning something. I'll give you a ride." He laid out the scheme for the following weekend as they walked to his car.

"Sounds like a lot of fun. How's Wingate coming?"

"I think we're about ready to start on the annual beds. After she finishes the rose garden." Connor kept chatting as he drove up the hill. After a brief stop at Wingate, he headed for the nursery.

The teens unloaded his car. Several drew Victor to see their handiwork while the others set out the paper plates. Connor got busy with the grill.

By the time they were ready to eat, the crowd had increased even more. The cabinet-makers and drywallers agreed to join the meal; Piper, Ashley and their husbands, along with Tatiana, appeared. Pierre and Esther, as well as several other employees, arrived with a huge strawberry shortcake. Even Laura Masters arrived. Quint and Kent used some paint cans and planks for benches and the group munched happily on Connor's burgers after Victor asked a blessing on the food.

Before the teens left for home, Rowena gave everyone a tour through her semifinished home. Connor felt a surge of satisfaction at their compliments. Slowly they drifted off until soon the only ones remaining were Rowena's two friends and their families, Laura and her father. The women returned inside to discuss decor. The men lounged on the patio, enjoying the rich coffee Rowena had insisted on brewing.

When Laura emerged from the house, she wore a troubled look. Victor quickly rose and hurried toward her. The two walked toward the greenhouse, obviously involved in some heated discussion. Connor caught a glimpse of them embracing.

"What do you suppose is going on there?" Jason murmured.

"I think she's why he's back." Connor saw agreement all

around. "And I think it's going to knock Rowena for a loop when she figures it out."

"That bothers you?"

"Yeah. A lot."

"Okay, then." Jason topped up his cup. "Good for you for getting the house into shape. That was generous."

"It was my uncles' idea."

"Uh-huh. They insisted on granite countertops, did they? And birch cupboards?" Michael raised an eyebrow. "I deal with wood, Connor. I know how much it costs."

"The kitchen was from another job that was canceled," he defended. "The cabinet guys gave me a discount on it."

"And the jet tub? Travertine shower? Hardwood floors?"

Heat traveled up his neck. Using skills he'd learned in the boardroom, Connor kept his face impassive. "So sue me," he said quietly.

Michael roared with laughter. Jason grinned like he'd just uncovered a new speedboat with his name on it.

"What's so funny, boys?" Piper glanced from one to the other. "Oh, it's a secret." She winked at Ashley.

"Really? A secret? The three of them? Hmm." She looped her arm through Michael's and turned on her megawatt smile. "Darling, you'll tell me later, won't you?"

"I—I—" Mick was no match for his wife's wiles.

"Of course you will. But we have to leave now. Tati's got her field trip tomorrow and she needs to get some rest."

"Just have to clean the grill," he muttered, tossing Jason a look that screamed "help."

"Yeah, we have to clean the grill," Jason parroted.

Revenge called. Connor grabbed it.

"No, I'll look after it. You two go on home with your wives. And thanks for coming. It was nice of you to volunteer to help out on Mother's Day. I know Rowena appreciates it."

"Yes, she does," Rowena said, stepping outside. "More than you know. Is everyone leaving already?"

"School night," Ashley told her.

"Where's Dad?" She glanced around, a frown marring her beauty.

"He went for a walk with Laura. Showing her the greenhouse, I think."

"Oh." Her smile faltered a little. "Well, thanks a lot, everyone. Are you two still coming over tomorrow night?"

"As if we'd miss girls' night out." Piper raised her brows. "I don't think so."

Connor hung back but they drew him in, included him as one of theirs.

"Hey, Connor, how come we don't have guys' night out?" Jason asked.

"Hey, good idea." He hoped.

"*Great* idea, you mean." Michael slapped Jason on the back. "You plan it for Friday night. We'll take out one of the houseboats if they're not rented. Connor can bring the food."

"Why me?" he asked, wondering if he dared go.

"'Cause you're the guy with the chef."

"I knew Pierre shouldn't have brought that cake."

They left, laughing and teasing. And then there was only Rowena and him left, standing in twilight.

"Tired?"

"Tired, exhilarated, worried."

"Worried?" He stared into her green gaze. "Why?"

"Connor, do you know why my father is here?"

"I think he wants to help with Mother's Day."

"Then he would have come on Saturday. I think it's something else."

"Maybe he's ready to move up here."

"Maybe."

But she didn't believe it and he couldn't find the words to assure her. The niggling whisper of concern was back and it was growing stronger.

"I'll clean the grill, then I'd better get going. I've got some forms to sign and Esther warned me she'd skin me alive if I didn't have them waiting for her."

"She's a tartar." Rowena gathered up the last bits of trash, bagged them, put the paint cans back inside and the boards where they belonged. "Thanks for helping. I enjoyed having that mob here, unfinished house and all."

"You make it a habit to enjoy people, don't you?" He closed the lid, hung the clean utensils. "You're like a magnet, Rowena. People always seem drawn to you. I think it's because you make them feel cared about."

She was standing so near, looking uncertain and worried. Connor couldn't help himself; he bent and brushed his lips across hers. It was every bit as delightful as the first time.

"Try not to worry too much. I'm sure that whatever your father has planned, it will be good news."

She touched her lips with her fingertips. "Good night."

"Good night." Connor climbed in his car and drove home, a snapshot of Rowena, teaching Shauna how to graft, burned into his brain.

"Is that love?" he asked as he peered into the night sky.

God was silent tonight.

Chapter Thirteen

"Do you know where Connor is, Dad?"

The nursery was teeming with people, each intent on buying the perfect flower. Rowena had been rushing around all week as people came in to pick up their gift for Mom. Thanks to Quint and Kent's unflagging efforts, a whole new array of baskets now hung, waiting for the next onslaught.

"I thought he went with one of those kids into the rooting shed," Victor said. He and Laura were making window baskets for one of his former clients.

"Thanks. I'll check." Poor Connor had been going nonstop ever since he'd gotten out of church. With a fresh pot of coffee brewing, Rowena intended to get him to rest for a minute.

The shed door was stuck and it took several shoves and finally Kent's shoulder to get the thing open. There was no one inside. That was odd.

"Connor?" She heard a sound on the other side of the refrigerator door. How had it gotten locked? She snapped the lock, dragged the door open. Connor huddled inside, his face paler than she'd ever seen. "Are you all right? What happened?"

He coughed several times, grabbed her hand as if it were

a lifeline. "C-can we go outside?" he stammered. His fingers were icy.

"Sure. Come on." Rowena slipped an arm around his waist and helped him out, carefully closing the doors behind her. He was shaking but at least those deep, gasping coughs were weakening. "How long were you in there?"

"Forever." The whispered response told her something was terribly wrong.

"Come on, sit on the deck in the sunshine. Good thing it's so warm today. You'll be sweating in no time. I've got coffee." She had to pry her fingers free. When she returned a little of the pastiness had left his face. "Take a drink of this."

He did, then cupped the big mug in his palms and held it against his cheek. "Oh, that feels good."

"Can you tell me what happened?"

"I got locked in. The pastor asked to see the cutting room the kids had been talking about and after he left I couldn't get it closed. I went inside to unstick it and it caught."

"But there's a safety latch." Even as she said the words Rowena shook her head, remembering it hadn't worked properly for ages. They'd talk about it later. Right now he needed to get warm. She went back inside, found an afghan and slid it over his shoulders. "I'm so sorry, Connor."

"N-not your fault." But his voice shook and his hands trembled.

Something else was going on.

"Connor?" She waited until he looked at her. "What's really wrong?"

He looked at his hands for a long time, then, eventually, lifted his head, looking everywhere but at her. His smile was self-mocking. "I'm a wimp."

"We both know that's not true."

"Yes, it is." He took a deep breath. "I'm kind of claustrophobic, Rowena. I never take an elevator, I fly as few places as I possibly can and I never go in any place I can't get out of."

A stiff north wind could have toppled her at his confession.

"But you climbed down the mine shaft."

"Over a cliff, into a valley. It wasn't closed in. Besides—" he coughed "—you were there."

What did that mean? That he felt safe with her near?

Rowena brushed her fingers through his hair, trying to communicate her apology.

"This is my fault. If you hadn't been trying to help me—" She shook her head, furious with herself.

Connor's eyes still bore a slight glaze; his fingers still trembled. And he didn't bother to try to stand.

"I'm so sorry," she repeated.

"It's not your fault. I've had the problem for a very long time. Usually I can deal with it." He sighed, closed his eyes for a moment. When he spoke again pain underlaid his words. "My mother locked me in my room sometimes. She heard these voices, you see. She was trying to protect me."

Rowena sat down at his feet and waited. There was more. She knew it.

"Usually I just waited it out. But this one time I was locked in and there was a fire. I couldn't get out. The smoke was so thick." As he spoke his voice weakened, took on a tone of fear. "I called and called for her to let me out. I thought I was going to die." He dredged up a smile. "Needless to say I didn't. It was just a pan on the stove. Nothing serious."

"Yes, it was. It was very serious. You must have hated her for leaving you like that."

"Hated her?" He frowned as if the idea had never come into his head.

"Hated her even though you loved her, I mean." She saw he didn't understand and wished she'd kept her mouth shut.

"Rowena, do we have any more of Pierre's cookies?" Quint stood at the edge of the patio, his gaze curious.

"If there aren't any left in the white boxes, they're all gone."

"Figures. I didn't get one of them. Things are starting to die down finally. Dad and I are going into town for dinner in an hour. Is that all right?"

"Of course. And thank you both for all your help."

Quint grinned. "It was worth it. I've never heard so much buzz about Wingate Manor since I got here." He turned his attention to Connor. "The whole county's going to show up for your grand opening."

"That's what we want," Rowena said. "Have a good meal."

Connor remained silent, probably lost in some childhood nightmare. She'd thought he was protected, coddled, a spoiled rich boy. And all the time he was dealing with a buried fear—and who knew what else?

Talk about judging by exteriors.

"You should help your customers."

"They're all being looked after." It was 5:00 p.m. She hadn't taken a break all day and she was bone weary. "I'm having a coffee break."

Rowena surveyed her kingdom with a sense of pride. Davis Nurseries was going to make it, thanks to her friends. Ash and Pip had revealed unknown talents as saleswomen extraordinaire, and wore the satisfied grins to prove it. Her father seemed to relish each conversation with his former customers and many new ones, as well, as he dredged up knowledge he'd kept stored away for years, with Laura hanging on his every word.

She'd done her job, brought the nursery back from the brink of disaster and given her father a place to start. She was broke, with only the few resources the nursery would bring in until fall, but that was all right. She'd go back to the city, get her old job back and start again.

Thank you for leading me here, God.

"Rowena?"

She turned, saw her father standing with Laura's hand tucked into his arm.

"Hi, you two. Thank you for helping. We got a little swamped for a while. Connor got locked in the rooting cooler so he's warming up."

"Oh, dear. Are you all right?" Laura listened to Connor's assurances but after a moment when she glanced at Victor she shook her head.

"Victor and I are going to leave now, if you're sure it's okay."

"Of course it's all right. You've done an awful lot. Thanks so much." She watched them walk away and realized that her father hadn't actually spent much time discussing the plants at all. Most of his moments had been spent beside Laura, talking about the past.

"Is something wrong? You're frowning."

Rowena glanced at Connor. "I guess I thought Dad would be more…I don't know, excited about the nursery."

"He's probably tired."

She shook her head, wishing the nagging headache at the back of her neck would recede.

"Even when he first got here, he was busy visiting, not checking the stock. You'd have to know my dad to know how unusual that is." She said the words that had lingered at the back of her mind for weeks. "Something isn't right."

"Can I ask you a question?"

She shrugged.

"Why did you come back here, spend all this time and effort on the nursery when you could have been living your dream?"

"This is my dream." She saw his confusion. "My father lost this place—his home, his livelihood—because of me. I wanted to be able to give it back to him, free and clear, to help him rebuild his life. To get him out of that convalescent home."

Connor finally shed the afghan as he met her gaze. His eyes softened.

"Feel free to hit me if you like, but what makes you so certain that he wants to get back on this land?"

"Are you kidding? Have you seen how he brightens up every time he comes? He's like a new man."

"That doesn't necessarily mean it's because of the nursery. You said he hasn't spent that much time here. Maybe he's just glad to be back among friends, in a place he loves."

"At first, yes. But once he settles in, you'll see. He'll be out here night and day. He's got it in his blood." She rose, stretched her arms over her head. "Kent shooed the kids home. Everyone's gone and I'm starved. What would you say to a pizza?"

"Hello, pizza." His eyes crinkled at the corners. "You had a very successful day today."

"Yes, I did. Thanks to my friends. To all of you."

"I was glad to help."

Something in his eyes had her blushing. She went inside and ordered the pizza. When she came out Connor was standing by the patio railing staring down into the valley.

"Feeling better?"

He nodded. "I was just thinking about your father. Maybe Victor's depression was caused by something other than losing the nursery. Maybe he was just lonely."

So he'd seen her father's interaction with Mrs. Masters, too. Probably everyone had.

"What do you mean?"

"Sometimes people get so lonely they go to extreme lengths to gain others' attention."

"What do you know about loneliness, Connor?" she scoffed. But his solemn gaze killed her laughter.

"I know a lot. I think Cecile must have been terribly lonely." His fingers gripped the handrail and he let out a pent-up sigh. "She kept trying to get my attention by planning nights out, but I didn't see it from her side. I thought she didn't understand my business, that she was trying to control me. I guess that's what makes me feel the most guilty—that I blurted out my feelings and upset her so much she ran out into the street and lost her life."

"You're assuming she ran out because of what you said. But you also told me she went after Tobias."

He nodded.

"Maybe you're putting the blame where it doesn't belong."

He turned, smiled at her. "Always trying to make things better, aren't you, Rowena? Believe me, she did it because of me. Tobias was her excuse."

"You can't know that."

"Can't I? I'd just told her that I didn't love her, that I never had, that I couldn't. She looked at me in that serious, thoughtful way she had and she said, 'Is it me you can't love, Connor, or is it that you can't allow yourself to care about anyone because they might hurt you?' I told her it was just her."

Rowena inhaled sharply, wondering why he was telling her this.

"You had to tell the truth."

"Was that the truth? Just before Tobias broke his leash she looked at me and her face was wet with tears." He swallowed, his Adam's apple bobbing up and down. "She whispered that she was sorry I'd used her. Then she was gone."

"Used her?"

"I met Cecile at a company function. She introduced me to her father. He became a very important client. In fact, a lot of my success was due to him."

"I see."

"I didn't use her to get ahead but I never had the chance to tell her so."

"I'm sorry."

"Anyway, I've had a lot of time to think about her, the way she died. I saw how lonely Cecile was but I ignored it. Since then I've come to understand how having someone else chases that feeling away." He smiled at her. "I believe that might have been at the root of your father's problem. But he seems to be doing fine now. I think Mrs. Masters has helped him."

Connor knew loneliness. Because he'd realized too late that he had loved Cecile?

"Have you thought about what you'll do if your father can't come back here right away—to work, I mean?"

"I guess I'll keep slugging."

"I think you should talk to him, ask him outright what his plans are, find out if he intends to come back here to stay. You can't keep your life on hold, waiting and wondering."

"No." But neither did she want to press him or force him into anything. It had to be his decision. The pizza arrived and Rowena decided to switch the conversation. "How about you? Figured your future out yet?"

He shook his head, averted his gaze. "No. I'm not getting a lot of direction on that yet. The uncles keep telling me to trust God, that He's got a plan, and I've been reading Scriptures that reinforce what they're saying. But beyond their return in September, I'm no more enlightened now than when I first came."

"And you hate that," she guessed.

He nodded.

"I've already admitted I'm a control freak. I like to know what I'm doing next Thursday at four but lately I can't even figure out what's on for tomorrow morning, especially since a certain landscape designer upset things."

"Delighted I could help." Rowena smothered her laughter.

"Go ahead, make fun of me. But September is a blank. There's no goal circled in red for me to aim for, not even a destination. It drives me nuts."

"Maybe that's the point."

"Huh?"

Rowena stretched out her legs, pointed her toes to the sky. "Maybe God's trying to teach you patience. You know, to rely on Him to work things out."

"You've been talking to Uncle Henry."

"No. Just a lot of personal experience. I think trust is the most difficult thing there is. I've been a Christian for most of my life and I still struggle with leaving things up to God." She waved a hand. "I mean, sure, I felt God wanted me to be here, but lately I've had no confirmation that I'm doing His will. That doesn't mean I'm not. I just have to keep walking by faith, trusting that He will show me the next path."

"We're a couple of blind bats," he joked.

"Thank heaven, literally, that we have a God who sees everything and will keep us from stumbling."

Connor rose, his face pensive. "Your faith amazes me, Rowena."

"Why? You believe the same things."

"Do I?" He shrugged. "I'm not sure I've ever trusted anyone. In fact, I've made it a tenet in my life to be independent so I never have to rely on anyone."

"Good luck with that. No one is independent. We need each other like flowers need sunshine. And rain," she muttered, glancing toward the sky. "God certainly answered my prayer to stop the rain. Now I wish He'd relent and give us a good shower."

"The heat's wearying, all right. But it's put the gardens in great shape. Just over two weeks and we'll open. Hard to believe, isn't it?"

She shook her head. "Not when you've got a ton of plants to get in the ground, it isn't."

"Which is my cue to get going. I'll see you tomorrow. Right?"

She caught a hint of uncertainty in the question, as if he wasn't quite sure she'd really forgiven him.

"I'll be there at the crack of dawn, Connor."

He made a face. "Oh, goody. To think I used to sleep till six."

She laughed, leaning on the patio railing and listening as he whistled for Tobias. The two of them walked down the lane toward Wingate Manor.

Have you thought about what you'll do if your father can't come back here right away?

No. She hadn't thought about that, hadn't even considered it. What made Connor even think he wouldn't come back? For years her father had reminisced about the Bay, the nursery, their life here. Coming back had always lurked unspoken behind his words.

"He'll be back on our land soon, digging in with Quint and Kent."

She'd meant to reassure herself. But Rowena couldn't stop one last plea.

"Please?" she whispered.

"You've canceled girls' night out one too many times," Piper scolded. "But since you've invited us to your swank new home I've decided to forgive you."

"You must adore living here." Ashley smoothed her hand over the elegant counter. "Everything is so beautiful."

Rowena nodded as if she agreed. But the truth was, she wasn't enjoying the house. Not at all. Instead she felt as if she were a visitor, and a grubby, interloping one at that.

"I hear a car. Are you expecting someone?"

"Actually, yes. I told Shauna and Trish they could come. You don't mind, do you?" she begged, hoping they'd understand. "They've been so good about organizing everything for their cut-a-thon when I haven't been able to help. When they heard about tonight and begged to come, I couldn't say no."

"It's fine, Row. They're nice girls. We'll enjoy ourselves." Pip went to answer the door while Rowena poured iced tea into five long, slim glasses. Connor had given her the set, along with new dishes, as a housewarming gift.

Elegant, delicate pieces—not like her at all.

"Gorgeous dishes, Row. I love the cracked-ice look on the bottom. And these slanted rims are really unusual. Where'd you find them?"

"A gift from Connor."

"He really knows you, doesn't he?" Trish plopped down on one of the stools, picked up a glass and grinned. "These are a perfect match to your personality."

Rowena blinked. "They are?" she squeaked.

"Uh-huh. Unique. Original, with a flair for the dramatic. And just a touch of whimsy."

"That's our Row," Ashley cheered.

"That's not me at all," Rowena felt obliged to argue. "I'm ordinary. There's certainly nothing dramatic about me."

"Are you kidding?" Trish drew her from behind the breakfast bar, marched her over to the bathroom mirror. "Look at that woman."

"Do I have to?"

"Yes." The order was unanimous from all four of her guests.

"You're beautiful," Shauna assured her.

"We've been telling you the same thing for years, Row." Pip sipped from her glass. "But you don't listen to us. Maybe Trish and Shauna can get through to you."

"She needs a haircut," Shauna murmured. "A proper one."

"One that emphasizes her eyes. They've always been her best feature."

"I just cut it," Rowena told them, feeling a little like a mannequin with everyone scrutinizing her.

"That explains a lot." Trish pushed her hair this way and that. "Got any ideas?" she asked Shauna.

"Yes. Get me some scissors."

Even Ash looked shocked. "You're going to cut her hair?"

"Yes." Shauna and Trish high-fived each other. "We were talking about the perfect look last night."

"Um, I don't want to sound ungrateful, but—" Rowena stepped back as she struggled to find a way to call a halt. Trish wasn't budging.

"Trust me, Rowena, you couldn't be in better hands," she said, planting her hands on her shoulders to stop further flight. "Shauna's going to train in aesthetics as soon as she's finished school, but she's already the best stylist this town has ever seen. Just give her a chance, okay?"

Rowena stared at the shaggy-haired woman staring back at her and thought about Wingate's grand opening in a week and a half. There would be reporters, Connor said, photographers, all kinds of media exposure. Did she really want the world to see her like this?

"Maybe you should let her try," Ash whispered.

Rowena drew in a deep breath of courage, squeezed her eyes shut and nodded. "Okay. Do it."

"Great!"

After allowing Shauna to cut her hair, and Ash, Pip and Trish to give her a manicure and pedicure, Rowena didn't think she could take any more pampering and started to fidget on the stool.

"Sit still," Shauna ordered. "I'm almost finished. You guys don't say anything until she sees for herself."

They nodded, went back to finishing their jobs after sharing a look that tightened Rowena's nerves a notch higher. Trish began sweeping up bits of hair that littered the porcelain tiles.

"There." Shauna removed the towel. "You can go and look now."

Rowena couldn't read the others' expressions so she walked to the bathroom, exhaled and stepped in front of the mirror.

They were right. Her eyes looked huge. Her hair framed her face like a wispy cap, the bangs long and spiky, the sides brushing against her cheeks, the back molding itself against her neck.

"Well? What do you think?"

"I look…frail."

"Not frail," Ash corrected. "Delicate. Dainty. Kind of Audrey Hepburnish in your own unique way."

"Who?" Trish and Shauna shared a look.

"Never mind. You look exactly like who you are, Row." Pip's full smile gave her opinion away. "A smart, hip, fantastically creative landscape designer who doesn't know the meaning of the word ordinary."

"Thank you." Rowena hugged each of them. "Thank you all for doing this."

"Now you'll be the belle of the ball at the grand opening." Trish giggled. "You've got something smashing to wear, haven't you? Something the color of your eyes."

"I haven't quite decided on my outfit yet," Rowena prevaricated. "But come on, this is supposed to be girls' night out, not Cinderella night. So far all you've done is waste your time on me. Let's take our tea, or in my case coffee, and our munchies, and go out on the deck and talk."

"About Connor?" Shauna winked. "He's so going to stare when he sees you."

They lit a little fire in the firepit, sat down and began to talk, one woman often interrupting the other. Rowena sat quietly, content to watch as the darkness fell and listen to them. Each one was full of plans for their futures.

Rowena had nothing to contribute.

"Yikes! It's after ten. My mom's going to ground me for life." Shauna jumped up, flung her arms around Pip and Ash. "Thank you so much for letting us come. This was way better than canoeing. And you, Rowena. You've been so quiet. I hope it's not because you don't like your hair."

Rowena hugged the two girls. "You did a great job and I appreciate it. I know how scruffy I've been looking."

Shauna hugged her back. "Pearls never look scruffy," she whispered. "They just hide inside their shells. Don't hide anymore, okay?"

"Hey! What's all the whispering?"

Rowena smiled. "Just some advice on how to fix my hair."

Once Shauna and Trish were gone, Pip and Ash carried the dishes inside, then left, too, promising to see her at the picnic on Saturday.

"And don't say you're not coming, because you are," Pip ordered before she and Ash drove off.

Rowena wandered back into the house, stood in front of the mirror.

She hadn't wanted to hurt anyone's feelings but truthfully she felt the hairstyle made her look weak, as if she wasn't up to a good day's work. Yes, her eyes were big—as though the world could look in them and see her neediness. Her nails were still short, though cleaner and well trimmed. Her toes, she decided, looked pretty good.

He's so going to stare when he sees you.

Rowena doubted that. Connor was far too involved in dealing with his own life to notice her as anything other than the woman who was putting the finishing touches on his uncles' project.

Sure, he'd kissed her twice. But it didn't mean anything except he was probably lonely and she was someone who could help him through the grieving he was so obviously going through.

Connor didn't see her. This house was proof of that. She'd left most of the decisions up to him; after all, he was footing the bill. The result was pure glitz, a gorgeous show home, the kind of place he could comfortably live in. But it only emphasized her grubbiness and she was constantly rubbing a towel over the granite, wiping up spots off the floor. Checking to be sure she hadn't left a coffee ring somewhere.

The house screamed money, exclusivity. And Rowena was common, ordinary, working class. The two couldn't be further apart. Kind of like her and Connor.

For those few moments he'd held her the other night she'd let herself imagine what it would be like to be wrapped in his arms when life's disappointments threatened. She'd leaned her head on his chest and imagined having the right to do that at any time, knowing he'd welcome her there, waiting to share the future.

It was only a dream, and not very realistic at that. She quickly washed the glasses, Connor's glasses. He'd been so cute, sending big white boxes with giant red ribbons by deliveryman so she couldn't argue. And then he'd called, pretending he had a question but really wanting to know if she got them, if she liked them. How sweet was that?

"Get back to reality, Rowena Davis. You have a lot of work to do before that grand opening, so stop daydreaming and get some rest."

With the house restored to order once more, she locked the door, and retired to her room. But she couldn't go to sleep without dreaming about a certain man.

Chapter Fourteen

"I don't think I've ever been to a Sunday-school picnic before," Connor admitted, determined to say something to fill the silence that had fallen between Rowena and him. "What do you do?"

"Eat. Watch the kids play games. Join the softball game if you want."

It was Rowena's voice, but the woman sitting beside him in his car wasn't Rowena. She had Rowena's eyes, her hair color, maybe even her sundress. But the warm woman he knew as Rowena had withdrawn.

"I think I'd rather go for a swim. This heat is becoming oppressive."

"You can probably do that, too," she said softly. "Though you'd better not tell Mick or Jason. If they go off with you, Ash and Pip will be furious." She grinned and he caught a glimpse of the old Rowena. "Trust me, those are two ladies you do not want to alienate."

"I'm learning that." He decided to broach the subject head-on. "You've done something to your hair. Is that why you've been hiding it under a baseball cap at work?"

"Do I need to?"

"Of course not. It looks gorgeous. Suits you, somehow. In an elfin, pixie kind of way." That hadn't been the right thing to say, judging by the downturn of her lips. "You look very lovely. I've never seen you in white before."

"Hazard in my kind of work." She stuck out her foot. "We had girls' night in on Thursday. I was the project. Shauna, one of the teens, cut my hair."

"She did a fantastic job. She obviously knows your personality."

"Funny." Rowena laughed. "She said that about you after she saw the glasses. Everyone loves them, you know."

"Do you?" he asked quietly.

"Yes."

"You weren't sure at first, though, were you?" He saw the surprise flare in her eyes. "You prefer something not so odd, right? I can take them back."

"I don't want to take them back. I love them. It's just—I've always looked at glasses as utilitarian, I guess."

"The ones I gave you hold liquid," he said indignantly.

Her light chuckle instantly lifted the tension. "They certainly do and with flair. I just meant that I've always made do with ordinary dishes."

"You say that a lot—make do. When we were discussing flooring you said you could make do with linoleum and carpet."

"I could have." She sounded defensive.

"Can't you 'make do' with what's there?"

"It's not the same." Rowena shifted, her hands moving as she struggled to explain. "I don't need luxury. You spent so much money on that house and I'm not the sort of person who can appreciate it."

"Why not?"

"Pardon?"

"Why can't you appreciate nice things?" He was tired of

hearing her debase herself. "Don't you like walking on cherry floors? Doesn't it feel good to climb into the jet tub and let the water ease your muscles?"

"I haven't tried it yet," she admitted.

"Why?" Connor squeezed his fingers around the wheel, trying to control his frustration. "You won't lose your work ethic if you enjoy that tub, Rowena."

A long silence stretched between them.

"It's hard," she whispered.

He pulled into a parking spot by the town park, switched off the motor and turned to face her. "No, it isn't. Use the house. Enjoy it."

"I'll get too used to it."

"That's silly."

"Sooner or later I'll have to leave, Connor. I'm only here to get the nursery going for Dad." Her hand slid over his, squeezed. "You were so generous and I really appreciate everything you did."

"But?"

She shook her head, the auburn strands moving like threads of silk before they settled into place once more. "I'm sorry. I shouldn't have said anything."

"You're entitled to say whatever you like." He climbed out, walked around to open her door, frustration chewing at his heels.

"Now you're angry."

"No, Rowena, I'm sad."

She frowned. "Why?"

Because I wanted to help.

"I hoped, prayed, the house would be a place where you could find solace, relax, rejuvenate. I thought if everything was modern, up-to-the-minute, you'd have to spend less time fixing and cleaning, and more time relaxing."

"I guess I'm not used to relaxing, especially in that splendor."

"Then get used to it," he grated. "You're not some hobo without a job, begging other people to toss you a dollar. You're a beautiful woman who's very accomplished in her field. The house is supposed to be a backdrop for you, not the other way around."

"I'm sorry."

"Stop apologizing!" Connor dragged a hand through his hair. "Look, I'm sorry. Let's forget about everything and enjoy the afternoon."

"Okay."

It wasn't exactly that easy. Many people complimented her on her new look but that only seemed to send Rowena further into her shell. The only time she truly relaxed was when the teens gathered round. Then her eyes sparkled, her face lit up and she shone.

"I'm glad to see you aren't letting the nursery cheat you out of a normal life," Victor told her after he and Laura sat down on the blanket Connor had brought. "If you let it, it will consume you."

"Victor, I'm sure Rowena enjoys a day off as much as the rest of us," Laura soothed. "How is Wingate coming, dear?"

"We're going full tilt next week. I hope to get all the bedding plants in by Thursday." Rowena searched her father's face. "Will you be available to give us a hand?"

"I guess I could stop by for a few hours."

A few hours—Connor knew that wasn't what she wanted to hear and once they'd finished their food he made an excuse about choosing their dessert and invited Victor to help. He was sick and tired of pussyfooting around.

"So what are your plans, Victor?"

"My plans?" The man looked startled.

"About the nursery, I mean. Are you going to partner with Rowena, make Davis Nurseries a name to remember?"

"Partner?" Victor laughed, chose a butter tart. "I'm too old to rebuild a nursery. I never thought Rowena should return, either. She should be carrying on with her career in the city, but she's old enough to decide her own life. I just hope she doesn't repeat my mistakes and let that place consume her so much she pushes everything else away."

What did that mean?

One of the teens, Greg, stopped Connor to ask about a book he wanted to borrow, allowing Victor to hurry back to Laura before Connor could ask more. The couple soon abandoned Rowena and wandered off to a park bench in the shade.

The teens had gathered around Rowena again and were deep into a discussion about trust. Connor handed her the dessert he'd chosen, tasted his own as he listened.

"We've been going through this in our youth group Bible study," one of them said. "You can't trust God unless you know Him, and the only way to get to know Him is through the Bible. The Bible says God is love, that He has plans for us, good plans to prosper us. So I guess what it really boils down to is are we going to believe what the Bible tells us and trust God, or are we going to keep fussing and fuming, trying to work things out for ourselves."

"It's a choice," Rowena agreed. "A tough one sometimes. God doesn't always work the way we expect. We must keep our minds open to His leading."

An announcement summoned those who wanted to play softball and the teens took off. Connor helped Rowena gather things up, then they moved to a bench to watch the little kids' games.

When a tyke tumbled in front of them during the sack race, she rose quickly, dusted off his knees and offered a bit of advice that dried his tears and sent him scurrying away to the finish line.

"What did you say to him?"

She glanced at him, then away. Her cheeks pinked. "I told him I thought he was going to be the winner, but he had to finish the race."

Good advice for all of them, Connor decided. But he couldn't help wondering how much finishing the race would cost Rowena.

"Did you ever expect to see so many people at this cut-a-thon?" Ashley said as she poured yet another glass of lemonade and made change for her customer. "Those kids sure spread the word about their contest."

"I just hope there's enough food to feed them all." Rowena glanced at Michael and Jason, busy manning her barbecue. "How many—"

"Rowena, this is Mr. Jones. He'd like to discuss having some work done. Do you have a minute?" Connor introduced them, then hurried away to talk to someone else. He was like a salesman on steroids today.

After promising to get an estimate to Mr. Jones, Rowena checked out the cutting shed. Greg, Shauna and Trish were giving demonstrations on cuttings. The pile of plants ready to hit the rooting powder was huge. She began moving them but Greg stopped her.

"I can do this. You go mingle. You've got about twenty minutes before the contest starts and I know that group of ladies by the greenhouse wants to discuss donating a fountain for in front of the veterans' building."

Compared to this, working at Wingate was a snap, she decided when Connor finally blew the whistle to call everyone to watch the contest. She'd been offered more work than she could possibly complete in the next few months. Unless her father came on board very soon.

Jason and Michael had set up three tables outside for each team to work on because there wasn't enough room in the cutting shed for the visitors to watch. With Quint, Kent and Victor ready to judge, Connor blew the whistle and the contest began.

The kids had learned well and the boxes of cuttings grew rapidly. After they were examined, each box was carried to the shed so the cuttings wouldn't dry out. By the time Connor blew the whistle again, Rowena knew they had far exceeded her goal for this year.

Greg's team was pronounced the victors and they flaunted their win over the others. Connor announced the total of funds raised for the orphanage, which made everyone cheer. He suggested the purchase of a soda and hamburger would increase that amount even more.

Then he encouraged those who needed plants to buy now, gave a short commercial for Rowena and Davis Nurseries, which had her blushing, and announced that Wingate Manor would be open to the public on June 2. He invited everyone to visit and see her work. After the teens effusively thanked her, the crowd began to shift. Quint and Kent went back to selling plants and Ashley and Piper doled out burgers and sodas galore.

"That went well, I think." Connor searched her face. "If you can hang on just a little longer, they'll leave soon and you can relax."

"I'll be fine." Rowena glanced around. "I never imagined so many people would show up. The whole town and the countryside seems to be here."

He grinned. "That was the idea. I think you can safely say Davis Nurseries is on the map."

"Thanks to all of you." Her father joined them. "Hi, Dad. Laura. Holding up all right? This heat is awful."

"I'll be fine once I get a drink and sit down for a few

minutes. Laura and I are heading to her house for that now. She has dinner ready."

"Oh. Good." Rowena summoned a smile. "Have a relaxing evening."

"You, too." He hugged her. "I'm really proud of you, honey. You've made this place a big success. I predict many years of the same."

"You helped," she murmured, wondering at the curious look Laura and her father shared. "All of you. Now if I can just get Wingate finished before Saturday, I'll be ecstatic. You are going to help us plant this week, aren't you, Dad? You don't have to go back yet."

Again with the funny looks. Her father and Laura both blushed.

"No, not yet," he murmured. They said goodbye and left, which seemed to be the signal for everyone else.

"All the cuttings are in the rooting room," Trish said. "There's one case of burgers left. Should we put them in your freezer?"

"I'll never eat that many. Why don't you take them, have a barbecue to celebrate. You guys did a great job. Thank you for all the work."

"Are you kidding?" Greg grinned. "This was a blast."

"We've got to go, Row. Michael's got a field trip with his class tomorrow and he needs to get some stuff ready." Ashley enveloped her in a hug. Somehow, despite all the burgers, she still smelled as fresh as ever.

"We have to leave, too," Pip said. "Jason's got an evening houseboat cruise down the bay and I need to prepare for a meeting on Monday."

"Thank you all, so much. I don't know how this could have happened without you." She hugged them all, waved them off.

Quint and Kent closed things up, then they, too, headed to town. There was only her and Connor left.

"Would you like some lemonade? We could go inside, into the air-conditioning?"

But Connor shook his head.

"I'm guessing you've been up since before dawn. I know you're going to push yourself to the limit this coming week, especially with that fountain—which, I'd like to reiterate, I think is perfectly fine the way it is."

She opened her mouth to argue but he put his fingers across her lips.

"I think you need to unwind this evening, pamper yourself and not be waiting on me or thinking about a bunch of metal spigots." He bent, brushed his lips against her brow. "For once just relax, Rowena. Try to forget about everything. Maybe even use that whirlpool tub."

"Maybe I will." She stared up at him and in that second the truth slammed into her so hard her heart stopped. She loved him—loved, adored—Connor Wingate. It wasn't infatuation, it was rooted deep inside, tucked away in the deepest recesses of her heart. When she thought of the future, he was there, beside her, teasing her, pushing her, loving her.

Until he left the Bay.

"Rowena?"

"Yes?" She blinked, grasped the threads of her shawl of composure and drew them tight. "I want to say thank you, Connor. You've gone above and beyond."

"So have you." He stood there staring at her, as if he wanted to say more but couldn't find the words. "I'm just glad it was a success."

"Yes."

Silence yawned between them like an invisible gap. Finally he broke it. "I'd better go. Bye."

"Bye, Connor."

She watched him until he disappeared behind the stand of

trees that led down to the road to Wingate. Then she touched her forehead in the exact place where he'd kissed her. Every nerve sang with joy, then screeched to a halt.

It was almost over.

Once she was finished at Wingate Manor she'd have no reason to see Connor every day. He'd be busy with his guests. Come the fall he'd leave, go back to his own world, and she'd move on to the next project. Whether that would be in Serenity Bay or Toronto depended entirely on her father. And he seemed more interested in Laura than the nursery.

Worry skittered up her spine but Rowena was too tired to think about it. Instead she walked inside, straight to the bathroom, and turned on the taps.

Connor was right. It was here. Why not use it? She lay for a long time letting the jets soothe her body as thoughts of Connor filled her brain. But eventually the water cooled, and she realized how foolish she was being. She couldn't love Connor. It was hopeless.

She climbed out, dried herself off and put on a light robe. With a glass of lemonade in one hand and her Bible in the other, she headed toward the window seat that looked down across the valley and offered just the slightest glimpse of Wingate Manor.

Maybe if she read long enough, she'd be able to figure out whatever God wanted her to do next.

It was finally done.

And now that she'd done everything she could for Wingate Manor, now that Connor had invited a host of people to this elaborate party to see the changes, now that the big night was here—Rowena found herself wishing she could go back.

If she could relive it all again she'd cherish each second, each hour with Connor. Time she'd never have again.

Her one disappointment was that the fountain wasn't operating properly.

"Are you excited?" Ashley and Piper met her at the bottom of Wingate Manor's big, yawning staircase, poised, elegant and as unruffled as usual.

"More like nervous. Do I look all right?" She waited for their inspection.

"You look perfect." Connor stood at the top of the stairs, elegant and heartbreakingly handsome in his white slacks and white silk shirt, waiting for her to join him. "You're late."

"Sorry."

"I'll forgive you." He took her hand and drew her forward to face the crowd that milled over the terraces, on the decks and even into the house.

"Ladies and gentlemen, I give you the designer and creator of the beauty that is Wingate Manor, Rowena Davis."

Suddenly she found herself in the spotlight, surrounded by people who were applauding. Rowena curtsied, then felt Connor's arm slip around her waist. He bent his head until his lips were millimeters from her ear.

"This next part is going to make the papers in Toronto, so smile," he ordered. As photographer's flashbulbs kept going off he turned to the crowd and commented on the many features Wingate Manor could now offer its clients, gallantly attributing the ingenuity of it all to Rowena. "Without her expertise, fantastic vision and intense demand for perfection, none of this would be possible. A toast to Rowena, master gardener and designer extraordinaire."

Punch glasses raised as the group cheered then drank to her. Lifting her hand, Connor pressed his lips against her knuckles in a public tribute, then, so softly no one else could possibly hear, he said, "Thank you."

"You're welcome."

His gaze held hers until a ripple of murmuring broke the connection.

"Mayor Franklin will now cut the ribbon officially opening Wingate Manor and then I invite you to stroll our well-lit grounds, sample a few of the treats Chef Pierre has prepared and plan your next visit with us."

Rowena stood beside him through the hoopla, pretending she was used to all the attention. Though she should be. The photographers had been here all of yesterday, poking and probing while she was trying to finesse the last bloom into place, and make sure no blade of grass stood out.

Finally the formalities were over. Connor turned to speak to her but someone garnered his attention and he left with a promise to return later. Several reporters asked for interviews and she spent more than an hour answering their questions, talking about her credentials and deflecting comments about past projects to highlight Wingate Manor and all it offered.

"I was particularly impressed by the fountain at the bottom of the garden. The music is a great asset, as are the changing colors. But knowing your past designs, I'd expected movement." A reporter from a national magazine geared toward landscapers asked the question Rowena had feared the most. "Is there some reason you chose not to do that here?"

"I—"

"Wingate Manor is all about meeting the clients' needs," Connor said from just behind her. His hands curved over her shoulders. "Ms. Davis has given us far beyond what we ever expected and we're delighted with every single feature she's created. Thank you all for coming. Now if you'd like to sample the cherry flambé, I believe Chef Pierre is about to light it. Please excuse us. Rowena and I have some other guests to speak to."

Connor flashed his model-white smile then drew her

toward the gazebo that she'd surrounded with baby's breath. The air was redolent with the scent of it, the blossoms fully open for the occasion.

"Who wants to talk to me?" she asked when he held out his hand to assist her up the stairs.

"I do." He led her toward one of the cushion-topped chairs, waited until she was seated before he drew a picnic basket from under the seat. "Coffee?"

"How did you know I was dying for a cup?" She accepted the chunky mug of rich, steaming brew gladly and took a sip. "Oh, that's perfect."

"No," he said quietly. "You are. Wingate is. This whole thing is due to you. I just wish the uncles could be here to see it all."

"So do I." She knew how hard he'd worked trying to get them here for the day but the doctors would not approve it. "But judging by the amount of pictures tonight, you'll have lots to show them when they come back."

"Yes." He sat down beside her, his face pensive. "I came here thinking I'd hate it but thanks to you, your friends, the community—I've enjoyed myself, Rowena." His fingers meshed with hers. "I've learned so much from you."

"Me?" She shook her head. "Like what?"

"Friendship, freedom, peace. How to stop anticipating tomorrow and enjoy today."

She quirked an eyebrow. "You've really learned that?"

He laughed. "Okay, let's say I'm working on it. I still don't know what the future holds. Part of me wishes I knew what I'd be doing in September, but I'm trying, thanks to your example, to keep looking to God for the answers."

"I'm glad." Outside, around them, voices talked and laughed. Music floated on the night breeze. Water trickled over rocks. And all she could think about was being here, with Connor.

For the last time.

"I've spent ages trying to think of a way I could show my appreciation for everything you've done," he said quietly.

"I haven't quite finished. That fountain is going to work if I have to die trying." She waited for his laughter. "Besides, I have the nursery up and running, a number of clients, that beautiful house. That's far more than we agreed on."

"I wanted to give you something from me, something personal." He withdrew a small black box from his jacket pocket. "I saw this and imagined you wearing it."

He opened the box. Inside was a delicate gold chain formed of a series of intricate knots. In the center of each knot lay a small green stone that resembled an emerald. The beauty of the piece made her catch her breath.

"Connor, it's too much," she whispered.

"No, it's hardly enough." He smiled, his eyes burning into hers. "May I put it on?"

"Please." She turned so he could fasten it behind her neck, felt the brush of his fingertips against her skin and shivered.

"Are you cold?" he whispered, his breath warming her neck as he turned her so he could look at her.

"No." She couldn't move, could barely breathe.

"Rowena?"

"Yes?"

He smiled, and touched his lips to hers in the lightest of touches, like the gossamer wing of a butterfly.

For once Rowena ignored the voice telling her this couldn't be, ignored everything but his touch. Leaning in, she placed her palm against his cheek to stop him from moving away, grazed her thumb across his lips.

And Connor, big, strong Connor who always had to be the boss, sat there with the oddest look in his eyes, waiting for her to make the next move.

The chance to kiss him might never come again after tonight. She had to take it, had to try and show him what was in her heart. Then maybe, maybe—

"Rowena?"

She jumped back; her hand dropped. Connor's face lost all expression as her father stepped into the gazebo.

"Oh, good. They said I'd find you here." Victor drew Laura in behind him, patted the seat motioning her to sit down.

Who else knew she was in the gazebo with Connor? Was the whole party watching them?

"Is there something wrong, Dad?"

"Not wrong, no. But I do need to talk to you."

"Now?"

"I've put it off too long already." He glanced at Laura, who nodded. "Honey, I've asked Laura to marry me and she's agreed. We're going to be partners in her shop."

Married? Partners? The words slid past her in a whir of confusion. Rowena wanted to deny it, demand he take it back, tell her he would start at the nursery on Monday.

She'd given up everything—everything! And he didn't even care!

As Rowena opened her mouth she felt Connor's hand wrap around hers, infusing her with a strength she desperately needed. She glanced at him, saw him smile and knew she could say none of it. A glance at her father told her how happy he was, how much he wanted her to say it was all right.

"Married? That's wonderful." Connor rose, drawing her up with him. He let go of her hand to shake her father's. "Congratulations. I think that for once, you've left your daughter speechless."

He was covering for her, giving her time.

Breaking free of her stupor, Rowena reached out and embraced her dad. "I'm very happy for you, Daddy," she whispered, using the name she hadn't used since her mother's death. "Congratulations. When are you getting married?"

"Right away," Laura said after accepting a hug. "We've thought about it long enough and we know what we're doing. The thing is—" She hesitated, glanced at Victor.

"We'd like to be married at the nursery. On the deck, if you don't mind." Victor wrapped his arm around Laura, his face glowing. "It—it has some special memories for us."

This blow was almost as hard as the first and Rowena sank down before she collapsed.

"Married—at the nursery," she repeated blankly.

"If you don't mind," Laura said.

"Hey, Wingate Manor is supposed to host the weddings now," Connor joked. "You'll have her cutting into my business."

She had to do this. Somehow her father had snapped out of that horrid depression that had kept him in its grip for so long. There was no way on earth she wanted him to go back to Toronto, to the blank walls and blank stares.

"Don't worry, Connor. I'll only be hosting one wedding. But it's going to be a good one." Rowena swallowed hard, hid behind the shield of business she'd used so often as her dreams went crashing down. "When?"

"Is a week from today too early?" Laura asked. "Nothing fancy, just a few friends, your gorgeous flowers and the minister. I'll have some canapés catered in. Maybe an evening ceremony?"

"That sounds lovely. Why don't we get the details nailed down tomorrow during lunch, after church?"

"Have lunch here. I hope you don't mind, but I want to be part of this, too." Connor smiled. "I know Pierre will jump at the chance to create a wedding cake and some hors d'oeuvres. Please?"

"Well, I don't know what to say. We never expected—"

Did that mean they'd expected her to argue about it? Rowena wondered. Didn't her father know her at all?

"Don't say anything, Laura. Just be ready to tell us what you'd like and we'll try to accommodate you." He reached out, grasped Rowena's hand. "I'd love to talk about it more but there are some people we really need to talk to."

"And we've intruded on your special night." Laura shook her head. "That was thoughtless. I'm very sorry, Rowena. But I agree with everyone else—you've done a marvelous job here."

"Thanks." The tug of Connor's warm fingers kept her centered, helped push back the hurt. "So I'll see you tomorrow. And I am really happy for you both." She hugged them then let Connor lead her away.

"You're doing fine. Just keep up the smile for a little while longer," he murmured as he led her back to the house. "We'll talk later. Okay?"

Did she nod? Rowena didn't know. She did joke and laugh with Ash and Pip. She modeled for the photographers beside the chocolate fountain. She even posed with Connor beneath the arch of climbing roses.

But inside she was dying. How could God do this to her?

While Pierre repeated his cherries flambé, Rowena escaped, abandoning her truck to walk up the hill to the house Connor had created. She went inside to change out of her dress but seeing her reflection only emphasized how deeply into the dream she'd fallen, how mistaken she'd been.

She wasn't a princess, this wasn't a castle and there was no Prince Charming.

Princesses didn't wear cotton sundresses, they wore silk and satin gowns. They didn't have calloused hands and sunburned cheeks. They wore glass slippers, not sandals with holes in the bottoms. She pulled the dress off, tossed it in the corner and pulled on her familiar T-shirt and torn jeans.

Princesses had kingdoms. She had a run-down, barely operational nursery that would drain every ounce of strength she could muster to bring it back to life. Princesses had fortunes. She'd blown her money making Wingate beautiful so she could give her father the desire of his heart.

Only she'd been wrong.

He didn't want the nursery. He wasn't interested in working with her. He wanted to start a whole new life.

Rowena made herself a cup of strong black instant coffee and went to sit on the patio. A billion stars lit up the night sky but she didn't feel a connection. She should have been celebrating tonight. Instead she mourned.

"How could You do this?" she whispered, tears falling unheeded. "I trusted You. I followed where I believed You led. And now I'm left with what? Pointless love and a plot of ground that I don't want. Why?"

She'd talked about faith in God, trusting, believing.

Tonight she didn't believe her own words.

Chapter Fifteen

"Rowena, it doesn't matter if the flowers aren't perfect. They don't see anyone but each other." It was probably the wrong thing to say but Connor was at a loss to reach her. A scant hour before the ceremony and she insisted on planting the last of her petunias and pansies around the burgeoning peonies.

"I want it to be perfect," she muttered, stabbing the flowers in like stakes.

"Okay, that's enough," he said after ten minutes, drawing her upright. "There's only a little while before the wedding. You need to get changed."

"Embarrassed, Connor?" She glared at him, her face red, her eyes brimming with anger. "I'm afraid this is who I am."

"I could never be embarrassed by you, Rowena. I'm too proud of you. I know this has been rough, but you're almost there. Just keep going. Hang on to me if it will help." He brushed his knuckles against her cheek. "Go have a shower and get changed. I'll look after everything else."

She was going to argue so he bent and kissed her. When he drew back she stared at him for a moment. "What was that for?"

"That was for me. Because I care about you and I want to help." He turned her toward the house. "Go."

"You're not my boss anymore." She tossed him a defiant glare then left.

He didn't want to be her boss. He wanted to be her friend, someone she counted on, could trust. No, Connor knew he wanted to be more than that. He wanted to have the right to support her through the next ten years when the nursery would test every skill she possessed. He wanted to protect her, surprise her, lavish her with all the things she wouldn't give herself.

He loved her.

The admission floored him at first, but then it took up space in his heart and stayed there. He'd been coming up here every night, no matter how busy Wingate was, because he needed to see her, needed to be near her, needed her to need him. Because he loved her! A smile lit up his heart.

Pierre appeared bearing the cake and the food, Laura's bouquet was delivered, guests started to arrive. Connor dealt with them all, choosing solutions that he hoped Rowena would prefer while nurturing his secret.

He could love—he *did* love her.

When Victor arrived in his suit, looking slightly dazed, Connor sent him into the house, told him to talk to Rowena. Maybe if the two of them could talk it out… But there wasn't enough time. The bride arrived ten minutes later, exactly on schedule, and the wedding began.

Rowena's beauty stunned Connor. She wore a green dress, soft, wispy, dappled like the shades of her nursery, her bouquet a mixture of delicate green and white. It was all Laura's choice but in his opinion perfect for the delicate woman by his side.

Connor wrapped Rowena's arm in his and walked beside her down the aisle. As witnesses for the happy couple they were required to play their part and he had no intention of leaving her side until the day was over. He could feel the strain under her facade of happiness and prayed for help from the One he was beginning to trust.

"You're beautiful, Rowena," he whispered as the groom kissed his new wife. "Just keep smiling. It will soon be over."

"Yes." She smiled at him but the shadows in her eyes didn't dissipate.

Most of the town had shown up to congratulate the couple. Connor envied them. He'd always kept himself too busy to feel lonely, but now Rowena's easy connection with the community was something he wanted. These people had known her as she'd grown up. They'd been there when she returned, quietly supportive, ready to help however they could now that she was home.

Home. That's what he'd been missing.

"I'd like to propose a toast." Rowena's fingers tightened around his before she drew them away. "To my dad and Laura. Happiness, joy and much love."

The couple embraced as the guests drank the iced fruit drink, but then Victor had his own toast. "To my beautiful daughter. I love you."

After a round of hugging and hand-shaking Connor knew he had to do something to break the tension.

"Pierre is going to make me pay dearly if that wedding cake isn't eaten." The atmosphere lightened. Rowena's hand slid back to nestle in his.

"Thank you," she murmured, standing on tiptoe to whisper in his ear.

He brushed a tendril of wispy hair from her eyes as love gushed up. He relished the sensation. It was nothing like the movies. It was better, so much better.

"For what, Rowena?"

"You know. For being here."

Connor wrapped his free arm around her waist and drew her close. "I'm always here for you. Whenever you want me."

"Until you leave in September." She rested her head against his chest for a few moments, then pulled away as someone interrupted them to ask for more punch. "I have to go."

"I'll go with you." He met her glare. "I'm not leaving your side, Rowena."

"Fine." She let him, even leaned on him when the bridal pair made their departure, after an emotional thank-you that made her cling to him so tightly he pressed her against his side to ensure she didn't collapse.

But when most of the guests were gone Rowena pulled away. She was putting up her barriers again, trying to keep him at arm's length. It wasn't just tonight; she'd been doing it all week, ever since her father's announcement. Connor didn't understand why but he intended to find out.

"I really appreciate your help, Connor," she whispered as her friends cleared away the remaining debris. "I don't think I could have gone through it without you."

His rush of elation quickly drowned when she moved beyond his reach.

"I'll get to work on the fountain on Monday. I've contacted the company and they gave me some ideas about how to fix it."

"There's no rush. It works fine. Everyone's enjoying it."

She shook her head. "I don't like unfinished projects."

"Whatever. I left a package on the kitchen counter. Did you get it?"

"No more presents, Connor." A flash of anger lit jade flecks in her eyes.

"It's not a present," he said, delighted to see her finger the chain he'd given her. "It's copies of the magazine articles about Wingate Manor and you."

"Oh."

"Come on. Let's go find it." The package had been tossed on a side table. He opened it, slid out the magazines. "I'll show you my favorite." Connor leafed through the thickest magazine, found the picture of her buried to her hips in a sea of dancing lupines, her smile as wide as all outdoors.

"Your favorite?" She glared at him. "I look like a ruffian. My shirt is dirty, my hair's a mess." She pawed through the magazine, set it aside and chose the next one. "There are hardly any from the grand opening."

"No. They mostly wanted candid shots that showed Wingate in daylight. He tracked her gaze to a double-page spread in the center of the landscaper's trade magazine. "That's my second favorite."

"Are you kidding me?" Tears welled in her eyes. "I'm sopping wet, the stupid fountain isn't working properly and every single person who works with gardens in this country will know I'm a failure when they see this. It's horrible!"

Connor took the book from her, looked at it. He shook his head.

"I don't see anything horrible when I look at this, Rowena. I see a woman with a love for what she does, completely comfortable in her skin whether she's working on a fountain or hosting her father's wedding."

"Nice try, but it only proves you don't really see *me* at all."

"Of course I see you."

Rowena shook her head. "No, Connor. You see who you imagine me to be. Who I really am is a gardener whose nursery probably isn't going to show a profit for years, if it even survives. I'm not exotic, like the house. I'm not classy or elegant like this dress. I'm just a plain gardener."

"You could never be plain, but—"

"I'm tired, Connor. Thank you for everything you've done,

for helping me and Dad and Laura. We really appreciate it." She stared at him. "Good night," she added when he didn't leave.

Longing to touch her, to hold her and soothe away the pain, Connor only allowed himself to touch her cheek. "Good night, Rowena. I'll see you tomorrow."

"No. I've got things planned. I'll be busy."

The tiny hesitation told him it was an excuse but the wobble in her voice made it clear she was exhausted.

He reached out, drew her into his arms and kissed her the way he'd been wanting to since he'd discovered he loved her. And wonder of wonders, Rowena kissed him back. For a moment. Then she stepped away, shook her head.

"Goodbye." She turned on her heel and walked inside the house, closing the door firmly behind her.

"It isn't goodbye," he said softly.

In the distance the thunder rumbled a warning over the hills surrounding Serenity Bay. Lightning zipped across the sky in a jagged flash that lit up the nursery around him. Lord willing, they might finally get some rain.

He drove home, switching on the wipers as the first fat droplets pinged against the windshield.

"I love her, God. I never thought it could happen to me. Never. But I love her." He grinned as he said the word over and over. But the joy faded when he recalled that firm, unarguable *goodbye*.

"You taught me to love," he whispered as he stood under the awning and watched the awesome show in the heavens. "Tell me what I'm supposed to do now."

"Rowena?"

It was after one a.m. She couldn't imagine why her father was calling now.

"Laura and I wanted to say thank you. It was a beautiful wedding, more than we ever imagined. Thank you for giving us that."

"You're welcome, Dad. Are you happy?"

"Happier than I've been in a very long time. What about you, honey? Why did you go back to the Bay? Can you tell me now?"

She couldn't tell him. It would ruin everything, spoil the joy he'd found with Laura. The nursery was hers. She'd have to figure out the next part of her life in the days to follow.

"It doesn't matter, Dad. This is home now." She had to ask, had to be certain. "Is the depression gone now? Completely?"

"I think it began to leave the first day I came back to Serenity Bay." He laughed, his voice light, carefree. "I knew for some time that I'd have to sell out sooner or later. I'd come to terms with that. But then I got hurt and I couldn't work and I started to feel useless. I came back to take one last stab at the nursery. Then I fell in love with Laura."

"I see."

"Your mom died a long time ago, Rowena. I was so lonely. But Laura brought the sun back. We were like teenagers. But I couldn't keep the nursery afloat and I knew it. I was also pretty certain I'd never get a decent job in the Bay. After all, what did I know?"

"You know a lot," she said loyally as the tears dripped off her cheeks.

"Thank you, sweetheart. Anyway, I tried at a couple of places but you know what it was like then, a summer town. Not much opportunity. So I had to leave."

"It's okay, Dad."

"I wandered around, dabbling in this and that, but I couldn't settle. Things got to me. I couldn't get Laura out of my mind but I realized I couldn't go back. I'd only be a liability to her. Her girls had troubles and she was trying to support them. I couldn't interfere with that so I stayed away."

"But still close—in Toronto."

"I hated it there. I had no friends, I couldn't find work. I got worse and worse, let despair take over. That was wrong, honey. I should have trusted God to see me through and I didn't. But then you decided to come back. That gave me an excuse to return. I can never thank you enough for that."

"I'm just glad you're better. And happy."

"I am now. Eventually, with Laura's help, I realized I'd almost given up a love that was worth saving, worth sharing. I don't know why you decided to get the nursery back by exchanging for work on Wingate Manor. I hated to see you slaving so hard, but I knew that once you'd made up your mind, nothing could change it." His voice cracked and he cleared his throat.

"Oh, Dad." He sounded alive, well, happy.

"I'm so proud of all you've done, sweetheart. Laura and I are in Niagara Falls. We're going to pack up my stuff on our way back and then I'm moving home for good. If you need a hand, you just ask."

"I'll be fine. You get off this phone and be with your bride. Give her a kiss for me."

"I love you."

"I love you, too, Dad." She hung up. So it had all been in her mind; the guilt about spending so much time in school wasn't the primary motivation behind her father's leaving. How could she have been so wrong?

A loud boom pierced the silence. Rowena wiped her eyes, moved to the doorway to watch the storm. Silver-blue streaks of lightning arced across the sky, dropping down to touch the earth.

"That was close." She stepped outside, held up a hand. "Where's the rain, Lord?"

Though a few drops spattered her face, there was only a minimal amount of wetness. Certainly not enough to provide the water her plants, lawns and trees needed—which meant two backbreaking hours of watering before she could even start work tomorrow. No, tomorrow was Sunday. Well, she'd work, anyway.

Defeated, Rowena turned to walk inside. Another lance cut through the night sky. She thought she saw an orange-yellow glow. Fear grabbed her throat. She broke into a run, racing across the yard, into the nursery, past the newly planted cuttings. Urgency sent her feet dashing past the pruned trees, into the forest that banded her property. Smoke began to billow toward her.

Forest fire! If it came this way she could lose everything.

The tractor sat where Quint had left it. She could climb on, begin making deep furrows that would act as firebreaks. But Wingate Manor might also be in danger if the wind changed. She had to alert someone.

Back she fled across the nursery, grabbing the phone inside the house and dialing the Department of Natural Resources. In a few descriptive sentences she gave the sleepy voice all the particulars, hung up, pulled on her boots, grabbed a jacket and hat and headed back out.

Rowena prayed the quirky engine would start and when it finally sputtered to life she heaved a sigh of relief. The wind was picking up. With painstaking slowness she made two furrows, double wide, which she hoped would stop the fire. But the heat was getting closer. Sparks carried by a freshening breeze singed her hair, tingled against her cheek.

But she kept going, praying desperately for a wind shift as the fire inched closer and closer. By the time her watch read five she'd done everything that she could. The fire burned hot and fast and it was closing in on the nursery. If she didn't work quickly everything she'd slaved for would be gone.

Rowena pulled the tractor into an open space and left it,

grabbed a shovel and began digging. She shoved the roots into a pail and lugged it to the root cellar, then repeated it over and over. Her arms ached, her shoulders screamed in pain. If only she hadn't told Quint and Kent to go home this weekend. If only she had help.

In the distance she could hear sounds and knew that the fire crews would have utilized the old logging roads on the other side of her property to start working on the fire. Their main concern had to be Wingate Manor and the town. She was alone.

"Rowena!"

She swiveled around, saw Connor racing toward her.

"You have to get out of here. The fire is moving this way—fast."

"I know." She kept working. Dig, put the tree in the bucket, carry it to the root cellar. He followed her, begging her to go with him. "No. I have to save what I can," she puffed as she strode back to the planting area. "If it spreads, it will kill everything. I'll lose it all."

"They're just trees, sweetheart. You can grow more."

The words infuriated her. "To you they're just trees but this is all I have left, Connor. I sank everything I owned into this place. Okay, my dad doesn't want it, but I can make it work. If I just work hard enough."

He forced her to stop what she was doing, to look at him.

"Rowena, I know you did this for your father. It was a totally selfless gesture designed to give him a better life and you took it on without a thought to yourself." His voice dropped, his fingers touched her sweaty face, brushed the hair off her brow. "I think that's one of the first things I loved about you. Your generosity. Nothing is ever too much. You just keep giving and giving."

"Love?"

Connor grinned. "I know. I was as stunned as you but that's

what I feel for you. Love. I realized it before your dad's wedding. I wanted to tell you last night but you pushed me away." He cupped her face, kissed her. "I love you, Rowena."

For a space in time she could do nothing but respond, losing herself in the glory of his embrace, the rightness of Connor's arms around her. Then reality returned.

"Connor, this isn't going to work. Anyway, you have to get out of here. Get all the sprinklers going at Wingate, soak the land down as much as you can."

He shook his head, pressed a finger against her lips. "Wingate is all taken care of. It's you we have to get out of here." Suddenly he frowned. "What do you mean it won't work?"

"You'll be leaving at the end of September."

"So?"

"I'm not going anywhere. I'll be here, trying to make this place work. To do that I need stock. These new planting are my future, Connor. They're all I have left." She stepped back, away from temptation. "Please go home."

"You can't stay, Rowena."

"I can't go. This is my life." She smiled. "I'll be fine, don't worry. I can always take refuge in the root cellar if it gets too bad. Please, go look after Wingate Manor."

"But—"

"Don't you understand? God didn't answer my prayers when He sent me here. He tricked me. If I lose this, it will have all been for nothing. You can move on, find a new project. I can't." She drew in a breath of courage. "I have nothing to offer."

"Are you nuts? You can start again, Rowena. If not here, then anywhere. I'll back you. I want to! I love you."

"I can't love you back, Connor. Not now. Not ever." She turned so she wouldn't have to see the hurt in his eyes. "Please just leave me alone. Go!"

He argued some more but she ignored him, kept working. His cell phone rang. He promised to come immediately.

"We're feeding some of the firefighters. They need help. I have to go. Please say you'll come."

She ignored him. Eventually Connor stopped pleading, whispered he loved her, then left.

A whoosh of wind caught her clothes, pulled hard. Rowena lifted her head, saw the flames advancing closer, felt the scorching heat. The greenhouse! If she could save some of the bedding plants maybe she could sell a few more, earn a few more pennies.

Rowena dashed inside, began to load the wheelbarrow with the most expensive stock. Unusual roses, the showy bulbs, the perennials. She was ten feet from the door when a sudden crack sounded above and a tree plummeted through the glass. It knocked a shelf against her, pushing her into a heavy iron fountain.

The crack of her leg breaking sounded as if in a vacuum. For a moment pain blocked out everything. All around the rush of the fire grew louder, smoke began to filter in through the broken panes. She struggled to free herself but the shelf was too heavy.

"I trusted You," she whispered as she faced the impossibility of her situation. "I believed You. You said, 'Give all your worries and cares to God, for He cares about what happens to you.'"

The familiar verse on which she'd based her decision to move back wouldn't stop playing in her head.

"I tried, Lord. I did my very best. Forgive me if that wasn't enough. There's only one thing—I wish I'd told Connor I loved him. If You truly do care about me, please let him know I love him. Please."

The air was thick, choking. The fountain still held some water. She soaked her jacket in it and pressed it over her mouth. Through the glass she could see the flames licking closer, devouring everything in their path.

She was going to die.

"Please help me, God. Please care about me."

A pane of glass shattered just behind her. She arranged everything to shield herself as best she could, but Rowena knew it was futile. The smoke was choking her. She hid her face and waited for the end.

Something nudged her arm. She lifted her head a fraction, saw Tobias.

"Go away, Tobias. Go find Connor."

"I'm right here, Rowena. I'm going to get you out of here. Stay still, I've got to move some things." Her heart sang praises as she watched him heft aside shelves, plants, anything that stood in his way.

The fire roared closer, the heat intense as it surged across her fireguard and ignited her trees. Was Connor going to die, too? Was that what God asked?

"Please, not him. Please?"

"Okay, here we go. Hang on tightly, sweetheart. What's wrong?" he asked as she gasped when he swung her up. "Your leg?"

"Broken. Connor, we have to get to the root cellar. It's our only chance."

His face was grimy with droplets of sweat clinging to his temples but his movie-star smile was all Connor.

"My darling Rowena, I love you very much. But not even for you am I willing to be locked in that cellar again. We're getting out of here. If my call went through, reinforcements should arrive at any moment." He kissed her then pushed his way outside, pressing constantly forward. "Keep the cloth over your mouth," he ordered as smoke enveloped them.

Rowena couldn't see where they were going; she only

knew Connor kept pressing ahead long after most men would have given up. He stumbled twice and she begged him to put her down, let her hobble.

"I've got you and I'm not letting you go," he whispered, his eyes sending a message she couldn't ignore. "I will not let you go, Rowena."

A moment later strong hands grabbed them, pulled them into the back of a vehicle. As it pulled away the smoke shifted and she caught a glimpse of her nursery. It was gone, all of it. Nothing but a blackened, smoking ruin sat where the house had been. The only thing remaining was the small plot of pansies, petunias and peonies she'd planted on her father's wedding day.

"Oh, Connor. Your house. I'm so sorry."

He squeezed her hand then asked to be let out at the bottom of the hill. Rowena remained silent as they sped over the rough road, downhill, away from the fire. Connor moved and she grabbed his arm.

"Where are you going?"

"You're going to the hospital for smoke inhalation and to get that leg set. I have to help at Wingate. Pierre's got his hands full." He leaned in to kiss her. "I'll come for you, Rowena. Wait for me."

She knew what he was asking and she was scared—too scared to believe it.

"Please?"

She nodded. He squeezed her hand, broke into a jog and headed toward Wingate. That's when she noticed her driver was Michael, her attendant, Jason.

"Thank you," she whispered as her eyes welled with tears.

"We aim to please," Jason said and saluted.

"What about Wingate Manor?"

"The wind is shifting. Looks like it will be spared. Now lie back and relax, Miss Davis. The good guys are in charge."

"Yes, they are." She did, because her heart was full. Connor was alive and safe. God had answered her prayer. Well, one of them, anyway.

"You're sure you're not upset," Connor repeated two days later.

"Upset? Try thrilled. Now get off this phone. You've got something to do."

"Yes, Uncle." He hung up, dropped the cell phone into his pocket and sized up Esther's SUV. He hoped it would work.

Rowena would be in a cast. Which meant he'd had to trade his vehicle for Esther's. He wasn't delighted at the thought of her driving his new BMW but what could you do. This plan was going to go off without a hitch, no matter what.

"I'm putting my future in Your hands," he whispered. "Please don't let me mess it up." Then he climbed out and walked into the hospital.

"I should have been discharged six hours ago. What is the problem?" Rowena was not a happy patient.

"I am," he said, walking in unannounced. "Ready to go?"

If looks could kill—

"Okay, we're off." Once she was seated in the wheelchair and the papers were signed he pushed her out of the hospital, lifted her into Esther's SUV and put the wheelchair in the back. "I apologize for being so late, Rowena. I had a few things I had to see to."

She didn't answer. Connor hid his smile, concentrated on steering the hulking vehicle out of town. *Don't let me mess this up.*

"I just realized, I don't have anyplace to live." She leaned forward. "Where are you going?"

"Wait." He continued to drive.

"But this is Wingate Manor. I'm not staying here."

"No one asked you to." He climbed out, fetched the wheel-chair and rolled it to her door. "Get in. I want to show you something."

"Connor, it's dinnertime. I missed lunch waiting for you. You haven't been to see me even once since I got there—"

He put his hand over her mouth. "Just wait."

She crossed her arms over her chest and harrumphed her displeasure. Connor pushed the wheelchair over the path, constantly heading downward.

"Thank you for making these paths wheelchair accessible," he said softly. "That was very intelligent of you."

Her glare required no translation.

Finally they reached the bottom terrace and the stone patio in front of her nemesis, the fountain she'd fought with so often.

"Yes, I see that the grounds escaped unscathed. I would have thought you'd have some patrons tonight but I suppose after the fire—" She stopped because he had his fingers over her lips again.

"Wait."

Rowena clamped her lips shut and stared straight ahead. He ached to explain but that would ruin everything, so Connor simply sat beside her and watched the gardens fall into twilight, listened as the birds chirped, smelled the soft, spicy fragrance of Persian roses blooming behind the fountain.

Hurry, hurry, he begged impatiently. Finally he heard the click. He narrowed his entire focus on her face.

At the same time that the fountain lights came on, the soft, haunting voice of Nat King Cole wafted through the speakers she'd encased in pillars, singing about a forever love.

Tears streamed down Rowena's face as she watched the delicate dance of the fountains jump and pirouette in time to the velvet voice then fade away at the end until darkness fell over the grounds and only the landscape lights cast a shadowed glow.

"Oh, Connor, what have you done?"

"Fallen in love with you," he said softly, wiping away the tears as he knelt before her. "I didn't think I could love anyone. I thought I was a misfit, that God was punishing me for not loving Cecile. And then I came here, and I met you."

He closed his eyes for a moment, remembered that first moment, savoring all that happened since.

"I've never known beauty like yours, Rowena."

"I'm not—"

He stopped the words with a shake of his head.

"You're beautiful and exactly the woman I believe God made for me. Look around, sweetheart. You're so full of beauty it pours out of you. You create beauty wherever you go. Wingate Manor is a testament to that beauty, but so is the youth group, your father, my uncles. You touch everyone, change their lives, not just because of how you look, though I adore how you look." He grinned at her blush. "Your beauty is deeper. It spills out from your beautiful heart."

For once Rowena was speechless. Connor grasped the opportunity to say what he wanted. He pulled out the small box he'd placed in his pocket just an hour ago and placed it in her palm, wrapping her fingers around it.

"Will you marry me, Rowena? Will you teach me how to give from the heart? Will you try to love me at least a fraction of the amount I love you? Will you wear my ring as a promise that you'll keep bringing beauty to my life?"

She was silent for so long his old fears threatened to take over. But Connor had placed his trust in God and he wasn't reneging on that.

"Rowena?"

She let the box fall into her lap, tucked her hands under her thighs. "I can't."

"Why not?" he whispered, desperate to hold her.

"Everything I have is gone, Connor." Her beautiful hazel eyes, awash in tears, stared back at him.

"Oh, my darling, that isn't true." He drew her hands out, opened them so he could place a kiss in each palm. "Everything that could be is just waiting for these hands to create it." She tried to pull away but he refused to let go. "I love your hands, Rowena."

"You do?"

He nodded. "These are the tools God has gifted you with to create unbelievable beauty. How could I not love them, or you?"

"But—you're leaving and I have to stay."

"I'm not leaving." His heart sang at the joy that flared in her eyes.

"You're not?"

"No. I know why God brought me here, Rowena. I'm buying Wingate Manor from the uncles. I'm going to run it. With you, if you'll say yes." He picked up the box. "Please, will you marry me and share my life? Please say you'll let me mark a date on my calendar, help me achieve my goal of Wingate Manor's first wedding—ours."

Rowena burst into tears, hid her face in her hands.

"Why does that make you cry?" he asked, frustrated by her lack of response. This wasn't going according to plan.

"I thought God had betrayed me," she bawled. "I thought He'd brought me up here, left me with the nursery and then let it be destroyed to play some cruel trick."

"That isn't God's way, Rowena."

"I know." She sniffed, dashed away the tears. "Now I see He kept me here to show me His goodness and mercy." She threw her arms around his neck, kissed him in a way he'd only dreamed of.

"I'm assuming this means you like the ring," he teased when they finally drew apart.

"I don't see a ring," Rowena said, staring at her hand. She sighed when he slid the square diamond onto her finger, kissed it in place. "It's far too big," she began, then grinned. "But I love it. Can we listen to Nat again and watch the fountain? I can't believe it's finally working. How'd you do it?"

He drew her out of her chair, wrapped his arms around her while they stood together, watching the water dance once more.

"It takes a community. That's another thing I learned from you. We owe a lot of favors, sweetheart. They're not going to be happy unless we invite them all to the wedding. Is that okay with you?"

"Yes, my darling," she whispered, leaning her head back against his chest as the final chords of the song died away.

"Darling?"

"Kiss me, Connor."

Epilogue

The wedding of Connor Wingate and Rowena Davis took place on the last day of September, on the grounds of Wingate Manor, at twilight. The youth group seated guests in no particular order, welcoming everyone with a program and a whisper. A hush fell on the group as music began to drift toward them.

Wearing elegant, gauzy gowns awash in bright flower patterns, the bride's two best friends walked slowly down a path lit by luminaries to the fountain at the bottom of the gardens. Ashley and Piper carried baskets filled with the last flowers of summer.

The soft flute music changed as the bride appeared above them on the arm of her father. The crowd gasped at their first glimpse of the fairy-princess dress that sparkled and shone when Rowena moved gracefully toward Connor. She carried a bouquet of cinnamon-tinted roses reputed to be chosen from the uncles' private rose garden.

As Ash and Pip took their places beside their husbands, Connor's best men, Victor gave his daughter's hand to her betrothed. Then the minister began the age-old ceremony that bound two lives for eternity. Each repeated the vows that had joined countless lives before theirs, each exchanged a gold band sealing their promise of love. A unanimous "ahh" rose upward as the groom embraced his new wife.

And then, to the amazement of the couple and the delight of the crowd, the fountain burst into a triumphant wedding chorus followed by an astounding show of fireworks managed by two elderly uncles who couldn't contain their joy.

Then the celebrations began.

"I feel like Cinderella," Rowena told Piper and Ashley a little later.

"Connor's car isn't going to turn into a pumpkin, so I think you're safe." Pip nudged Ash. "Ask her."

"Ask me what?"

"What about the nursery, Rowena? Are you going to rebuild?"

She shrugged. "I don't know the future, girls. I just know God's going to see me through it. And that's all I need to know."

"Amen."

"You do realize the Bayside Trio is going to have to change its name," Michael said, coming up behind his wife.

"That is, if the membership isn't too steep," Jason mused.

"We can work something out." The three ladies shared a wink.

Rowena and Connor sampled Pierre's delicious food, received many toasts as his punch creation disappeared and gladly shared a kiss or two to the tinkling of glasses. Finally they cut the five-tiered wedding cake the kitchen staff had insisted on creating.

When the cake was passed out and no more duties pressed, Connor caught Rowena's hand. "Come with me?" he whispered.

"Anywhere."

He helped her into his car, drove up to the nursery. It was

still burned and devastated, but Rowena caught a glimpse of flickering light.

"What is that?"

"That, my darling wife, is how I see our future."

Rowena glanced around, wrinkled her nose. "Really?"

He looped his arm around her waist.

"Not that. That," he said, pointing straight ahead. "It's our promise for the future from God, a promise of love and hope, blooming in spite of everything that's happened." He led her to the plot of still-blossoming flowers that had lasted from her father's wedding to her own. "Look."

"It's amazing they've survived, let alone still bloom," she whispered, snuggling again his side. "They're spring flowers."

"Spring flowers for a summer love. I can hardly wait to see what God has in store for us for the rest of our seasons together."

"I can wait," Rowena murmured. "A certain man taught me that waiting is worthwhile."

"I love you, Rowena."

"I love you, Connor."

Their kiss was interrupted by a boom and several flashes.

"The uncles are into the fireworks again."

They finished their kiss then settled in to watch the show.

Dear Reader,

I'm so glad you could return to Serenity Bay for another visit. The lure of lapping water, the sweet giggles of children in search of sea shells, the whisper of night winds through the forest all remind me of my own happy hours by the water. Somehow when you're at the lake, cares seem to dissolve and life becomes so much clearer, so much simpler.

Actually, simplicity was God's original plan for us so it's no wonder we crave it. Like Rowena we often think we know God's plan, and when life takes a twist we become frustrated and unhappy. Isn't it wonderful to be able to turn to the One who loves us, give Him our cares and rest, knowing He has it all under control?

I hope you'll write and tell me how you like the story. Address your letters to me at Box 639, Nipawin, Saskatchewan, Canada, S0E 1E0. I'm on the Web at www.loisricher.com, or e-mail at loisricher@yahoo.com.

I wish you peace, contentment and the joy of knowing that no one can love you more than your heavenly Father.

Blessings,

Lois
Richer

QUESTIONS FOR DISCUSSION

1. Rowena made a huge decision based on her love for her father and her belief that God was leading her back to Serenity Bay. Have you ever found yourself believing God was leading you and found subsequent events made you question that belief? Is it possible to trust God wrongly?

2. It's hard to speak the truth when it hurts others. Connor told his fiancée that he didn't love her, then blamed himself when she died. Are there ways to be brutally honest and yet still minimize hurt feelings?

3. Connor took it upon himself to keep and care for his fiancée's dog, Tobias. Why do you think he did so? Would you have done so in his place? How did Tobias help Connor go on with his life?

4. Piper, Ashley and Rowena shared a friendship for many years. Friendships support and sustain all of us through life's difficulties. Discuss how to cultivate and build new friendships while sustaining those we already have.

5. Connor told Rowena her hands were instruments given by God to create beauty. Choose a friend. Each of you make a list of all the abilities and gifts you believe the other has. Now make a list of your own. Compare the two lists. Discuss the similarities and differences. Do you agree?

6. As Shauna cut Rowena's hair, she commented on today's tendency to copy those in the media. Discuss our need to follow celebrity trends.

7. Rowena's father was felled by depression after the death of his wife and the fall of his business. How did Rowena try to help him beat his illness? What would you have done differently?

8. Connor found a strong connection in the Serenity Bay community. How can Christians foster this in their own cities and towns through individual efforts? Can individuals reach more people than organized groups?

9. Some people find verbalizing prayers difficult, as Connor did. Does God hear those prayers that are hidden deep in our hearts but never spoken aloud? Discuss why we need to pray.

10. Fire is a powerful, destructive force, but it can also cleanse the forest of deadly pests and disease, purify silver and hone steel. Fire often represents God's spirit. Discuss times when you thought God took away what you wanted most. What were the positives and negatives of such times?

REQUEST YOUR FREE BOOKS!

2 FREE INSPIRATIONAL NOVELS
PLUS 2
FREE
MYSTERY GIFTS

Love Inspired

YES! Please send me 2 FREE Love Inspired® novels and my 2 FREE mystery gifts. After receiving them, if I don't wish to receive any more books, I can return the shipping statement marked "cancel." If I don't cancel, I will receive 4 brand-new novels every month and be billed just $3.99 per book in the U.S., or $4.74 per book in Canada, plus 25¢ shipping and handling per book and applicable taxes, if any*. That's a savings of 20% off the cover price! I understand that accepting the 2 free books and gifts places me under no obligation to buy anything. I can always return a shipment and cancel at any time. Even if I never buy another book from Steeple Hill, the two free books and gifts are mine to keep forever.

113 IDN EF26   313 IDN EF27

Name	(PLEASE PRINT)	
Address		Apt. #
City	State/Prov.	Zip/Postal Code

Signature (if under 18, a parent or guardian must sign)

Order online at www.LoveInspiredBooks.com

Or mail to Steeple Hill Reader Service™:

IN U.S.A.: P.O. Box 1867, Buffalo, NY 14240-1867
IN CANADA: P.O. Box 609, Fort Erie, Ontario L2A 5X3

Not valid to current Love Inspired subscribers.

Want to try two free books from another series?
Call 1-800-873-8635 or visit www.morefreebooks.com

* Terms and prices subject to change without notice. NY residents add applicable sales tax. Canadian residents will be charged applicable provincial taxes and GST. This offer is limited to one order per household. All orders subject to approval. Credit or debit balances in a customer's account(s) may be offset by any other outstanding balance owed by or to the customer. Please allow 4 to 6 weeks for delivery.

Your Privacy: Steeple Hill is committed to protecting your privacy. Our Privacy Policy is available online at www.eHarlequin.com or upon request from the Reader Service. From time to time we make our lists of customers available to reputable firms who may have a product or service of interest to you. If you would prefer we not share your name and address, please check here. ☐

LIREG07

TITLES AVAILABLE NEXT MONTH

Don't miss these four stories in May